Hauntings AND House Witchery

COLLEEN DELANEY

Hauntings AND House Witchery

COLLEEN DELANEY

CITY OWL
PRESS

HAUNTINGS AND HOUSE WITCHERY
The Witches of Star Island, Book 3

CITY OWL PRESS
www.cityowlpress.com

Cover Design by MiblArt. All stock photos licensed appropriately.

Edited by Tee Tate.

For information on subsidiary rights, please contact the publisher at info@cityowlpress.com.

Print Edition ISBN: 978-1-64898-542-3

Digital Edition ISBN: 978-1-64898-541-6

Printed in the United States of America

To Jackie and Maddie.
How I wish we'd had a great aunt bestow an island cottage upon us.

Praise for Colleen Delaney

"Delaney casts a spell with the first in *The Witches of Star Island* paranormal series. The love story is endearing and the supernatural twists propel the story forward at an exciting clip. The ending leaves many questions unanswered... but Delaney's sturdy worldbuilding ensures this series has plenty of places to go. This is a strong start." — *Publisher's Weekly*

"Family relationships, soulmate relationships, past lives, and incredibly well done magical elements keep you turning the pages of this one." — *HJ Reviews*

"*Finding His Mate* is an interesting story in a dystopian future where different paranormal creatures rule the world. The characters are so damaged and so resilient, and the next book promises more of the same. Highly recommend for fans of shifter romance with fated mates, especially if darker backstories are your thing." — *Jaycee Jarvis, author of The Hands of Destin series*

"*The Hedge Witch* is a fast-paced and delightful read with a heavy dash of spice as well. I recommend this to fans of a good witchy romance, particularly if you enjoy a suspenseful plot to go along with it." — *Your Book Friend Blog*

Also by Colleen Delaney

THE WOLVES OF LUVEN

Finding His Mate

Waiting for His Mate

Stealing His Mate

Protecting His Mate

Aching for His Mate

THE WITCHES OF STAR ISLAND

The Hedge Witch

Bewitching Rosemary

Hauntings and House Witchery

Nine Years Earlier

In a cottage home to five witches, there were a few rules that even the old gods respected: a sprig of mugwort tied around a doorknob meant caution to any who crossed that threshold, a harvest moon was good for more than farming, and a younger sister should never, ever compare her fashion sense to her older sister's.

"Is that what you're wearing?" Verbena leaned away from the vanity mirror in her bedroom and caught a vision of Rosemary walking through the hallway.

"Of course, why?" Rosemary answered, hands on her hips.

Verbena glanced down at her outfit. She had on jean shorts, a white tank top that said "HOMEBODY" in black cursive lettering, and purple flip-flops. Her hair was how she always wore it: down, curly in the back, wavy in the front. Getting her hair to do anything else took ages, especially in the summer. She had been a little bold and put on mascara and some pale pink lipstick, but she definitely looked casual.

Rosemary, on the other hand, was wearing...lingerie? It was black and lacy and left little to the imagination in terms of the exact number of freckles she had on her entire body. Her hair was done up like Bridgette Bardot, and she was wearing sandals with straps that wound up to her knees like some sort of Greek goddess.

"You look gorgeous, Verbena. Remember though: I'm twenty-three and you're seventeen. We are going to this little shindig with very different plans in mind. With all hope, I won't be coming home until the sun is on the eastern horizon." Rosemary flitted down the stairs, leaving Verbena with her reflection.

"Try not to pay attention to Rosemary," Laurel interjected.

Verbena cast a glance at another older sister. Laurel was wearing a black, Victorian-style, high-necked dress that fell just above her ankles and Doc Martens. Her hair was freshly dyed black, her face powdered white with intense black eye makeup and dark purple lipstick. She looked like widow from 1890. Who had murdered her husband.

If Verbena had learned anything from being the fourth of five sisters, it was that they all had very different opinions on fashion. And magic. And, honestly, life in general.

Verbena finished up and walked downstairs. She was excited. It was the first year Star Island was doing a Summerfest, and she was ready to have some company other than her sisters. It wasn't that Verbena didn't have friends, only that most of their parents didn't feel comfortable allowing their kids to come hang out at the Bay cottage with a twenty-four-year-old as the guardian. Lavender was beyond the straight and narrow, but she was still in her early twenties. Parents saw her and assumed that the Bay cottage had an unlocked, fully stocked liquor cabinet and bowls of condoms decorating the parlor. In their defense, if Rosemary was her guardian, the vibe wouldn't have been far off. But Lavender took her role as caregiver extremely seriously. Verbena had a curfew of ten-thirty on the weekends, and boys were not allowed in the house once the sun went down, and that included full adult Rosemary. But tonight, Verbena was finally getting a chance to hang out with her friends, and not just until the diner closed and sent them all home.

"Let me stay home." Sage sat at the dining table, her face stuck in a grimace.

"No. I don't feel comfortable with you being home alone at night."

"Lavender, I'm not a baby. I'm fucking fifteen!" Sage seethed.

"Watch your mouth," Lavender replied evenly. "Yes, you are fifteen. You also live in a slightly haunted three-hundred-year-old cottage in the middle of nowhere on an island in the middle of the ocean. There could be an electrical fire. Or an intruder. Or a malicious ghost. You can sulk in the corner, but you have to come."

"I hate this." Sage pushed back from the table and stomped toward the door. She flopped onto the ground to pull on her sneakers.

"You'll grow out of it. Hey, at least we know the food will be good." Lavender had supplied all the desserts for the party, and Mr. and Mrs. Convito, who ran the Italian place in town, were providing dinner. The food would be delicious, but Verbena was much more excited for the company.

She shook her hands nervously as she walked outside. There was something…crackling in the air tonight. She didn't know if it was nerves or something else, but she pushed it away, determined nothing would ruin her good time at Summerfest.

"And then, and then!" Danielle panted, grabbing Verbena's forearm. "Sara told Tom that she didn't want to be exclusive anymore—can you believe it? Who on earth is Sara going to hook up with other than Tom? Paul's with Mari, Caden has that girlfriend from Boston, Jim would never date her, and Robbie is totally in love with Mari. We aren't swimming in available romantic partners here." Danielle rolled her eyes.

Verbena laughed. When your class only had twenty-two kids in it, and fifteen of them were girls, there weren't tons of dating options in high school. Sometimes Verbena wished they had stayed in Ohio after their parents died. She could have gone to a normal high school with more than one hundred kids in her class and stuff like clubs and organized sports that didn't involve a ferry ride. But she had to admit Star Island was pretty great. All the drawbacks were countered with beautiful views, a big piece of land, a gorgeous home, and lots of space for witchcraft without the prying eyes of neighbors. In Ohio their witchy room had been their musty basement, which didn't hold a candle to a sprawling attic. Plus, the neighbors had basically been on top of them. Here they had a bonfire every summer solstice.

"Holy crap," Danielle breathed. "Who is that?"

Verbena looked over her shoulder in the general direction of Danielle gawking.

There—walking out of the diner—was a guy Verbena had never seen before. He was tall and thin, built like he played soccer at whatever school he went to. His blond hair was a little long on top, and he pushed it off his forehead as he descended the stairs toward the party. He had an ease to the way he walked, like he floated on air rather than stomped on the earth like the rest of humanity.

Verbena felt her heart fall to her stomach, and her entire body buzzed like every muscle had fallen asleep. Her hands gripped the sides of her jean shorts, fisting the already tight fabric. She swayed.

Him.

That was *him*.

She'd found her soulmate.

Verbena searched the crowd wildly. She needed to find one of her sisters. Lavender, preferably, but Rosemary or Laurel would do in a pinch. Her soulmate had just walked out of the diner, and she had no idea what to do. She should run away, right? Hide in a bush and observe him for a while? Hide anywhere?

And now he was looking at her. And smiling. And walking in her direction.

Shit. She was done for.

"Hey, Earth to Luke!"

Luke looked up from the soapy water in the sink.

"We're closing for the festival tonight. You should come." His boss, Julio, slipped off his apron and hung it on a hook in the kitchen.

"Yeah, maybe." Luke looked back at the water. He was nearly finished with the dishes, but the floor still needed mopping.

"Star Island isn't New York City, but we still have fun. There'll be a lot of people you haven't had a chance to meet yet," he called over his shoulder. "See you there!"

Luke sighed and switched off the water.

He'd been on Star Island for just under a week, had this job for five days, and in ten days he'd be able to put a deposit down on one of the shittier apartments the island offered. For now, he was camping. But he was lucky—the Star Island campsite wasn't overcrowded and had showers. It was also practically free to camp there, since the person who was supposed to collect money barely ever showed up to work. He'd been there for five nights and only paid for two.

Luke finished the dishes, dried off, and stretched his arms over his head, then got to mopping. The din of the celebration carried over his steady work, beckoning him out of the restaurant and into the night air. Maybe it would be good to socialize a little. All that was waiting for him at the campsite was a pile of clothes that needed handwashing, a threadbare sleeping bag, and a night staring at the stars. Maybe he'd get lucky and someone would buy him a beer. Or better yet, some food.

Luke stepped down the diner stairs and glanced around. There were more people than he imagined this small island could muster for a street festival. Sure, a lot of them were tourists, but still. He'd expected a couple dozen and was met with about a hundred.

He had come to Star Island to turn over a new leaf. He was sick of barely making ends meet in a big city and living in rat-infested apartments with a bunch of guys who tried to steal from him. Luke had landed in the city as a place to disappear from his old life, but there was nothing in the fine print that said you couldn't disappear in a more affordable place with better rent prices. He figured a spit of land in the Atlantic was about as different as he could get from anywhere he'd lived before.

Luke scanned the street, looking for Julio or anyone else who worked in the diner. He counted himself as friendly, but he was tired and didn't necessarily feel like going up to a stranger to strum up some conversation.

A woman caught his eye like he was a fish on a hook willingly being reeled in to his demise. Once he saw her, he couldn't take his eyes off her. It was like the opposite of a car accident—she was too perfect to look away. A mess of unruly brown hair tossing in the breeze, sun-kissed skin glimmering under the streetlights. She smiled nervously in his direction as she chatted with a friend, then turned to really look at him.

His heart switched on.

He had to talk to her.

Luke had never felt so compelled in his life, but the moment he saw that woman, he knew he couldn't let her pass by. She was someone, someone important. He felt it in his bones, his heart, his brain, and, bizarrely, in his teeth. This woman was part of his life. It was like seeing an old friend after years apart, but he was certain they'd never met before.

He closed the distance between them before she could disappear into the crowd and away from him forever. What if she was a tourist? She could walk out of his life as quickly as she'd walked into it.

"Hi, I'm Luke." He wished he had come up with something clever to say to her other than his name, but he hadn't, so that was all he had. He'd try to be charming from now on.

"Hi," she answered slowly. "I'm Verbena."

"Verbena?" he repeated.

"Yup. Like lemon verbena, the herb, candle, soap scent." The girl next to her nudged her. "Oh, this is Danielle." The other girl was grinning ear to ear.

Luke glanced at her for a moment, but his eyes shifted back to Verbena. That name would be seared into his brain for the rest of his life.

"So, Luke," Verbena began, "did you just move here or are you on vacation?" She leaned against a lamp post and tucked her hands behind the small of her back. Her eyes searched beyond him for a minute, then settled back on his face.

Luke couldn't help but do a full sweep of her, head to toe. She was gorgeous. Her legs were long, strong and looked fantastic in her shorts. She was on the thin side. She looked like she might have been a runner of some sort.

"Moved here," he answered, finally. "Few days ago."

"Welcome." She looked over his shoulder. "I think I need to find one of my sisters."

"Can I come with you?" *Shit*, he thought. That was way too forward, but he really didn't want to lose her in the crowd. He needed to talk to her more and figure out where she worked or lived. He didn't have a phone and wasn't planning to have one for a while, but he knew he needed to see her again.

"Oh, hell, I'll see you later," Danielle said to Verbena and stomped away. Verbena tried to smother a smile.

"Sorry. Don't want to lose you yet. If I'm bothering you, I'll go away."

"No! No, you're not bothering me." She smiled and visibly relaxed.

"Actually, you want to go somewhere and talk? There are a lot of gossips around here." She motioned to the crowds. "Not much else to talk about."

"Of course," Luke answered, knowing full well if she asked him to swim back to the mainland with her, he'd do it. Hell, he'd walk to California right now if she was next to him. He could definitely leave Summerfest.

"Favorite color?"

"Gray," Verbena answered.

"Gray?" Luke laughed. "Who on earth calls gray a favorite color?"

"Verbena Bay, that's who," she said defensively. "It's so calming. It's the color of the ocean in winter, the sky in winter. No one is agitated by gray. It's a lovely color."

"I'm guessing you really like winter." Luke shifted a little closer to her. She'd taken him to the park a little bit away from the festival in the street. It was quieter here, so they could really talk. People still walked by occasionally, but overall, they were alone.

She'd thrown caution to the wind and foregone finding an older sister for guidance. Luke was her soulmate, she knew it. She was safe with him. Soulmates protected each other. They would never hurt each other. Hell, she was probably going to be dating him by the end of the night.

"I do like winter. It's the perfect season to stay inside and be cozy. And it's quiet here in the winter. No tourists or summer-home people, no loud drunks crowding the beaches. It's really peaceful. Only the real Celestials are here in January."

"Celestials?"

"Oh." Verbena felt color rise to her cheeks. "That's what we called year-round Star Islanders. I think I've earned the title. We moved here four years ago."

"We?" Luke prompted.

"My sisters and I." She thought for a moment whether to tell him that their parents' untimely death had prompted the move, but she decided against it. "We inherited a cottage from our great-aunt. It's been in our family for a while."

"Cool."

Their conversation settled into silence, but it wasn't awkward. It felt like a comfortable, well-earned silence, the calm that two people enjoy after being together for a long time.

Verbena's mind began to wander, thinking about her future with Luke. She was only seventeen. She still had a year of high school to finish. It wasn't like she could move in with Luke tomorrow. But if she could, well, that would be perfect. No more waiting, wondering what her life was going to be like. Her soulmate was here. She didn't have to trip through the rest of her young-adult years trying to figure out what direction her life would take. Everything was settling into place so early.

She slowed her train of thought. Move in with him? Was she crazy? Lavender would slap her silly if she brought it up. He might be her soulmate, but they were teenagers. And Lavender was her legal guardian.

But still, it was so exciting! She'd never have to date or try things out with guys she knew weren't going to be around for the long haul. She was so lucky, getting to meet Luke this early.

Verbena was about ten the first time her mom sat her down and had the soulmate conversation. It was sort of like having the sex talk. It came in waves. She didn't get all the information that day, but she got a general gist. The rest came in other conversations over several years. Verbena was told not to expect her soulmate to show up until she was in her twenties. There were very few witches who knew their soulmates in childhood.

Yet, here she was, the summer between her junior and senior year of high school, sitting next to her soulmate.

"I feel like I should tell you something," Luke started slowly.

Verbena turned toward him, tucking her fist beneath her chin and resting her elbow against the picnic table.

"I swear this isn't a line." He smiled, his dimples making a quick appearance. "I feel connected to you, like we're going to be really good friends, or something."

"Or something," Verbena echoed. She looked at him now, really looked at him. His hair was dirty blond, a little on the long side with some waves in the front. His eyes were hazel with sparks of gold throughout, gleaming like sunspots. He had a relaxed energy to him, as if he didn't have a care in the world. It was so easy, talking to him, being with him. It wouldn't take much for her to lean in and kiss him. For the first time in her life, she was dying to know what someone's lips tasted like.

Verbena moved her knee until it rested against his. Just that simple meeting of knees, skin against skin, and she could feel her heart race.

"Verbena," he breathed. He slid his hand into hers and leaned closer until there was only an inch between their lips. For a moment, they were completely still—a breath away from touching—until she couldn't take it. She pressed her lips against his and buried her hand in his hair. She gasped against his lips, completely unprepared for the raw need that came from deep within her. Excitement and desire bubbled in her chest, turning to white heat. She threw her arms around his neck and grasped at his back, her fingers tangling in the cotton of his t-shirt.

She had never wanted anything as much as she wanted Luke in this moment. Not only to kiss him, but everything—it didn't make any sense. She was picturing all the emotions life had to offer with a boy she'd met a couple hours ago.

This was a whole new horizon. Verbena had kissed a boy before, but nothing like this. This was power and fate and desire and pure need. Her head felt like she'd taken some of Rosemary's herbs, dizzy and giddy.

Luke pulled away from her mouth and let his lips move to her neck, then her collarbone.

Suddenly, Verbena heard the park gate swing shut. Her eyes snapped open.

"What time is it?" she blurted out.

"I don't know," Luke answered, his voice husky against her skin. "Maybe eleven?"

"Shit!" Verbena untangled herself from him and jumped to her feet. "My sister is going to kill me!"

"What do you mean?" His brow furrowed.

"Lavender, my oldest sister, she's my guardian, and she takes the job very seriously. I was supposed to meet her back at the car at ten-thirty. No later. Damn, she is going to be so mad at me." She leaned back toward him, hoping she could sneak one last kiss before heading to the car to be yelled at, but he ducked out of the way.

"Your guardian?" He pushed her to the side and stood up, then paced back and forth in front of her.

"Yeah," she answered slowly. "What's wrong?" She sat on the bench, leaning against the table.

He stopped his pacing and rubbed his hand over his forehead.

"Verbena, how old are you?"

She felt her stomach sink.

"Seventeen," she answered quietly. There was no point in lying. She couldn't lie to him. He was her soulmate. Even if she did, he'd figure it out sooner or later.

"Seventeen?" he repeated. "Fuck!" He turned away, walking back toward the festival.

"Luke! Wait!" she called after him, clamoring to her feet. She couldn't let him go. He was her soulmate. They were destined to be together. They just needed to talk, to figure it out.

She raced to catch him and tried to thread her fingers through his, but he shook her off as if her touch burned him.

"Luke, stop! Come on, please." She ran to keep up with his long strides.

He stopped walking and turned toward her. "Verbena. I'm twenty-two." He shook his head, then jogged away, leaving her alone in the street.

Luke didn't stop running until he reached the campsite. He couldn't risk her catching up with him. He didn't want to be mean to her but...he couldn't be near her. He skidded to a stop at his makeshift home: a hammock strung between two trees with his backpack stashed in the bushes. He grabbed his bag, then turned on his heels and raced toward the showers.

"Fuck," he hissed, letting cold water rush over him. His clothes, hastily removed in his fury, were in a pile outside the stall.

What the hell was wrong with him? Seventeen. Verbena was seventeen years old. She was a child and he'd been about to...he'd wanted to...*oh God*.

He shook his head and turned the water colder, as if to punish himself.

He wasn't like that. He wasn't a guy who believed that if someone looked older they should be treated as such. Luke may have had to grow up fast when he was younger, but he never had an adult prey on him in that way.

"Damn it!" he shouted, water pouring down his face. He'd never felt anything like that before, like they were about to consume each other. He could have kissed her for hours and hours and hours, simply in awe of being in her arms. He wanted her so badly it felt like a need.

His mind raced. Why did he feel like this? He didn't know her. She was just some girl. Why did everything feel so intense?

A moment of clarity washed over him in the cold water. A vision of her—Verbena. But she was different. And he was there, but different. They were somewhere else, someone else. A loud ocean, a brutally cold wind...

Great. Now he was losing his mind too. What was he going to do?

His teeth started to chatter, and he slowly turned the water to cool instead of cold. He needed to keep himself preoccupied. He would finish showering, wash all his clothes and hang them to dry, organize his stuff. Maybe he'd try to build a fire by hand. Sleep probably wouldn't come, but he only had a few more days until he had a paycheck in his hand. He could try to look at some apartments tomorrow, find something small to rent. One thing was for sure: Luke Karnes would not be seeing Verbena Bay for a long time.

Verbena lay in her bed, curled in on herself, trying to stop her body from shaking.

Twenty-two?! Verbena thought he might be older than her, maybe nineteen, but twenty-two? Five whole years older? They couldn't be together, not legally at least, until the end of November. She rolled onto her back, holding her head in her hands.

"This isn't fair," she moaned. She needed him, needed to be with him. He was her soulmate, after all. They were supposed to be together. Two hundred years ago it would have been no big deal that she was seventeen. Hell, they could have gotten married tonight. He would probably have been considered a little young for her. But now...now...

Her mind began to race. Could she entice him into being with her even if it was illegal? She shook her head hard. He could get arrested. And Lavender would kill her.

Verbena choked back a sob. She felt awful right now, like her insides were twisting on themselves, like she'd swallowed a length of barbed wire. How was she going to live like this? It seemed impossible.

A week passed, and it only got worse. Verbena couldn't eat, sleep, or do anything but think about Luke. She tried to sketch ideas for kitchens, something that always calmed her, but she could only draw a house for her and Luke. She had picked up a knitting project, but as soon as the stitches became rhythmic, Luke clouded her vision.

She felt like she was losing her mind.

"Verbena?" Lavender knocked softly on her door. "Do you want some lunch?"

"No," she answered shortly, pulling her quilt around her. It was the blanket she'd had as a baby and toddler, something her mom had tucked her under again and again.

"You need to eat." Now, Lavender sounded insistent.

"Leave me alone, Lavender."

"No. I won't leave you alone. Unlock your door."

Verbena didn't answer. Maybe if she gave her the silent treatment, she would go away.

"Verbena," Lavender began calmly, "open your door right now or I will kick it down and take it off the hinges. You will have no door on your bedroom, and your only privacy will be when you are using the bathroom."

Verbena scrunched her nose. Lavender wasn't one to make idle threats. Verbena slid off her bed and unlocked the door, then got back in bed.

Lavender pushed open the door, her brows creased in worry.

"What happened?"

"I don't want to talk about it."

"I know you don't, but you have to tell me. Is this normal bad, like you had a fight with a friend or a boy embarrassed you, or is this really bad? Like trauma bad?"

She looked at her oldest sister, her brow creased with worry.

Verbena shook her head. "No one did anything bad to me." That was true. Luke may have run away from her, but he didn't do anything terrible.

"Then what is going on? You don't sulk. You don't get moody. You're the one sister I can always count on to leave the dramatics alone."

"I have a lot on my mind. I need to figure it out."

"Can I help?"

Verbena pulled her quilt up to her chin. "No. I have to figure it out on my own."

"Okay. But you have to eat. Something. I'll make whatever you want."

"Seafood paella," Verbena answered quickly. That would take Lavender a couple hours, and she would definitely have to go to the store. The rest of her sisters would leave her alone. Verbena just bought herself an afternoon in peace.

"All right, fancy-pants. You better have two to three servings."

"I will."

Verbena kept her word and ate heaps of dinner, but around two in the morning, when she was still awake, she snuck up to the attic. She tore down books, looking for some sort of heart-hardening spell. There was no way she could handle pining over Luke for seven months before she could do anything about it.

And what if they slipped up? If the wanting became too much? He could go to jail. She needed to take care of this, as a witch.

Verbena had never done a big spell by herself before. She'd done little ones, brightened up different rooms in the house, arranged the furniture in ways to make the room feel inviting or bring good fortune. She always decorated their front porch depending on the season, but that kind of magic was trivial in comparison to what she was looking for now.

Their personal library was huge and unorganized, and after an hour of looking through books on halomancy, astrology, jumping the hedge, and hexing, she collapsed in the middle of the floor and put her face in her hands.

This was hopeless. Verbena lay down on her side and squeezed her eyes shut as hard as she could.

"I want my mom," she sobbed, letting every feeling of loneliness and despair finally escape. Her crying came violently, wracking her body. She hadn't cried with such fervor since her parents died, but it made sense. This was the first time she'd really *needed* her mom. She would have the answer.

A loud bang across the room gave her a start and she sat up, whipping her head toward the noise. The window on the far side of the attic was fogged up as if the temperature inside had suddenly skyrocketed and the outside was freezing. Verbena walked over to investigate.

Letters appeared, written in the fog, as if someone was scribbling advice.

Call Mable for help.

"Who's Mable?" Verbena whispered.

A book fell off one of the shelves, the pages furiously turning. Then, they abruptly stopped. Verbena hurried to the book.

It was her great-aunt June's address book.

"Mable Silver," Verbena read. Her phone number and address were listed, as well as "Hearth Witch" scribbled beside her entry.

Verbena glanced around the empty attic. The window wasn't foggy anymore. There were no signs of anything.

"Thanks, Aunt June," she whispered.

Chapter One

Verbena stirred before the sun broke the horizon. By four-forty, she was completely awake, popping out of bed to set her eye mask on her bedside table and immediately straightening her blankets until her room looked five-star-hotel-worthy. She started her morning in the exact same way every single day, whether it was a workday, weekend, or holiday. Verbena liked order, she liked to be in control, and there was nothing like a strict morning routine to set a precedent for the day to go exactly as she planned.

She finished piling her decorative pillows on her bed and slipped into yoga clothes. Without an opening meditation, she jumped straight into her Vinyasa practice. A succession of sun salutations, a crow pose, headstand prep, and a quick pigeon pose on both sides, and she was off. Verbena usually skipped savasana if she wasn't in a traditional class. She didn't see much point to lying prostate and seeing what thoughts tried to weasel their way into her brain while actively forcing quiet. Better to move on.

Verbena rolled up her mat and tucked it into the straw basket she had bought for this specific purpose, then walked into the bathroom, where she showered, dried her hair, and did her perfect makeup in under twenty minutes flat. No room for dillydallying in the morning. She put on one of her more relaxed outfits—a simple pair of black pencil pants with a white blouse—and tucked in her shirt. She added a thin necklace and two bracelets, then checked her manicure for chips. Her look was complete, so she exited her bedroom, magic tingling at her fingertips.

A large oak armoire in her living room that looked like it held china was home to all her witchcraft supplies. Verbena's wasn't as extensive a collection as the Bay cottage attic held, but she did just fine. She had candles in every color of the rainbow, her most-used herbs, a few cloudy vials of premade potions, her ceremonial knife, her personal spell book, and a few of her favorite books on house magic that she had snagged from the Bay cottage library. She also had a large broom, but that was kept in the back of the coat closet where it actually fit.

She pulled out two vials filled with potions of her own creation, a circle of lemon balm that slipped around her wrist comfortably, her knife, and a piece of jade. She set everything on her table, grabbed her salt from the kitchen, and then returned.

"In the early time of the Sabbath's eve, a protection spell I begin to weave," she murmured, drawing a circle of salt around the two vials. "Keep us apart so that we may stay content, for hearts unconnected cannot be broken or bent." The liquid in the vials shimmered for a moment before returning to its clear form. Verbena picked up her knife and drew four tick marks in the salt, one in each of the cardinal directions. "Protect him, protect me, as I speak it, it will be."

She set the knife down and brushed the salt into her hand, then tossed it into a glass of water. She grabbed one of the vials, popped the cork, and downed the liquid, grimacing slightly. No matter how many times she drank that murky liquid, it always tasted like charcoal.

Verbena picked up the other vial and put it in her purse, then tidied her workspace. She checked that her hair tools were unplugged, her bedroom lights off, and then left, locking the door behind her.

The streets of Star Island were always empty at six in the morning on Friday. Her sister Lavender was the only business owner currently in her shop, but even the bakery didn't open until seven on Fridays. Still, she kept to the shadows as much as possible on a sunny summer morning. She didn't need the gossips of Star Island chattering about why Verbena Bay, a realtor, was walking around town far too early for a showing.

Verbena turned down the alley, as she did once a week every Friday morning for the past four years. She walked to the backdoor of Luke's bar and pressed her palm against the handle and concentrated.

The lock clicked open.

She ducked in quickly, her head down. In a swift motion, she pulled the vial out of her purse and poured it into the coffee pot, then escaped through the backdoor and locked it behind her with a press of her palm.

A few hours and three showings later, Verbena strolled through town on her way to the title company office. Verbena had a closing in fifteen minutes, an inspection this afternoon, and four showings around dinnertime. It was set to be a busy day.

"Hey, Verbena!" Luke called from the doorway of his bar. "Beautiful day!"

Verbena plastered a smile on her face and waved. "Lovely," she answered. He was radiant in the sunlight, his blond hair catching errant rays, his smile wide and true. He wore a dark blue t-shirt and low-slung jeans, his thumbs tucked into the belt loops.

She didn't stop. She didn't stare. She didn't let the thud of her heart distract her. It would pass, it always did. Though it took longer now. When she was still a teenager, her heart didn't do anything when she saw him, heard his voice. It was as calm as any other time. But now, now it was starting to rebel. Starting to have a mind of its own.

Verbena shook her head slightly. Luke Karnes was her old neighbor and an acquaintance, nothing more.

The potions she prepared made certain of that.

After a particularly vexing week of work, Verbena went home to the Bay cottage. True, she didn't live there anymore, but the cottage would always *feel* like home to her. She had her reasons for moving out, and they were important and healthy reasons for her own mental state, but nevertheless, the small, comfortable apartment she rented in town was just temporary.

This cottage was a generational home, and she didn't have to be a house witch to feel the gravity in that.

As a house witch, Verbena's sense of "home" was much stronger than most, but any regular human would approach that two-hundred-year-old house and know that it was a truly good place. From Rosemary's gardens and Sage's fields to Lavender's cooking and Laurel's tarot cards, the cottage was *home*.

Verbena parked in front, close to the walk but not blocking it, and ambled her way to the front door. The front garden, which had been the setting of an intense battle between Rosemary and Ivan Stoch a week earlier, had recovered and looked completely normal again.

"Hello?" she called as she walked through the front door.

"In the kitchen," Lavender answered. The cottage was quieter now. Laurel had moved into an apartment with Owen, her soulmate, and Rosemary was spending nearly every night with her soulmate, Asher, even if she hadn't officially moved out of the cottage.

The kitchen was an explosive disaster of baking supplies. Lavender had more than a dozen jars littering the countertops and a pot on every burner. There were stripes of salt and dried herbs spilled over from their containers, and about seven spoons of different sizes strategically placed throughout.

"Lavender, what on earth are you doing?" Verbena started putting the tops back on the jars.

"Verbena! Stop! Don't put anything away. I know it goes against every grain of your body to allow a mess, but don't touch anything." She turned back to the pots. "I'm working on a spell."

"What kind of spell?" Verbena closed her eyes and inhaled. "It smells like...regret?"

"That would be the frankincense." Lavender grabbed a handful of salt and added it to a pot, causing a defeated belch. "Damn it." She turned the flame off on that one. "I'm trying to reverse the Fortworth curse. If I can just figure out the right ingredients, I'm sure I can remove the blood curse on our family."

"With boiling?"

"It's my lane." Lavender sighed. "Just like you can protect a home or property, I can whip something up in the kitchen and use it in my craft." Lavender grabbed a dish towel and dried her hands. "Nothing is working so far. I even found graveyard moss. I don't know how to fix this." She shook her head hard. "Don't worry, I'll figure it out."

"For the time being, we've got Morana and Ivan taken care of. Now we just have to wait—"

"For Miloslav—a chaos warlock—to show up? Sure, can't wait." Lavender turned off the rest of the burners. She rubbed the bridge of her nose and leaned against the sink. Her sister looked exhausted. "In the meantime, you can put the jars away. If you want to help."

"Of course."

They tidied up the kitchen space, and then Verbena moved on to the parlor. She couldn't help it. A clean space was a workable space. Too much clutter made the energy in the house off. None of the other sisters felt the same way, so Verbena took it upon herself to keep the Bay cottage in well working order.

"Verbena?"

She looked up from the couch. Lavender was sitting quietly at the dining table, watching her tinker around the parlor.

"Hm?"

"Are you okay?"

"Of course I'm okay." Verbena moved to the bookcase, rearranging picture frames and their non-witchcraft books. The complete works of Colleen McCullough was her favorite collection down here. They'd found the majority of them when they inherited the house and had never stopped adding new titles.

"Your...your energy is very disturbed," Lavender said.

"Disturbed?" Verbena repeated. She turned to Lavender and crossed her arms. "How on earth can you read my energy? You don't do that."

"Laurel mentioned—"

"Laurel? Are you having meetings about me?" Verbena suddenly felt very defensive. Yes, she had moved out, but she was supposed to be included in all family meetings. Were her sisters gossiping about her when she wasn't there?

"No! No," she said firmly. "Laurel came to me privately. She thought it would be best coming from me. I know...well, we both know there can be side effects."

"Did you tell her?"

"Of course not. I would never tell anyone. But," she inhaled, "it's been way too long. You promised you were going to stop all this eight years ago. I know why you didn't then, but, Verbena, the last five years, you've had no excuse. This cannot be healthy, for either of you." Lavender paused. "You don't have to follow fate, but if living here without your potion is terrible, it might be time to leave. I don't want you to leave Star Island, but I do want you to be safe. And maybe...Star Island might not be your home anymore, if you don't feel safe here."

Verbena started to dig her nails into her palms, then stopped. Lavender was right. The only thing keeping the charade going was her fear. She prided herself on being able to face any scary thing that came her way, when in reality she'd been hiding behind her fears for years.

"I'll stop," she mumbled, sinking down to sit on the couch.

"No more? Starting today?"

Verbena nodded. "We haven't been dosed in six days. Next Tuesday, it'll be out of our systems."

"Good." Lavender smiled. "It's better this way. You know I'm not one to push anyone toward their destiny, but you can't keep...medicating both of you like this."

"I know." Verbena took a deep breath. "I should go home."

"You don't need to. You can stay a little longer, even spend the night if you want to. We all...I want you to be happy. And I miss hanging out with you."

Verbena shook her head. "I can't. Especially now that I know I won't have this protection anymore. I can't be this close." She stood up and grabbed her purse. "I'll stop by again in a few days. At night, when I know he isn't home."

"He's home right now?"

"Yeah. And it's a bit...much."

"Go ahead. Text me later, just so I know you are doing okay."

"I'll be fine. But I will." Verbena hurried to the front door. "See you later."

"Bye!" Lavender called after her as she hurried down the front steps.

Verbena got into her car and pulled out of the driveway, the gravel crunching beneath her tires. She needed to get back to her apartment, back to her organized life. Life was going to change, but she could still get a few moments of peace before it did.

She couldn't help but glance in the direction of Luke's house as she passed.

He was standing on the porch, as if waiting for her to drive by so they could lock eyes, if only for a breath.

He raised his hand in greeting, a smile on his face.

Verbena quickly waved, then turned her face to the road and sped away. Her hands started to buzz, exactly like they had when she met him nine years earlier. She banged them on the steering wheel, willing it to stop.

What a mess.

Chapter Two

Luke's alarm blared at nine. Like every morning, he swatted at his phone until it eventually silenced. He wanted to roll deep into the covers, climb within the mattress, and get at least ninety more minutes of sleep, but his dogs, Jaeger and Whiskey, bounded onto the bed, anxious for their morning piss, followed by laps around the yard.

"All right, all right, I'm getting up," Luke said, swinging his feet to the ground.

He opened the back door for them and watched as they clamored out into the yard. It wasn't fenced, but the dogs knew not to wander. There were some woods on the borders, a particularly dense pack of trees between his property and the Bay property, and a small creek on the far edge.

He walked back into the kitchen of his cabin and put the coffee on. He was a religious coffee drinker, being that most mornings he woke up wishing it wasn't quite time to go to work. In the winter the bar was much quieter and he had shorter hours, but during the busy summer months there were tourists wanting a drink at ten in the morning right through midnight. Sometimes they were the same people.

He poured his dogs some breakfast, then made himself a bowl of cereal to go with his black coffee. He liked having this chance to sit and think without a million things bombarding him for attention.

He usually thought about Verbena.

Verbena Bay was the most amazing woman he had ever met. She was beautiful, obviously. She had eyes like a stormy sky, and her hair had been wild and brown, but now it was straight and blonde. He liked it both ways. But it was the way she carried herself that really drew him to her. She was insanely confident, super successful, and always friendly and helpful to every person she met on the street. If Star Island had a face, it was Verbena Bay.

He tried, over the past few years, to initiate something with her. After their rocky start, he'd felt terrible about it for a week or so. Mostly he'd felt like he'd never stop wanting her. But it disappeared. It was almost like his mind had slapped his heart and told him to cool it until she was older.

Well, she was older now. Thirty-one and twenty-six didn't seem too far apart anymore. She wasn't a teen, and he wasn't a brand-new adult sleeping outside. He had a house, owned a small business that stayed firmly in the black, and was ready to take on something serious.

But she wasn't. At least not with him.

The last time Luke had attempted to talk to Verbena, she'd smiled politely and immediately excused herself. For someone who was always the picture of confidence, she was sure anxious around him. The only thing he could think of was that she was still mad about that kiss from nearly a decade ago. He should have handled it better, not bolted and then kept his distance for five years, but he was twenty-two and an idiot.

Luke yelled for the dogs to come back in, finished getting ready for the day while they settled, then headed to work. It looked like rain, which promised either a packed bar or an empty one. Tourists would already be in town and spend the afternoon drinking and staying dry, or the rain would start before they went out, and it would be him and a handful of locals shooting the breeze.

This Thursday morning, Luke would be the only one in until noon, when his two summer waiters would come in to help with the afternoon rush. They were local kids, Cormac and Erin, who had just graduated high school and were looking to earn some money before heading off the island to college in the fall. He had one full-time year-round employee, Derrick, who was cranky, fifty-two, and liked to sit behind the bar and mope until someone forced him to pour them a drink. And lastly was Diana, his short-order cook. She was a summer employee but a year-round resident who had taught high-school literature for the past thirty years and was even better at making comfort food. During the off-season, Luke could manage the menu on his own, but when there were tourists pouring in, he liked having a specific cook.

Luke walked in through the back, switched on the lights and the coffee maker, and set to opening for the day.

That afternoon, Star Island was hit with a gale of a summer storm. Being a spit of land in the Atlantic, it was often rocked by crazy weather, summer, autumn, winter, or spring. By three o'clock, the only people in the bar were Luke, Cormac, Erin, Mrs. Fitzpatrick enjoying her weekly mint julep, and Jake the mailman, who'd decided to duck in out of the rain for a stretch before getting back to work. While the slow periods weren't great for business, Luke didn't mind those quieter days at the bar. From October to April this was what the bar was: a place for locals to have a nice, quiet chat alongside a beverage of their choice and a plate of something delicious. The warm months were like a burst of extra income. Those months helped him move out of the upstairs apartment and put the down payment on his house and, two years earlier, add on a pretty amazing deck.

A blur of bright blue and white rushed to the overhang in front of the bar. Luke squinted through the foggy glass, trying to figure out who it was. He kept a stash of cheap umbrellas behind the bar for occasions like this, so he grabbed one and headed out to bestow it upon some unlucky tourist.

"I thought you could use this," he began.

The soaked blonde whipped her head around, spraying droplets in his direction.

"Luke!" Verbena exclaimed.

"Verbena! Come inside, it's coming down in sheets." He opened the door for her. She hesitated for a moment, her expression like a rabbit going into a fox den for safety, then walked through the door. She had on a blue top and some white jeans, which were slick against her.

He could see every curve of her body.

"Do you want a towel?" he asked. He sneaked past her to take his position behind the bar, his forearm brushing against her bare shoulder. Her skin was damp from the rain, and he couldn't help but want to make her more comfortable.

"Sure, that would be nice." She stayed by the door, standing in an ever-expanding puddle.

"You can sit down," he offered, handing her one of his clean bar towels. Her fingers brushed over his as she took it, and she quickly pulled away, like touching him was something she did not want to do today. She patted down her arms, collecting rivulets of water as they snaked down her skin.

"I don't want to get your seats all wet." Verbena looked behind her out the window. It was like she was keeping her gaze on anything but him.

"Waiting for someone?" he asked.

She shook her head. "On my way home. Thought I could beat the rain."

"Thought wrong," he teased.

She looked at him and pulled a smile, then set to toweling her hair.

"Work busy?" he asked.

"Normal."

Damn it, Luke thought. Why was it that in the presence of Verbena he lost all ability to carry on an interesting conversation? He could talk to anyone. He was a bartender, after all. But this woman, this beautiful, soaking wet woman, made him a tongue-tied mess.

Luke turned back to the bar and busied himself with reorganizing already clean glasses, searching the recesses of his brain for something interesting to say.

He looked up to ask her about her Fourth of July, but before he could say a word, he caught her staring at him. Intensely. She was looking at him like she was trying to memorize the way his hands moved when he cleaned the bar.

"Oh," she mumbled as she noticed him looking up.

"Woo! That's a storm!" Owen Davies exclaimed, jumping into the bar and out of the rain. He stood at the door for a minute, shaking out his shirt.

"You want a towel?" Luke busied himself turning toward the pile to hand one to him.

"Nah, I don't mind the wet. I'll do my best not to drip all over your bar." Owen looked over to Verbena. "Hey! Didn't expect you to be here." His gaze flashed at Luke.

"I was leaving. Just popped in to get a break from the rain." Verbena stood, folded the towel she'd been using, and handed it back to Luke. His knuckles brushed against her fingertips as she gave it to him. She felt cold. Too cold for a July afternoon. She needed to get warm. Something panged in him, like there'd been a thousand times she was too cold and he'd never been able to warm her. What the hell was that?

"Thank you for the towel and the roof. It looks much better now." She smoothed her shirt and turned to the door.

"Are you sure?" He didn't want her back out in the storm. It could be dangerous. Or windy. Or simply wet.

"Verbena, it's almost a hurricane," Owen pointed out. "No harm in staying dry a little longer."

"I'll be fine."

"Some big real estate emergency happening?" Owen teased. "You could sit down and have a meal with me? Locals say it's the best place for a good drink and a hot meal."

She shook her head. "I have to go." She looked at Luke, their glances meeting for a moment, then shot out of the bar and down the street.

Luke shook his head clear, then turned to Owen. "What can I get you?"

"Burger and fries. Thanks, man."

Luke scribbled the order on the ticket, then handed it to Diana. Then he pulled out the half-full ketchup bottles. Nothing like a mindless task to keep him from obsessing about a woman who clearly wanted nothing to do with him.

The rest of the evening went quietly. The worst of the storm had passed, but it still rained lightly. Around eight, Luke sent Cormac and Erin home, figuring if there was some huge rush, he'd be able to handle it. He had, after all, run the bar alone for the first year he owned it. But that was back when the only food on the menu was a bag of potato chips or a bowl of peanuts. Now there were things like a deep fryer in the kitchen.

Diana closed the kitchen, and the two local barflies flew home not long after. Luke was taking his time, wiping down the tables and rearranging the salt and pepper shakers for tomorrow, when a flash of light caught his eye outside.

He glanced up and, at that precise moment, Verbena Bay walked past the bar. She had her umbrella open now. It was one of those clear ones and must have caught a headlight or something.

She paused for a moment in front of the bar, then brought a hand up to her eyes. Was she crying? But just as quickly as she had stopped, she was off again, walking like she had somewhere to be at that exact moment.

Luke could run out there, try to talk to her again, get to a point where he could ask her out... He looked back at the half-finished bar.

Or he could go back to work and refrain from hassling a woman on a dark street after midnight. A woman who was clearly uninterested in him.

"Pull it together," he chided himself. He should go to the mainland next week. Download Tinder again for a day away from home. It would do him some good to try and think about someone other than Verbena.

Chapter Three

Verbena sat in the walled garden, fidgeting. Her potions were finally out of her system, and she was feeling the effects. It wasn't like they were opiates—more like if someone had two cups of coffee with three sugars every morning for nine years and then quit cold turkey. Her body had gotten used to it. Her mind relied on the comfort. She wanted her boost.

It was like her soul was laid bare now, stripped of any protection. It made her want to obsessively rip her hair out so she could feel anything besides vulnerability.

It had been seven and a half days since her last dose.

Verbena always knew when she began the regimen that one day it would end and she would suffer the consequences. Luke would be suffering too by now, but he had no idea why he was suddenly feeling like his chest was sinking in on itself and all his muscles were achy.

She leaned back against the magnolia tree and exhaled. It would be okay. She needed to survive for the next week or so. Then things would get better. At least, in terms of the side effects. She had no idea what her relationship with Luke would look like then. But it was her fault, her mess. She deserved it.

A rustling in the undergrowth perked Verbena's ears. A soft bark accompanied the rustling, and Verbena smiled and slid into a crouch.

"Hood?" she whispered.

Verbena's familiar, a beautiful red fox with a streak of white down her left side, bounded out of the shrubs and into her arms.

"Hood! Where have you been?"

The fox yipped in response and licked her face a few times. Verbena rubbed her neck, finding her familiar's favorite spots to be petted and enjoying the fur beneath her hands.

Hood and Verbena were linked, familiar and witch, but they didn't live together anymore. When Verbena moved into her apartment, she could hardly ask Hood to become a town fox. There were far too many people for her taste, and dangers that came with living in town. More traffic and humans in general could lead to the demise of a fox. Plus, Hood liked running in the woods, coming to the Bay property for a quick "hi" and some love. She valued her freedom, just like Verbena who could never trap her familiar, not when Hood was meant to be wild.

Verbena wrapped her arms around her little fox, pulling her close. "I needed this cuddle," she admitted and pressed a kiss to her brow. Hood rubbed her muzzle against Verbena's neck and snuggled into her arms.

Verbena smiled and let the feeling of comfort wash over her. Sometimes she wished she could keep Hood as a pet, buy her a little dog bed and plop it next to her bed. But it wasn't the way of things. Plus, the Bays were very serious about keeping their witch status secret, and if the island's most popular realtor started keeping a fox in her apartment, it might raise a few eyebrows and warrant a call to animal control.

"Verbena?" Lavender called over to the garden. "Everyone's here so we can start."

Verbena gave Hood a few more rubs, then stood up. "See you soon, Hood. Don't be a stranger." With a quick nod, her lovely fox darted back into the garden, completely camouflaged in seconds.

Back in the house, Rosemary and Asher were on the couch, entwined as usual. Rosemary wasn't shy when it came to showing affection to her soulmate, and it was overly clear that both of their love languages were physical touch. Lavender and Sage were at the table, and Laurel and Owen were bringing drinks from the kitchen.

"Booze or booze-free?" Laurel asked.

"Booze for me!" Rosemary giggled. "And booze-free for the guy who has work tonight." Asher had given notice at the police department that he was leaving, but he'd agreed to stay on until a replacement was found for the officer taking over the role of sheriff.

Laurel passed out drinks, taking a booze-free one for herself.

"No alcohol for Laurel?" Rosemary exclaimed. "What? What? Do we have an announcement?" she nearly shrieked.

"Announcement?" Laurel's brow furrowed. "Oh, good goddess, no. I'm going to jump the hedge tonight, and I need a clear head. My uterus is empty, thank you very much. We live in a tiny one-bedroom apartment."

"I don't think a uterus is ever really empty," Sage cut in. "Isn't there always, like, tissue and blood floating around?"

"Okay!" Lavender interrupted. "Let's come to the table and discuss what we are here to discuss—the Stochs and the curse." Verbena had to admire her oldest sister's sense of organization. "We're not discussing what's in any of our uteruses. Uteri? Uteri. That's it. Moving on. While Morana and Ivan are currently imprisoned and safe-ish with the Guardians, I think it's obvious that their older brother, Miloslav, will probably be paying us a visit soon. I imagine he and Ivan were in constant communication after Morana's disappearance, so we can assume he knows our addresses and most likely all our places of work. Verbena, can you keep up the protection spells around the house and pretty much all of town? I'd like to be on the safe side. No use in being protected at work if we can't pop into the market."

"The market will be tricky, but I can put a magical violence block around it. So, don't willingly go to a secondary location if anyone approaches you in the produce aisle. Call the police to come and get him to leave." She'd already been refreshing the spells on a weekly basis. The house was the easiest to protect—she could speak loudly, brandish her knife, and had no need to hide anything. Town was trickier, but she made do.

"Thanks. Onto the curse. I've been trying with no luck to counteract it," Lavender admitted. "Anyone else?"

"Tonight I'm going to try to unweave it in the Hedge World," Laurel explained. "I've tried six times here, but...I don't know. It's almost like whenever I attempt to break it, it becomes stronger. The curse I put on

Morana felt like it was woven in wool. This feels like steel to me. Maybe it will be different in the Hedge World."

"Are you okay going back there?" Verbena asked. A few months earlier, Morana Stoch had dragged Laurel into the Hedge World and almost killed her there.

Laurel glanced at Owen. "I'll be okay. Owen will watch over me. He knows what to do if something goes wrong. I don't know if I'll ever love going there like I used to, but I can do it." Owen slipped his arm loosely around Laurel's shoulder, and Verbena felt her heart thud.

She had to stay focused. Seeing her sister with her soulmate could not sidetrack her. She took a deep breath.

"I have no idea how to break or cast a curse," Rosemary said.

"Same here," Sage added.

The Bays all looked at Verbena.

"I tried but...I can't even see it. When I try to call the curse to my mind, I get nothing. Only endless darkness," she answered. Verbena felt extremely useless when it came to the awful curse on their line. While she was great at casting protection spells, she had no idea how to undo something laid down to steal all the magic in her line.

"Okay. Keep trying everyone. We're bound to figure out something soon. Hopefully."

"No kidding," Asher said, tightening his grip on Rosemary. "The sooner the Stochs are out of our lives, the better. I don't want Ivan or his siblings anywhere near Rosemary ever again."

"Anything else before we leave?" Lavender asked.

"Yes." Rosemary mocked raising her hand. "I have something to add."

"Go ahead, Rosie."

"I was thinking last night, as I laid in the embrace of my soulmate after a particularly satisfying and very athletic roll between the sheets—"

"Keep it moving, Rosemary," Lavender reminded.

"I was thinking," she continued, "the voice said between the greening and the harvest of the year we'd have basically a lot of shit and a lot of love. It's almost August, and while we've had some shit, it's mostly been attached to Laurel and I, as we've found our soulmates. And we've both had some past life business with a Stoch. Are there Stochs we don't know about? It's just the three of you, Lavender, Verbena, and Sage, are left. Your soulmates aren't sitting around this table, and you haven't had a run-in with a Stoch either. Are we sure there aren't five Stochs? It would make more sense."

Verbena tossed it over in her mind. It would make sense if one of them lined up with each of the Stochs. But maybe they had lucked out. Or maybe they had some secret siblings no one knew about.

"Their parents are dead," Lavender said. "I'll go through the book tonight and see if I can find any distant cousins. I'm pretty sure that they were the only Stochs in the book, but I'll double check."

"So, who's shacking up with their soulmate next?" Rosemary asked. Verbena's eyes flicked to Lavender's, silently telling her to keep her mouth shut.

"Probably me," Sage bemoaned. "Oof. I'm going to have to start shaving my legs more regularly. Or not. Owen, Asher, would you have cared if Laurel and Rosemary had hairy legs when you first met them?"

All five sisters whipped their heads toward the two men in the room.

"I fully expect there to be days when I don't shave my face, so I would never expect Laurel to shave her legs on a consistent basis throughout our relationship," Owen answered quickly.

"Ditto," Asher added, rubbing his beard. "And with that, I've got to get home before I get too tired to study before work." He leaned down and kissed Rosemary like he was going on a walkabout for a year and not just to patrol their small island. "Verbena, would you mind giving Rosemary a lift home?"

"No problem," she said.

"We're going to leave too," Laurel added. "I need to get in my headspace for jumping the hedge. I want to have at least an hour of yoga beforehand to prepare, maybe draw some cards. Give myself a real chance at it."

Everyone said goodbye to Laurel, Owen, and Asher, and the four remaining sisters retired to the screened porch with glasses of iced tea. It was a hot, sticky night, with air so thick Verbena felt like her emotions were pulling out of her body to hang in front of her. She rolled her neck a few times, trying to work out the ache that she knew wasn't muscular.

"Sage, what are you most excited about when it comes to meeting your soulmate?" Rosemary asked. She was clearly a little tipsy and enjoyed goading her sisters into divulging secrets.

"Honestly? An orgasm I don't have to do any work for."

Verbena nearly spit out her iced tea.

"Hell, Sage," Lavender mumbled, staring at her glass of wine. "Don't mince words or anything."

"What? Farming is hard work. I'm looking forward to just laying back and enjoying myself without feeling like I'm going to get carpal tunnel."

"Sage!" Verbena couldn't help but giggle.

"I'm going to order you a vibrator just in case your soulmate doesn't show up until October." Rosemary pulled out her phone as she spoke. "No reason you should cause yourself overuse injuries while you're waiting. And now that I've pretty much moved out, you've got the room to yourself every night." Rosemary giggled.

"Good Goddess," Verbena shook her head. Her sisters were the most motley crew, but, hell, she loved them.

"Verbena, what about you?"

"What about me? I don't have carpal tunnel."

"No, what are you most excited about when it comes to your soulmate?"

"I don't know." Verbena took another big sip of her iced tea.

"Non-stop sex? Mind-blowing orgasms? Someone to snuggle? The deep connection? Knowing you've got your person?"

"Rosemary, do you still have your IUD?" Lavender interrupted.

"Of course. I'm not an idiot."

Verbena shot Lavender a look of thanksgiving, but it was too late.

She had to get out of there.

She could feel his presence. Even if he wasn't home, his scent was in the night, his soul was imprinted on the land just across their property line. It would be easy—so easy—to run through the woods, wait for him to get home. Beg him to...

"I have to go," she blurted out. She stood up, took her glass to the kitchen and rinsed it, then beelined for the door. She needed to get off the Bay property and put some space between herself and Luke's home. His presence was too overwhelming. If she didn't leave soon, there was no telling what she would do.

"Verbena! Wait! You're giving me a ride!" Rosemary clamored after her.

"Hurry up," Verbena called back, not bothering to turn around. She hopped down the front stairs, jumped into her car, and turned it on, tapping her fingers impatiently as she waited for Rosemary to catch up.

"What the hell? I barely got to say goodbye."

"You'll see them tomorrow," Verbena chided, already reversing out of the driveway.

"Verbena," Rosemary started slowly. "Verbena!"

"What?" She feigned ignorance as to why her sister would be shouting at her. It wasn't like she was driving sixty miles an hour down their winding back road. She was going forty-five.

"Slow down! You're going to hit an animal." That did reach Verbena, who immediately slowed to a more appropriate thirty. "What is with you?"

"Nothing, I just need to get home," she lied.

"Bullshit." Rosemary crossed her arms and looked at her. "I have tried to be nice and leave it alone, but it's like you get weirder and weirder the longer you live alone. Do you need to move back home? There's no shame in it."

"Absolutely not. I am fine in my apartment, and I would like to be there right now."

"Is your apartment some sort of magic bubble that protects you from your inner demons, because right now I'm wondering if you are on drugs."

"I'm not on drugs, Rosemary."

"Well, you are acting like you are." Rosemary turned back toward the road but kept her arms crossed. "Are you in trouble?"

"Not in any sort of tangible way."

"See? That is not a normal response! Is a ghost bothering you?"

"Not at the moment."

"Is it something with Luke? I know you don't like to talk about it, but someday—"

"Look," Verbena slowed the car to a stop at an intersection, "I don't want to talk about it. I'll figure it out on my own, but I really don't want to talk about it."

Rosemary nodded once. "Fine. But please don't drive like a maniac, whether or not I'm in the car."

"Deal."

They spent the rest of the car ride in relative silence. Rosemary gave Verbena a quick squeeze before hopping out of the car.

"You'll be okay. Sometimes you need to allow fate to happen. It's the only thing you can't control."

"I know."

"Also, sex is very stress-relieving, so if you aren't sleeping with Luke yet you should probably rub one out yourself tonight."

"Goodbye, Rosemary."

Rosemary winked and squeezed her shoulder. "Good night, Verbena."

Chapter Four

Once four in the morning rolled around, Luke resigned himself to a sleepless night and got up. He'd been flopping around his bed like a fish for the last two hours, but it looked like dreams were going to be out of reach tonight.

His entire body ached, and he couldn't ignore the terrible sinking feeling in his chest. It was like he was waiting for something horrible to happen.

But he had no idea what.

Luke searched every recess of his brain, trying to find something, anything he could be anxious about, but he came up empty-handed. Was he just getting sick? July was a strange time to pick up the flu.

He walked into his living room, a cozy spot with a leather couch and a beat-up recliner he'd gotten second-hand a year after he moved to Star Island. Luke did well now, financially speaking, but he liked to keep some of his favorite things from rougher days to remind him of how he'd managed to climb out of the darkness. In the deepest pit of his personal hell at seventeen, he never would have believed he'd own a house and a business before he turned thirty. He had thought he'd bounce around the country for his entire adulthood and probably land himself in prison at some point.

But he was lucky, and things had worked out. Julio had hired him at the diner without any references. His landlord, Janice, had given him a break on the rent that first month and only charged him half. The people of Star Island had opened their arms and given him a place in their quirky little world, and he hadn't squandered it. Luke knew not to waste chances. They were in short supply.

He unlocked his phone and opened his email, expecting to have some notices of deals from websites he purchased a solitary item from four years ago.

"Oh my God." He had an email from Taylor. He quickly opened it, his heart pounding so hard it sounded like blood was rushing in his ears.

Hey Luke

Hope you're doing okay. I wanted to let you know, Danny came by here a couple days ago. He was in a bad place. I let him crash with me and Jenny for a couple nights, but with the kids and how he was acting, I couldn't let him stay. I looked up your address and gave him some cash to get there. I hope you don't mind. He's a good kid, but he still hasn't been able to find his place.

Hope everything with the bar is good. Chloe is four now and Zac is two. And I didn't tell Danny, but Jenny's pregnant, due in December. One of these days I'll figure out how she keeps getting knocked up, lol.

Can't believe I'm going to have three kids. Going to be a wild ride.

Talk to you soon—

Taylor

Luke chewed on his thumbnail.

It looked like Danny was coming to Star Island. Unless he took the cash and split, but Luke didn't see him doing that. Danny *was* a good kid. He had to be around twenty-four now, not really a kid anymore, but Luke would always see him as a little brother. They'd gotten through the worst part of their lives together, the three of them, and they were bonded for life because of it. If Danny or Taylor ever needed Luke, he would be there. They'd survived together, and they'd always have each other's backs.

Luke threw on his sweatshirt and walked out to the porch, careful not to let the screen door bang shut. He loved his dogs, but for the moment, he wanted to be alone with his thoughts.

He didn't let his mind wander to that time often, but those five years on Boris' chicken farm were hell, no mincing words about it. They'd been worked to the bone, day and night, when they were just kids. Boris was the worst man Luke had ever met, and as the oldest of the group, Luke was inclined to protect the younger kids. He did, and he bore a few terrible scars from it—some physical, but mostly festering wounds on his soul.

Luke and Taylor were lucky. Boris was their sort of uncle, while Danny was his actual son. Though Boris had always bitched that Danny wasn't really his son, that his whore mom had dropped him off even though she'd been sleeping with half the town before she disappeared to California. Luke rubbed his forehead. He would help Danny any way he could. Forever.

He stepped off the porch and into the pitch dark. In half an hour, the sky would start to lighten to purples and pinks before bursting into glorious orange and blue. But for now, he was alone in his dark world.

It was something a kid with his upbringing felt all too often, that singular, oppressive loneliness that never truly disappeared. No matter how many years or miles he stuck between himself and his past, it was always there, lurking and waiting for him in the dark and quiet moments. He wished he could stuff his life full of family, push the darkness out, but it hadn't worked out yet.

Whiskey pushed through the screen door and collapsed on the porch.

"Hey, Whisk," he murmured. "Did I wake you?" She grumbled a few times in response before falling back asleep. Luke climbed back to the porch and settled in the rocking chair beside his sleeping pup.

Danny would have a home—a family—with Luke as long as he wanted. There was a small apartment above the bar that Luke had lived in when he first moved to Star Island, and again when he'd bought the bar. He didn't have much in there anymore, a twin mattress on the floor and an old kitchen table. When he bought his house, he'd gotten a queen-sized bed and never bothered with bringing the twin over. He'd always parked that in the someday file, when he needed a guest room. He made a mental note to bring over some sheets and towels, fill the fridge and get some toiletries. If Danny showed up, he'd have a place to stay, a place of his own.

The sun rose, and rather than wallow around his house any longer, Luke decided to head to town much earlier than he usually did. He could set up the apartment for Danny and get some tedious work done around the bar. His body still felt really achy, so he popped a couple Tylenol and hoped that would do the trick.

The streets were still quiet as Luke walked carrying supplies for Danny. It was faster to get to the apartment from the front door of the bar than the back, so he shifted the pile to reach his keys out of his front pocket.

A gasp behind him had Luke whipping around, his bags falling to the ground.

Verbena.

"Hi," Luke breathed, feeling like a weight on his chest was concurrently released and slamming against his lungs.

"Morning," she answered, her eyes on the concrete.

Luke flailed. He didn't want her to leave. He needed to keep her by him, even if only for a few moments, so they could talk. It was like she was air and he was desperately gasping. He would do anything to reach her.

"Do you want to come in for some breakfast?" he blurted out. He could fire up the grill, and they had some brunchy items on the menu he could make without fucking up too badly. Eggs were hardly rocket science.

"I shouldn't," she brushed past him, her shoulder barely skimming his bicep. He followed her lines, the space she took up beside him. His fingers flexed as he had to stop his hand from running up her arm.

"Wait," he managed. He needed to talk to her. He needed to figure out a way for them to have a conversation that was more than a friendly hello. More than a good morning or good night. He wanted to ask her a million questions, talk to her all day and night. He wanted so much more than this.

She stopped and turned back to him.

"Yeah?" she prompted. Her eyes were wide, her lips slightly parted.

This was it. He had her, and she wasn't running away. There was a question on his mind, one that he played over and over every single time she brushed past or ran away. One he needed answered.

"Are you still mad at me about that night?"

There it was. Luke couldn't pull those words back into his mouth even if he wanted to. It had been trapped in his mind for nine years, and now it was out in the open.

"Excuse me?" Verbena met his gaze now, her eyes wide with shock.

"Are you still mad that I blew you off when you were a minor? It wasn't because I didn't like you. I liked you too much, way too much, and you were just a kid—"

"I was *not* a kid," she retorted. "I was five years younger than you. Same five years that stand between us still."

"Legally, you were a kid," he answered. "And I was twenty-two. Most twenty-two-year-olds are idiots. I didn't know how to handle it better. And then I never said anything, and I'm sorry if I hurt your feelings."

"I don't think we should talk about it," she said quietly. She grasped her hands in front of her waist and twisted her fingers hard. It looked painful. "It was a long time ago."

"I do want to talk about it." Why was he getting upset? Luke took a deep breath. "Sorry. The thing is, I like you, I've liked you. And I would really like to spend more time with you, but whenever I try to talk to you, it's like a wall of ice goes around you and I can't get anything more than a pleasantry you'd give a stranger."

"I'm not cold." She crossed her arms in front of her chest, and her whole demeanor changed. She went from shocked to annoyed with one sentence out of his mouth. But God, even when she was pissed, Verbena looked gorgeous. He wanted to smooth the furrow between her eyebrows with his thumb until she smiled.

Don't do that, he thought.

"You're only cold with me. You keep your distance like you don't want to say anything more than niceties. You are friendlier to every other resident and tourist on this island. Did I piss you off that badly? It was nine years ago. As I said before, I was twenty-two and an idiot."

Verbena's entire face crumbled, her eyes closing slowly. "I can't do this," she breathed and shook her head. "I can't."

"Are you okay?" He stepped to her, cupping her elbow with his hand.

She jumped at his touch.

"I didn't mean to scare you." He pulled his hand away and took a step back. Hell, the last thing he wanted to do was make her feel worse.

"I'm sorry," she whispered, then turned and ran, full-out ran, away from him.

Luke picked up the bags as quickly as he could, unlocked the bar, and slammed himself inside.

"What the hell?" he mumbled.

That had gone absolutely terrible.

Chapter Five

Verbena had never unlocked her building door as easily as she did while Luke watched her from a block away. She rushed up the stairs to her unit, unlocked that door, stumbled over the threshold, and locked the door behind her.

She took a breath. Probably the first breath she had taken in two blocks. Luke.

"Fuck," Verbena exhaled and collapsed onto her couch, burying her face in her hands. She had him, right there, right in front of her. She could have...

She could have taken one damn moment and spoken with him. Hell, he had asked her in for breakfast. He was being so kind to her.

What was wrong with her?

Panic had seized her, and her flight instinct flew to the forefront of her mind. She needed to get away from him. She couldn't control herself when she was near him. She had to escape.

So, she'd been rude and almost burst into tears. Great impression to make on a soulmate.

Verbena grabbed her throw from the back of her couch and wrapped herself up in it. Once she was ensconced in the white plush, her heart rate began to slow. Her fingers danced over the soft fabric, and her mind started to settle.

She needed to calm down. This was normal, she reminded herself. She'd been self-medicating, keeping her feelings for Luke pushed down so deep they couldn't breathe. But now, the floodgates were opening.

She shuffled across the room and grabbed her purse, fishing her phone out, then walked into her meticulously designed bedroom. Her bed was piled with no less than seven pillows, which she very ungracefully flopped onto, still wrapped in her throw like a burrito. She scrolled through her phone and pressed on Mable's name. It was early, but Mable wouldn't mind.

"Everything okay?" Mable answered after one ring.

"In a general sense, yes," Verbena said, pulling her blanket up to her chin. Mable gave good advice. Mable would know what to do.

"In the more specific sense, then? You don't usually call before eight in the morning. Rowan and I are in bed watching *Downton Abbey*."

"I thought you finished that last year."

"We're rewatching. My cat can't help it. She adores Lady Mary's bitchiness. She's a feline in human form."

Verbena hummed a laugh. "I should watch it again. If only for the interior design porn."

"I don't think you called to discuss how much you adore a well-decorated English country house," Mable interjected. "What is really wrong?"

"I stopped the potions."

"Mm. For just yourself or Luke as well?"

"Both of us. With the prophecy thing going on...it didn't seem wise to continue." Verbena let a beat pass. "It's really hard."

"Listen, darling, I've been trying to get you to quit those for years. When I gave you that spell, you were a heartbroken seventeen-year-old who, might I remind you, promised you would only use it for one year so you could finish high school without distraction. It's been nine. You needed to stop."

"I feel absolutely awful. Like I'm getting the flu but also having a panic attack just below the surface for twenty-four hours a day."

"Well, I don't know anyone who has used this for longer than five years, but I don't think panicking is a side effect. The flu symptoms are more likely a form of withdrawal and will clear up within the next week." Verbena heard Mable start walking. "I'll get the spell right now so we can go over likely related side effects, but I think you know why you are feeling panicked. Care to enlighten me?"

Verbena squeezed her eyes shut.

"He's going to hate me. I basically drugged him for nine years. There's no way he'll ever forgive me. He'll be so mad, rightfully so. Why did I have to meet him then? Why couldn't I have met him when we were both old enough?"

"Why couldn't you stop this business the week before you turned eighteen? You made choices too, Verbena. You can't blame fate for all of it. You were angry and wanted to control a situation, and now you have to deal with the consequences."

"I know," Verbena admitted roughly. "It still sucks."

"Indeed, it does suck. Let's see." A large thud let Verbena know Mable had located the spell book. "To block the feelings of soulmates," Mable mumbled. "It says here that some achy feelings are to be expected after long-term usage. It also says that this is not a permanent solution and the author, Ms. Mary Martin of Chesapeake, recommends murdering one's soulmate if the witch cannot abide their company." Mable snorted. "The nineteenth century was a wild time."

"I'm not going to murder Luke, I lo—" She stopped herself, her hand flying over her mouth.

"I won't force you to complete that sentence, but I'm going to give you a few pieces of advice before Rowan and I get back to Lady Mary's sass. First, take a bath with some lavender oil, and when you get out, try to spend at least an hour resting. No tidying, no spells. Read a fiction book that has nothing to do with witches or watch a show you love. Secondly, tell him. Everything. You already feel crappy right now, just rip the Band-Aid off. You think he's going to be mad? Might as well tell him you're a witch, you've drugged him, how many years you've wasted because you were afraid of being with him, the Fortworth curse, your sisters having brushes with death, all of it. Get it over with, that way he can forgive you all at once, and the two of you can move on." Mable exhaled.

"You're right," Verbena answered quietly. "I didn't even ask how you are doing. How are you?" Mable's soulmate and husband of forty-two years had died six months earlier. Verbena had gone to the funeral and stayed a few days to help out. Mable was resilient though, and she seemed to bounce back relatively well.

"I'll be just fine. You're still coming for Yule, though, right?"

"I would not miss it. I'll be there the day before for baking, and the day after for laying on the couch unable to move after eating so much."

"Perfect. Now, you go relax. It's going to work out. I promise."

"Thanks, Mable. I miss you."

"Miss you too, darling."

Verbena did exactly what Mable advised, right down to sitting on her couch with her face full of Regency drama and beautifully decorated ballrooms.

Once the show ended, she popped open her laptop to check her work email. She could get a smidge of work done before she talked to Luke. After all, he was at work. It wasn't like she could bust into his place of employment and turn his world upside down. Not if she wanted him to forgive her in a timely manner.

> *Dear Ms. Bay,*
>
> *You were recommended to me by a colleague. My firm is looking into developing a property on Star Island. We are still starting out, and therefore the prices in the south of the island are too high for us to turn a profit at this time. There is a piece of land for sale on Sirius Point, 53-59 Ring Road, that I would like to build a few houses on. I would pitch them as artists' retreat-like vacation homes, away from the hustle and bustle of Solaris, but still a close enough distance to enjoy dinner out if needed. If zoned, I'd love to also put a building for meetings etc. on the property.*
>
> *I've only seen the singular picture the owner has listed. I am wondering if you could visit, take a few more pictures, and let me know if you think it's suitable for what I have in mind.*
>
> *Thanks,*
>
> *Brian Lennox*

"Nice," Verbena mumbled. She opened up her maps app and typed in the address, then zoomed in. "Oh, that place." She knew it. It was pretty desolate. There were areas of Sirius Point that were quiet, and then there were places that were downright eerie. This piece of land was definitely in the eerie column.

"No harm checking it out," she said. There weren't any official artists' retreats on the island yet, but they definitely had the setting for it. And "desolate" tended to sway "secluded" when it came to people who were trying to focus on creating.

Mr. Lennox
Thank you for reaching out to me. I would love to take a look at the property for you and send pictures along. I'll be in contact with the owner today and will hopefully have pictures for you by tomorrow.
Feel free to contact me with any other questions.
Verbena Bay

Good, a project. Verbena looked up the owner, Madelynn Skado. She wasn't a current Star Island resident, so she shot her an email rather than showing up at her door. The land had been for sale for over twelve years, which was insane in a market like Star Island's had been for the past five. Verbena was losing confidence in this piece of land and guessed it was inhabitable for some reason.

She packed up her things and tried to stay focused on work, but the pit in her stomach was impossible to ignore.

Tonight was the night.

Luke Karnes would finally know that he had a soulmate. And that she was a pretty terrible person who had...done spell work on him without his knowledge, kept them apart years longer than needed, and had some serious magical stuff going on in her life.

Now, her stomach really hurt.

Chapter Six

Luke was irritated. After his morning run-in with Verbena, he'd tried to go home and nap, but he hadn't really slept. Now, he had a full day of work staring him down and got wind that there would be two bachelorette parties coming in around five. It wasn't that Luke didn't like bachelorette parties. He would never bite the hand that fed him. But he didn't want to deal with a group of drunk women tonight. He got in around one and started messing up orders and failing to turn on the charm to customers immediately.

"Derrick, I'll be in my office for an hour or so. Knock if there's a rush," he called, then slunk into the back.

Luke's office was basically a closet he'd converted into a place where he could have space to do the books without spilling alcohol or ketchup on his tax documents. He collapsed into the desk chair and stared at the ceiling. He felt so off, like his body wasn't his own. Sure, he was upset about his run-in with Verbena, but that couldn't be what was causing his physical discomfort.

He checked his email, but there wasn't anything other than a message from the busybody who owned the tiny bookstore, saying she thought everyone needed to wait until October 1st to put up Halloween décor this year. Luke grumbled. He didn't complain that she blared Christmas music on November 1st.

With nothing from Taylor or Danny, Luke started to wonder whether Danny would show up.

In a flash, his brain flooded with memories of the five years of hell on Boris' farm. Danny crying in the corner while Luke tried to get between Boris and Taylor. Those memories came in snatches, always grayish and fuzzy, like a nightmare a few minutes after waking. But Danny's cries—those were always clear.

Luke rubbed his forehead. Sometimes these memories wouldn't stay down, even if he was at work. They rose to the surface like horrid, dank things hidden in water.

Luke checked back in with Derrick and Diana, and it was still quiet, so he decided to go for a walk. He didn't want to spend the rest of the day half-thinking about Boris. If his brain needed to work through it, which it did on occasion, he would get it done in an hour, not steal moments here and there all day long.

When Boris Varga, the worst man Luke ever met, agreed to take on Luke, he had no idea what sort of hell he was in for. Luke's mom had thought she could trust his dad's cousin to watch over her son, give him some manly discipline and influence. It didn't matter that Luke's dad had been dead for ten years and never even had a relationship with his cousin. She'd needed out of motherhood, and this way, she could come and go if she wanted. No pesky government agencies getting involved.

Taylor was already there when he arrived, ten years old but looking like he was seven. He'd been there for a year, living with his uncle and spending most of his days working instead of enjoying his childhood. Danny didn't show up until about six months after Luke got there, at five years old. His mom came late one night, screaming at Boris and saying he was the one who knocked her up and owed her. By morning, she was gone and Danny was sleeping on the couch.

Over the next five years, they all took turns being Boris' least favorite of the day. Taylor was the worst, goading Boris into bad moods, getting him riled up while Luke and Danny tried to keep their heads down.

"Fuck him," Taylor used to say. "Soon we'll all be bigger than him and stronger than him, and he won't be able to push us around anymore. We could kill him with our bare hands, if we wanted to."

"Hey, Luke!" Sandra Convito's voice jolted him out of his funk for a moment.

"Hey there, Sandra." Luke smiled and tried to keep his face neutral. His past was his past, and he liked to keep it there. There wasn't a soul from this life who knew anything about his years with Boris or the year in the group home or even about his mom. It wasn't exactly a cheery conversation to have with new friends, and after years of living here, it felt like a strange thing to bring up. As far as anyone knew, his life began when he stepped onto Star Island.

Luke rubbed his lower back a couple times. He could feel that thick band of puckered white flesh even through his t-shirt. That reminder would never go away. Shittiest night of his life. The day had been hell, he was sixteen and recently learned to drive so he could do deliveries for Boris. He came up with a plan to steal Boris' truck and get the three of them out of Indiana. He figured once they crossed state borders, they could pretend to be brothers, he could get a job, they'd find a place to live.

Didn't happen, obviously. Luke had been an idiot for thinking he could pull something like that off. Even if they'd managed to get off the property, he was sixteen, he didn't know how to take care of the other boys or make enough money to support three people. They were all just kids.

That image of Boris, outlined in the headlights, shotgun raised at him—he shuddered. He was a thirty-one-year-old man now, but that sort of fear didn't go away.

They'd gotten the crap beaten out of them that night, Taylor first. Luke had held it together watching him, but when Boris started beating Danny, little nine-year-old Danny, he'd lost it. He'd attacked Boris, jumped on his back, and was almost immediately slammed to the ground. He hit his head so hard he saw stars for the rest of the night. He could barely move. He definitely couldn't run away, even when he saw the bright red crowbar coming.

A family brushed past him, kids chattering and laughing, and Luke turned his face toward the trees. He needed to get out of his head. He couldn't stay in those memories too long. They brought nothing but pain and horror to the surface.

He turned around and jogged back to work. That was enough reliving the past for one day. He needed distraction.

The day passed, a blur of drinks and customers and chatting with locals while Luke tried to stay in the present. As much as he wanted to push Boris out of every corner of his mind, that man still had a hold on him, even fourteen years after he died. He sagged with relief once the bar was closed and everyone else had left, glad to have some moments of peace as the night ended.

Luke pulled into his driveway and left the car out. He had a garage, but on summer nights when he was really tired, he liked to park right next to the pathway, instead of having to make the walk from his detached garage. Tonight, he couldn't wait to hit the bed and pass out.

"Hey," a voice called softly from the porch.

Luke jumped a mile, then squinted toward the singular porch light he'd left on. "Verbena?"

She stood up from the seat and walked further into the light.

"What are you doing here?" He didn't want to have it out with her tonight. He was too tired to form his thoughts into words, too stuck in the past to do anything but wallow until he passed out.

She sighed and looked down at her feet, as if she was resigning herself to something terrible.

"We need to talk. Can I come in?"

Chapter Seven

Verbena followed Luke into his house and was immediately hit with a rush of warmth from the tips of her fingers and toes, straight to her trunk. She tried to shake it off. She needed to keep her head clear and not let her heart overwhelm her with feelings of home.

But it was like walking into her childhood bedroom, the one in Ohio, with her mother poised to tuck her beneath her quilt and read her a chapter of *The Secret Garden* before she drifted to sleep.

This place was Luke's, but in her soul, she knew it was theirs.

She'd known it the moment he bought it. Made her life hell by moving in, his scent drifting through humid nights to settle against her bedroom window. The feel of him surrounding her four walls, pressing against her skin every waking moment, seeping into her dreams.

Luke stopped and turned toward her, his brow still furrowed.

"Do you want to sit? Or can I get you something to drink?"

"I'll stand," she answered quickly. "But you might want a drink and to sit," she added, forcing a laugh.

"What on earth...are you all right?"

"Fine, just trying to lighten the mood."

"For Christ's sake, Verbena. Yesterday I see you and you basically panicked and couldn't wait to get away from me, and now you're standing in my living room trying to joke? What is going on?" Luke's face was stern, set like stone.

She took a deep breath. It was now or never. She couldn't run away and pretend none of this ever happened. She had to rip the Band-Aid off finally. She'd been taping it back on for too many years.

"I'm a witch," she blurted out, with no introduction or easing into it whatsoever.

"Yeah, I know," Luke said. He sat on his couch and leaned back, folding his arms across his chest.

Verbena felt a cool rush down her chest, like all the heat that had been building was suddenly doused. "You know? How?"

"I live next door to your family. I can hear you and your sisters when you're chanting or whatever at night. You get very loud."

"So, you think I'm a...religious witch," she said slowly.

"Is there another kind?"

"Luke, I'm a real witch. Real magic and all that. I can do stuff that no one else can."

"What can you do?" he asked, looking thoroughly unconvinced.

"Well," she leaned against the leather chair, "most of what I can do is sort of hard to just show. I can't snap my fingers and make fire, if that's what you were hoping for."

He snickered.

"The most impressive stuff I can do is banish ghosts, change the metallic makeup of materials, protect properties, and turn a house into a home."

Luke exhaled and rubbed the back of his head, a firm smirk on his face.

"After the first three, turning a house into a home is definitely less impressive."

"Ever wonder why I'm such a good realtor?" she countered. "That is why." She sighed. "Do I need to prove it to you?"

"I mean, if you want me to suddenly believe you, yeah, I'd appreciate some proof."

Verbena looked around the house, trying to get an idea. She looked back at Luke.

"I'm going to go outside and stand on the porch. Lock your front door."

"Why?" he asked as she exited.

"Just do it."

Verbena waited on the porch, listening for the telltale lock-click to puncture over the din of the crickets. What was taking him so long? He probably thought she was insane. He was probably calling Sage right now to come pick her up. He was probably calling Asher—

It clicked.

Verbena waved her hand over the lock, and in less than a second, it slid open, and she walked through the door.

"What the—" Luke said. "Did you pick the lock?"

"Honestly, no one alive can pick a lock that fast. Your house would never lock me out. I can unlock it whenever I want." For now, she left out that she could do the same at the bar. And anywhere Luke had ever lived, including his old apartment.

"I don't know." He still looked skeptical.

She had a better idea. "Do you have something that is metal but unimportant? Like a penny?"

Luke walked into his kitchen and pulled a jar filled with coins from a darkened corner.

"No penny, but will a nickel do?"

"Yup." He dropped the nickel into her open palm. Verbena shut her eyes tight.

It had been only a couple weeks since she'd managed to turn their water heater and furnace into plastic to keep Ivan Stoch from controlling them. Before that there'd been little things, like visualizing, that worked. A pair of curtains she really wished were dark blue instead of dark green suddenly started looking blue in certain lights. Floors that looked like faux wood in pictures were suddenly hardwood in person. But it wasn't until she and Rosemary were in actual danger that her alchemical powers truly stepped to the forefront.

She concentrated on the coin, the mixture of copper and nickel settling against her skin. She wove herself into the metal, snuck between the alloys, and commanded it to become...

Paper.

"What the hell?" Luke breathed. "How...I don't understand." He shook his head in disbelief. "I always knew there was something about you...the way you..." he drifted off. He looked over her shoulder, his eyes glazing.

Verbena waited. She'd give him a minute to process before throwing another log onto the fire. After all, he'd just learned the world he thought he lived in was merely a shade of the magical one.

"So, you're a witch," he said finally, refocusing on her face. "Any reason you decided on telling me tonight rather than one of the hundreds of other times we've seen each other over the past nine years?"

"Yeah." She licked her lips nervously and set the paper nickel on the end table.

She wanted to stay in this moment with him. He looked so happy, so relieved. She hated that by the end of this conversation it would all be gone.

"I need to confess something to you."

"Other than being a witch?"

"Yes." She took a deep breath. This was it. There was no going back.

Verbena stayed on her feet. For this, she wanted her full height, which was only five feet six inches, but still, standing made her feel less small.

"We are soulmates," she spat the words out, much too fast. "You are my soulmate. We've most likely lived other lives before, and been in love then, but we're destined to be together, be in love, whatever. Unable to fight it. You're my soulmate. Okay?"

Luke stared. He simply stared. He didn't gawk or roll his eyes or make some grand gesture in her direction. He only looked at her.

"It's a witch thing, knowing who your soulmate is," she continued. "Regular humans can have soulmates, but they only feel extremely strong toward the other person. There isn't any innate knowledge."

Luke still didn't speak. His expression didn't change but stayed blank. He didn't move, and for a moment Verbena wondered if he was even breathing at this point.

"Are you going to say anything?" she finally prompted when it felt like too much time had passed.

He looked down at Jaeger, who was nudging his legs, then back up at Verbena. He walked right by her, opened the door, and whistled for the dogs to head into the yard.

He walked back into the kitchen, opened the fridge and pulled out a bottle of vodka, took a swig, then replaced it.

"Is this why I felt like I was on fire after I met you?"

She nodded furiously. Good, he felt it too. She wasn't going to have to convince him of it.

"And why lately I've been trying to ask you out, trying to spend any time with you, even though you keep shooting me down?"

"Yes," she whispered. Maybe that was it. Maybe he would simply believe her, and they could move on. She met his gaze and softened hers.

He raised an eyebrow. "Why didn't it feel like that all the time? Just when we met and then now? A year ago, I didn't think much of you, to be honest. You were the nice realtor next door. Pretty and all, but nothing that made me want to make a fool of myself."

Fuck, Verbena thought.

"I did something to help us." There. That was enough. Right?

"Help us?" Luke repeated. "What do you mean?"

Apparently not.

Verbena twisted her hands together and tried to think of the best way to tell him. Damn, she should have written him a well-edited letter. She should have prepared something when she wasn't staring at her soulmate in a darkened room.

Goddess, she wanted him. All those years of tamping it down, of pushing her feelings into her core and locking them tight, were bubbling forward now. She felt as if all the love and desire and wanting would burst from her.

"Verbena, what did you do?" His voice was low and serious, as if he somehow knew every horrible thing she'd done.

"I did a spell. It made us not feel what we were feeling." Luke looked at her with horror. "I had to! You saw us that first night, there was no way we would have lasted until I turned eighteen. I would have fucked you on the picnic table if you'd asked. Hell, I would have run away, abandoned my family. I would have done anything to be with you. And a place like Star Island? Everyone is in everyone's business. You could have gone to jail!" She spat the words out as fast as she could, hoping that in convincing Luke she could finally convince herself that all her choices were the right ones.

"How did the spell work?" he asked slowly. "Did you curse me or something?"

"It...it was a potion. We both took it."

"Verbena, how the hell did I take a potion without knowing it? Did you erase my memory?"

"No! No. I wouldn't mess with your memories." She took a deep breath. "It was harder at first. That's why you used to see me more. I would sneak it into your drinks whenever I could. But," she hesitated. He was going to be very angry. "After you bought the bar, it was easier. I could just put it in your coffee pot before you got to work."

"Verbena, you've been breaking into my bar and poisoning me? What the hell is wrong with you?" She'd never seen that look of his before. It was hurt, anger, disgust. No trace of any positive emotions toward her.

"It wasn't poison! Just herbs. Herbs that separate and, without my spell, would do nothing to you. If anyone else drank the coffee, nothing would have happened. They were completely harmless. I made sure they wouldn't affect anyone else." She paused for a minute, hating the way he was looking at her, like he'd been completely betrayed. "I had to...I had to. It was to keep us safe. To keep you safe. I would never have forgiven myself if something happened and you were punished. Please, Luke. Please. I was seventeen. You said it yourself. You were an adult and I was a child." She hated her voice like this, so pleading and weak, crumbling under the weight of her choices.

Luke marched into the kitchen, putting distance between the two of them. He looked all around the room, anywhere but at her.

"You turned eighteen eight years ago." He stared right at her. "Eight years. Eight fucking years, Verbena. Why on earth didn't you stop this sooner? I've been walking around like an idiot pining after you, and you knew the whole time?"

Verbena met his eyes now, unflinching. He was hurting, so it made sense that she hurt too. Nothing like dredging up the past to knife her own heart. Nothing hurt like eight years ago. "Do you remember eight years ago?"

Luke searched his memory until his eyebrows relaxed as it dawned on him.

"Jess."

"Jess." Verbena bit her lip to keep her nerve. "I had been so excited for months. We were almost there. I had decided to wait until I graduated high school. I knew it was going to be impossible to concentrate once the potions stopped." She paused. "But then two months before that you suddenly had Jess."

"Fuck." Luke looked at his feet.

Three years. Luke and Jess dated for three years. Verbena may have been protected from the soulmate craze that could take a person over, but it still stung. He was having fun with her. And while he dated Jess, Verbena made a handful of so-so decisions that involved the ferry to the mainland, getting drunk, and usually some very banal sex with a stranger to try to soothe the pain. But somehow every time made it a little bit worse.

"You chose Jess. For three years, you chose Jess. You liked her enough to spend three whole years with her." Verbena shrugged, defeated. "And I was... I was nothing."

"After Jess?" Luke asked. "I haven't been with her for almost five years."

Verbena shook her head. "That's my fault. I...I was mad at you. And really hurt. I didn't want to reward you as soon as you broke up with Jess. Part of me had hoped that even with the potion, you'd be into me. Even if I was twenty-one and you were twenty-six. I wanted you to want me, still."

Luke rubbed his hand across his face. He walked to the back door, opened it, and called the dogs in. They scampered into the house, all happiness and wagging tails, no idea what they just walked into. He kept his gaze away from her, staring at the wall rather than her face.

"I think you should go," Luke said to her. "I want you to go. I need...I need a couple days."

Verbena nodded quickly and hurried to the door, relieved that no matter what came next, she had told him. It was over.

"Hey," he called after her. She froze, one hand on the knob, but turned toward him.

"You were the first bright spot of sun I'd had in years, you know, back then. I wondered why you faded to gray." He exhaled hard. "Even without the spell or poison or potion, I wouldn't have touched you. You meant too much to me."

He turned and walked into the hall, disappearing through one of the doors.

Verbena stood in his living room, alone, the world fading into smudges around her. Whiskey brushed against her leg, then settled into a spot on the floor beside the couch. She looked at the crumpled paper nickel on the end table and burst into tears.

She hadn't even told him about the curse yet.

Chapter Eight

L uke waited in his bedroom until he heard the front door shut and footsteps descend the stairs. He'd heard her gasp a sob, but only one, before she shuffled out of the house and away from him.

Because, right now, that is where he wanted her.

Away from him.

Nine years she'd known they were soulmates.

The witch thing...that was whatever it was, and it would take him some time to get used to the idea, because he really couldn't turn his brain to it at the moment.

Verbena had been drugging him for nine years.

He was angry, pissed off, but above all, so irrefutably hurt.

Luke hadn't seen Verbena's car in his driveway, so she was either walking back to the Bay cottage or all the way back to town. Either way, he was going to give her a minute to get off his property before he let go of the rage bubbling within him.

He sat calmly on the edge of his bed, watching his clock tick upward from one-thirty. Once it hit one-forty-five, he admitted there was a slight chance she was still hanging around, but most likely she was gone.

"What the fuck?" he yelled as loudly as he could. Whiskey and Jaeger both regarded him with shock, but they simply padded into the second bedroom.

He stomped into the kitchen, his hands itching to break something, anything, to quell the storm building inside him.

Because right now he wanted to yell at Verbena. He wanted to tell her every damn thing she'd done wrong, and he wanted her to apologize. He wanted her to beg for his forgiveness, and at this moment, he wanted to withhold it. He wanted her to suffer for this.

But he wouldn't.

Luke didn't yell at people. He didn't yell at anyone. Once he'd been yelled at for five straight years, the idea of raising his voice at another human made his stomach turn.

"What the fuck?" he whispered, then heaved into an angry fit of tears.

The next morning, life looked as gray as it had the night before. Only now, Luke was sleep-deprived and still had to go to work.

He'd spent the night wrapped in his sheets, wrestling with every bit of rage, sadness, and deep hurt, to no avail. Nothing was better this morning. No magical solutions had appeared to him overnight. It all remained complete shit.

He showered and forced down a bowl of cereal, then opened the door so the dogs could run around for a bit before he headed out for the day.

Instead of running straight back, Jaeger and Whiskey beelined to the front of the house, both of them barking up a storm.

"Oh shit," Luke muttered, quickly dashing out after them. There was either an animal or the mail carrier out front, and his dogs were making the intruder's presence known. Luke ran out onto the porch, hoping he might cut the dogs off or at least warn whoever might be encroaching on his property.

"Whoa!" Luke heard and skidded to a stop.

"Hey there, big brother."

"Danny!" Luke called out. He jogged off the porch and threw his arms around his little brother, gripping hard to make sure he was truly there. "How are you?" Luke looked him over. Danny was skin and bones, but then again, he'd always been. Luke wasn't sure if Danny was perpetually underfed or if he was just built that way. He always looked like he needed a good dose of hamburger and fries. But his white-blond hair was recently cut, and his eyes were focused and clear, which was a relief. Luke didn't want to add Danny turning to drugs to his list of worries right now.

"You know, I'm okay. Still trying to find a place to land." He shrugged. "But look at this house! I can't believe you and Taylor both live in big houses."

"Come on in, let's have breakfast." Luke motioned him back toward the open door. "I was just about to make another pot of coffee and some eggs and sausage." Luke usually wasn't one for a huge breakfast, but there was no way he wasn't going to immediately feed Danny. He'd been in rough straits enough times to know that a meal, especially a shared one and not a pity one, was always welcome.

"You're eating breakfast a bit late," Danny commented, following him through the door. "Late night?"

"Almost every night is a late one for me now. Working at the bar, I basically have the hours of a teenager. Well, one who chooses their own hours." Luke walked into the kitchen, trying to keep his mind from what his night had entailed. "Grab a seat."

Danny looked around the room for a minute before sitting at the counter. "You've got a real nice place, Luke. Real nice. Shit, man. This place is like a dream."

"Perks of your thirties," Luke chuckled. "Not quite as wild or fun as the twenties, but you usually can figure out some sort of stable living environment." Luke paused. It was as good a segue as any. "You still living in Indiana?"

"Naw, not for, what is it now, three years? Mostly been on the East Coast. Lived in New York for a bit, then made my way to Philly for a little while. Lately I've been in Providence. Had a girl there for a while, but it didn't work out."

"Could I give you some big brother advice, which you are free to disregard completely?" Luke pulled the sausages and eggs out of the fridge and grabbed a loaf of bread from the cabinet.

"Sure thing."

"Leave the big cities behind. They're too expensive. Small towns, rural areas, they've got more to offer. If you can find a job there, before you know it, you'll have a place of your own and can leave roommates behind."

Danny hummed a laugh. "I do have experience chicken farming."

Luke stopped midway between cracking eggs. He looked up from the food and at Danny.

"It was a joke, Luke. I'd never step foot on another chicken farm as long as I live. I don't even like to eat chicken."

"Should I throw away the eggs? We can have sausages and toast," Luke offered.

"No. Don't waste it. We've got no idea how hard someone worked for those eggs."

Luke nodded. He tended to treat all food with a sort of reverence after his upbringing. The sweat of someone else provided all his meals, and he was thankful.

"You want anything with your eggs? Ketchup? Salsa?"

"I'm simple, just a bit of salt." Danny leaned back in his chair. "So, what's going on with you? A house and two dogs—is there a Mrs. Luke?"

Luke grimaced, then recovered. No need to bring Danny into his troubles. He had enough of his own. "Nope, no wife or girlfriend. Just me and Jaeger and Whiskey."

"You named your dogs after kinds of alcohol?"

"I'm a bartender. I had to. Plus, they remind me of the drinks. Whiskey is a nice even-keeled girl. She listens, likes sitting on the porch and enjoying the sunset, and mixes well with others. Jaeger is like an insane nineteen-year-old who's blasted out of his mind and about to jump off a roof into a half-empty pool."

Danny let out a laugh, and Luke was transported in time. It was just like being back on one of those good nights, when Boris used to go God knows where, and the boys would shoot the breeze while Luke cooked. Those nights made the rest of it all bearable.

Luke handed him a plate of steaming eggs with a couple of sausages. He decided not to ask and put four slices of bread in the toaster oven. Danny would eat it if it was in front of him.

"I should really be asking how you are. I mean it, how are you, really?"

"I'll be fine. I need to figure it out."

"What needs figuring?" Luke asked. He got himself a plate even though he wasn't all that hungry. He could eat again, especially if it made Danny feel more comfortable.

"Job. House. Womanly company that lasts more than a night or two."

"Well, I don't have much advice for the last one, but I can help you with the first two." Luke took a forkful of eggs.

"I'm not moving in with you, Luke."

"Nope, you're not. But I could use some help at the bar, and I've got an empty apartment upstairs."

"I don't want charity."

"It's not charity." Luke sighed. "Danny, as far as I'm concerned, you're my brother. I'm a small business owner, and family hires family. Work for me for a month or two, just while you try to figure out where you want to live. It's my old apartment, first one I had here. Lots of people gave me a break that helped me land on my feet. Let me give you one."

Danny looked down at his plate like he hadn't known it was full. The toaster dinged and before Danny could protest, Luke threw two pieces of toast on his brother's plate and handed him a jar of strawberry jam. If he could wolf down food without even noticing, Danny needed a job. He needed a meal and a place to stay.

"You really need someone?"

"I do. And it's not going to be fun work. I don't need a bartender. I need someone to bus tables and help in the kitchen. My cook, Diana, can also be a bit of a pain. She'll leave you to clean up most of the mess ninety percent of the time. But she makes really good mozzarella sticks, so I have to keep her around."

Danny let a small smile escape.

"The apartment isn't nice, so don't get your hopes up. And if you're still living there in four months, I'll start charging you rent. But for now, try to save. Give yourself a bit of a cushion."

"All right. I guess that'd be okay," Danny relented.

"Good. Finish up, I'll take you over to the bar and get you trained today. And we'll set up the apartment too. It's a little worse for the wear right now, but we'll get it ready."

"Thanks, Luke," Danny said, staring back at his plate before lifting his toast.

"Course."

The day flew by and before Luke knew it, he had Danny in his apartment for the night, complete with sheets and a blanket, towels, a few toiletries, a fridge half-full of groceries, a new phone charger, and a deck of cards. The apartment didn't have a TV, and Danny's phone was a beat-up flip phone from years past, but he insisted he could pass the time with a few rousing games of solitaire. As Luke had been in similar straits before, he knew there wasn't a chance in hell Danny wasn't falling asleep as soon as he fixed himself something to eat and showered.

Luke locked up, and as he drove past Verbena's apartment, he saw her walking up the steps, her head low, her hair hanging in her face.

His stomach lurched, and he couldn't tell whether it was because his anger was so close to the surface it ached, or because he wanted to wrap his arms around her and forget the past.

Either way, he drove home without a second look back.

Chapter Nine

"Deep breaths, inhale and exhale. Find yourself in the fray. Your thoughts are your choice. You are at home within your own body. Let a surge of calm wash over you."

Verbena sat in the middle of a circle of dried lavender with a bowl of chamomile in front of her. She'd searched the Haberdashery for grounding and relaxing rituals and had printed out a script to follow. She had cleared a space in her apartment for this particular ritual, which was not working.

She hissed out a breath and tapped her fingers against the floor.

"Okay, what's next," she muttered, jumping to her feet. She went to her witchcraft armoire, pulled out a bit of dried lemon balm, and brought it to the kitchen. Maybe a nice tea would help?

She put her kettle on, then quickly got out a mug and set it on the counter.

It sure was taking her water a long time to boil.

Perfect, Verbena thought. She could do a couple sun salutations.

She hurried over to her yoga mat and whipped through five before the kettle whistled. In a quick scurry, she was back in the kitchen, steeping her lemon balm and furiously blowing on the hot water.

Her phone buzzed from across the room, and she sprang into action to retrieve it.

"Laurel! Hey, what's up?" she answered, as chipper as possible.

"What the hell is going on up there?" her sister said sharply.

"What do you mean *up there*?"

"I'm standing outside your apartment building on my way to the post office, and I can feel your energy from here." Laurel lowered her voice a few octaves. "Can I come up?"

"Sure! Ring and I'll buzz you."

Verbena tidied the circle of herbs on the ground and set the bowl of chamomile flowers as a centerpiece on her table while she waited for Laurel to appear at her door.

"Hi!" Verbena said, opening the door for her sister, who, in contrast, looked like a rain cloud.

"Don't," Laurel said, pushing past her. She eyed the room, then grabbed a fistful of dried lavender off the end table. "What the hell is going on inside your brain right now?"

"Nothing. Just normal stuff. I was about to start some work, I've done a lot of yoga, just made myself a cup of tea—"

"Save it!" Laurel interrupted. "Your energy is usually, like, a pretty gray. Sometimes it has bits of red along the edges, usually right before you get upset. But you are normally a relatively subdued person when it comes to your energy. Right now, you are like if a rainbow was emo. Does that make sense? You're exploding emotions, and most of them are not the good ones."

"I don't appear to be exploding emotions," Verbena countered.

"Oh, no. You've mastered masking your feelings. I don't know how, but you have. But there's one person you can't mask your feelings from, and it's me. Because I am magic." Laurel flopped onto the couch and patted the seat next to her. "Come here. Talk your big sister about it."

"No."

"Verbena, you'll feel better."

"Laurel, I won't. Rehashing the shitty stuff won't make things better."

"Here's the thing. We've all done shitty stuff, some of it magic-related."

"You haven't." Sure, Laurel had trapped an evil hedge witch in another realm, but that wasn't the same as drugging one's soulmate for years. "Not like me." She paused and narrowed her eyes. "Do you know?"

Laurel shrugged. "I had a vision."

Verbena felt blood rise to her face. "What did the vision show you?"

"This one? This one showed you putting a potion in Luke's coffee. And I saw you do it a dozen times, so I'm guessing it's been going on a while." She smirked. "Other visions...let's see. The two of you happy. A random one of you sitting on his porch."

"You don't understand. He'll never forgive me. You haven't done anything like this."

"Me, Laurel Bay? Not really. But me, my soul? I did curse Morana to years upon years of unhappiness. That was shitty. Even though she accused me of witchcraft and pretty much orchestrated my death in that life...I'm getting sidetracked. Was it a bad idea to drug Luke for years to keep the two of you apart? Probably. Did teenage Verbena have good intentions? Definitely. But, you made a mistake by letting it go on too long. It's fine. Luke will get over it."

"You didn't see him. He was so betrayed."

"Eh. I hate to be stereotypical, but he's going to start...needing you. Forgiveness will come then."

"I don't think I can rely on my wiles to get him to forgive me for casting spells on him for a decade."

"You'd be surprised. You've only been off the herbs yourself for what, ten days? Get ready to get hit with a ton of sexual frustration. Ask Rosemary if you have questions." Laurel stood up. "Good luck, Verbena. Also, go home if you want. This apartment is nice and all, but we've got more books, more space, and a lot more support."

"You don't even live there anymore."

"True. But I did when I met Owen, and it helped. And with that, I'm off." Laurel walked to the front door. "You're not a bad person, you're just a witch. Luke will see that. Give him time."

Verbena waited until the door shut before closing her eyes and putting both hands on her heart.

"I can do this. I can wait," she whispered. She only half believed it at the moment, but that was better than nothing.

Instead of talking about Luke with any of her sisters or calling Mable, Verbena decided to completely rearrange every room in her apartment. She flipped her dining space and living space in her open-concept kitchen-dining-living room and rolled up her rug and stashed it in the front hall closet, figuring hardwood floors might be the way to go for a while.

Then she switched the wall her bed was on, flipped her unmatched bedside tables, and moved her bedside lamp to her desk and ordered a new lamp for her bedroom.

She was at the point of contemplating painting the entire apartment a myriad of colors other than her uniform gray when thankfully her phone buzzed and shook her out of her mind.

"Phew," Verbena exclaimed, looking around her apartment. That could have gotten out of control. She had a new email, so she opened her laptop and checked on a few work-related items. She didn't have a response from Madelynn Skado, who owned the piece of land on Sirius, which was a little concerning. That land was appearing more and more unavailable as the days ticked on.

She put a reminder in her phone to contact Brian Lennox about possible other locations in two days. If Ms. Skado didn't reach out before then, she would consider it a lost cause.

"Good, this is good. I'm fine," Verbena insisted.

The image of Luke's back walking away from her flashed in her mind, and she felt her mood deflate.

"No," she announced to no one in particular. Verbena set her laptop aside and strode into the bathroom.

She was tired of waiting. She was going to see Luke, and she was going to look hot as hell when she did.

Verbena's phone buzzed as she was laying out dresses to wear. She needed to look hot enough to entice Luke to talk to her, but also keep her classic style. It was a quirk, but in the summer she only liked to wear red, white, and blue. She never knew when a potential client would see her, and she needed to be on and, basically, the symbol of a New England summer.

"Sage?" she answered.

"Hey, yeah."

Sage never called her. Their interactions were usually left for family meetings.

"Are you okay?" Verbena prompted.

"I'm fine. I want to know what the hell is going on with you. Lavender and Laurel were all whispery about you this morning, and when I walked in they said it wasn't their place to tell, so what the hell happened? Are you dying?"

"I am not dying." Verbena sighed. "I gave Luke a potion for nine years without him knowing, and he's mad about it."

Sage was silent for a moment. "Our neighbor? Why?"

"So we wouldn't be attracted to each other."

"What?" Verbena could almost taste Sage's confusion over the phone. "Oh shit. Is he your soulmate?"

"Yes."

"What the hell? I walk his dogs, for crying out loud. Why didn't anyone tell me? Don't answer that." Sage huffed. "Well. Whatever. Good luck. I don't necessarily want to hear any more about any of this." Sage hung up, and Verbena tossed her phone next to her clothing options.

Thirty minutes later, Verbena's hair was freshly straightened, her make-up perfect, her white dress snug and cut low. She slipped on a pair of black heels, readjusted her boobs, and smiled.

She was ready.

She sauntered down the street, her realtor smile plastered on her face, swinging her purse and waving to everyone she knew. She pulled her confidence out and put it on display.

Verbena pushed open the door to The Muse. It was a bit crowded but not jammed. There weren't any big parties, but the tables were full and only a few seats at the bar didn't have occupants.

She slid onto a bar stool and set her purse in front of her. It wasn't ideal, what with the loud chatter making it almost impossible to talk without halfway shouting, but it would do. Last time, she'd showed up at his house unannounced. This time, they would be in a public place. It would keep the tone pleasant and probably stop her from crying.

Luke caught her eye as he scribbled someone else's order, and Verbena flashed him a smile.

In an instant, Luke excused himself from the customer, walked the length of the bar, and stood in front of her.

"No," he said before she had a chance to speak.

Verbena felt the color drain from her cheeks. "What do you mean?"

"No. Not here. Get out of my bar. I'll tell you when I'm ready."

"Luke, come on. Can I at least have a drink? Riesling?"

Luke shook his head.

"That fancy Fourth of July martini?"

"Nope," he answered. His jaw worked a little in his grimace, which she took as a good sign.

"What if I ordered the most expensive thing on your menu?" she retorted.

"You want a party platter of wings for one hundred people? Sure, I can tell Diane to get started on it. It'll be about a four-hour wait though. We usually ask people give us a few days' notice on orders like that." He paused and picked up a stray napkin from farther down the bar. "Get out of here, Verbena."

Verbena started to refute him, tell him that he wasn't in charge of her or where she went, but he was gone before she could open her mouth, swallowed up by customers.

Verbena felt like the entire bar was staring at her, thrown out by the owner. She grabbed her purse and fled, trying to leave as quickly as possible. She burst onto the street, the din of the bar quieting behind her as she got farther and farther away.

So much for Laurel's advice that he would need her. As far as she could tell, Luke Karnes wanted nothing to do with her.

Chapter Ten

"**Y**ou okay, boss?" Danny asked, peering at Luke as he helped rearrange the tables.

"Please, never call me boss again."

"You got it, sir."

"Danny," he warned. After Verbena showing up during the lunch rush, Luke was in a foul mood.

"All right, I'm just shooting the shit with you," Danny chuckled. "But you've been wiping that same spot for a few minutes."

"Oh. Thanks." Luke stopped rubbing a hole in the counter and walked behind the bar, doing a quick check of their most popular bottles. It was boiling today, at least by Star Island standards, so beer would be the drink of choice once the evening crowd picked up, but there were always a few who still wanted mixed drinks.

Luke looked up to tell Danny he could head back to the kitchen and start on some prep for dinner, but he stopped before he could say anything. Danny was completely rigid, fingertips on the table beside him, his eyes focused on the wall.

Luke looked past him, expecting to see a spider or something, but there was nothing. Not even a spot on the wood paneling.

"Danny?" he said slowly.

Danny shook his head hard, then looked over at Luke. "Yeah?"

"Are you all right?"

"I'm fine. What next?"

Luke furrowed his brow but didn't push it. "You can head back and start prepping for the salads. Grate the carrots, chop the celery and romaine, and start hard-boiling the eggs."

"Got it."

Danny disappeared into the kitchen, whistling as he went.

Luke had noticed a lot of things about Danny over the years. He was prone to running away from problems, had a hard time forming relationships, and would cower in the presence of loud noises. But Luke had never seen Danny check out like that before. Maybe that's what had concerned Taylor.

Was it a seizure? It was pretty fast, and he had returned to normal almost immediately. Luke had never seen anything like that in his life.

Luke added keeping an eye on Danny to his list of problems at the forefront of his brain, right next to avoiding Verbena Bay for the next two days. He needed to get his mind sorted before he talked to her.

"Hey, Luke? I can't find the eggs," Danny called from the kitchen.

"Be right there," Luke answered and disappeared into the back.

Danny appeared fine the rest of the day. Luke told him he was off at eight, and let him know the diner was open until ten and the beach officially closed at nine. Danny surprised him by heading straight upstairs, grilled cheese and fries in hand. After putting "a woman who sticks around longer than a couple nights" on his list of wants, Luke thought Danny might attempt to meet someone. But food and sleep trumped all.

Still, his earlier behavior niggled in the back of Luke's mind. The last thing Danny probably wanted was his big brother insisting he see a doctor when money was nonexistent. Maybe he'd offer to take Danny in a week or so, sooner if he noticed it again.

Luke dealt with a handsy bachelorette party for most of the night, a group of women in their late thirties and early forties, which was not the usual demo. They were loud, half wearing wedding rings, all looking to have a bit of fun with a bartender, and he was not in the mood. He was mad at Verbena and worried about Danny. Pretending to flirt with women slipping wedding rings into their pockets was more than work, it was unbearable. Thankfully, around midnight the bride-to-be announced she needed to go home and go to bed, and they all followed her out like a line of ducks.

Around one in the morning, Luke flipped the sign on the door to closed and turned toward the bar to do a bit of clean up. They'd been quiet the last hour, so he was nearly ready to go home.

He heard a knock on the window and could have ignored it, but he decided to let the person know he'd already closed the register for the evening.

"Sorry, we're—" He stopped abruptly when he noticed Owen Davies was standing outside. Luke unlocked the door.

"Care to talk?" Owen asked, his head cocked to the side.

"Come in," Luke said quickly, then relocked the door.

"So, Verbena told you she's a witch. And you're her soulmate," Owen began. He pulled out a stool at the bar and turned toward Luke. "Any questions?"

"Yeah, one. Did Laurel drug you for a decade?"

Owen winced. "That was shitty of her. Believe me, I'm not here to defend that, in any way."

"So, I take it Laurel didn't do any spells on you or anything like that?"

"Not that I know of, but Laurel and I haven't known each other that long. There've been some spells I've participated in, but she hasn't done any behind my back. Rosemary, on the other hand, she did a spell on Asher, before they were really together."

"What kind of spell?"

"Um, well, it was a sex spell, and I think I'll just leave it at that."

Luke chuckled. "I think I would have preferred a sex spell. I would have gotten a fun hour or so out of that. Instead I have nine years' of what the fuck." He collapsed onto a stool beside Owen. "I'm so mad at her."

"You should be. If it makes you feel better, she's a mess."

"Good. It doesn't make me feel better, but it seems fair."

"You know," Owen said, "you can't really fight the whole soulmate thing. You can be mad as hell at her for as long as you want, but you, like your heart and soul, won't let you ignore her forever. Walking away from a soulmate is nearly impossible."

"I don't know if I want to forgive her."

"That's something you're going to have to wrestle with on your own."

"What's it like being with a witch?" Luke asked, genuinely curious.

"Ah, not as weird for me as you might think. I'm a sonofawitch."

"What?" Luke was starting to wonder if there was a lot about this world he'd been living in that he didn't understand. "Are you a wizard?"

"No," Owen shook his head laughing. "I don't have any true power. Nothing useful at least. And men in our line are referred to as warlocks if they do have powers, not wizards."

"What are wizards?"

"I don't know if wizards are real. They might be, I don't discount anything, but I've never met one."

"So, there's no like school you all go to?"

"Nope. Regular old school. It's hereditary too. Witches and warlocks don't just pop out of nowhere."

Luke exhaled. It was a lot to take in. The woman he'd been interested in for a long time was a witch, his new friend had a witch mom, and no matter how mad he was at Verbena, he wasn't going to be able to be free of her. Ever.

"Fuck."

"Fuck, indeed." Owen clapped him on the shoulder. "It'll be okay. Fate and the gods and all that, they do fuck with us, but there's a lot of good to make up for it. I can't imagine my life without Laurel, and I met her in May. It's crazy, really. To go from strangers to forever in a flash." He paused. "I'm sorry you met Verbena when she was a minor. That must have sucked."

Luke shook his head. "It was only bad for me for a couple days. And I stayed away from her."

Owen nodded slowly. "The spell was good for one thing, then. Good luck, buddy. It's bound to be a shitty next couple of days or weeks, depending on how long you and Verbena stay apart."

"Thanks," Luke grumbled.

"I'll see you tomorrow. It's my night to cook, so I'll be grabbing takeout."

Luke stayed at the bar for a long time after Owen left, letting the silence of his loneliness settle around him. No matter what he did, Verbena kept pushing into his thoughts. And not all bad stuff. Moments from years ago when they'd had friendly conversations. The sound of her laughing with her sisters sitting at the bar.

He still wasn't ready to talk to her, but he was already tired of being mad.

Chapter Eleven

"Is there anything specific we need to talk about?" Verbena asked as she grabbed a chair at the table. Sage was still in the shower and Rosemary wasn't there yet, but Laurel and Lavender were waiting for her.

"I don't have any news," Laurel answered.

"Me neither," Lavender added.

"Then why are we meeting? Does Rosemary or Sage have some big revelation? Or should I say, does Rosemary? I can't imagine Sage has been spending her free time researching."

"It's just a meeting, a chance for us all to get together." Laurel stood up and walked into the kitchen. "I'll make a pot of tea, get out the fancy teacups."

Verbena narrowed her eyes at Lavender. "Did you do this? Is this just some excuse to get me cornered so everyone can force me to talk about...him?"

"Luke? Your soulmate and our neighbor? No. This is an attempt to lend support to a sister who is currently floundering."

"I am not floundering!"

"Laurel said she can feel your energy from blocks away, Verbena. It's okay to ask for help."

"You never do," she shot back.

"Well, do as I say, not as I do." Lavender sighed. "What are you afraid of? That we won't help you?"

Verbena tossed it over in her mind. What was she afraid of? A million things, of course, but she'd never let the world see that. Verbena thrived on well-orchestrated situations. She liked to know exactly how things would land *before* she threw them. It was orderly.

But it wasn't just that. When she thought of Luke, her thoughts went red and scary. She chewed on the inside of her lip, searching her brain for the most terrifying thing she could think of.

"What if he never forgives me?" she spat out. She tried to keep her eyes away from meeting Lavender's. Suddenly, the lamp on the table needed her full attention. It was covered in dust. How did they live like that?

"Verbena," Lavender said softly, setting her hand on her forearm. They weren't a big physical touch family. It just wasn't their love language as sisters. They showed their affection with kind words and undying support for one another. "Even if he never forgives you, you'll survive."

"Without my soulmate?"

"Many before you have. It's doable."

"That sounds miserable." Verbena rubbed her hands over her face then let her head rest on the table. "What am I going to do?"

"You," Laurel's voice joined them, "are going to have a cup of Happy-Go-Lucky and relax."

"That will make me too high to drive home," Verbena pointed out.

"I'll drive you home, and Owen can pick me up from your place. Do you have any extremely pressing realtor things to do tonight?"

"Not really," Verbena answered. She could always check out the property tomorrow morning. It would probably be better to see it during the day. She didn't want to traipse around private property in the failing light. A nosy neighbor could call the police, and then she'd have to apologize to Asher for making him drive all the way to Sirius Point.

"Then, huzzah! You and Lavender are getting reeee-laxed!" Laurel cheered.

"Lavender is joining me?"

"I could use a night of unwinding. Sage also mentioned she was interested in a dreamless sleep, so she'll join us too."

"Looks like we're getting a little wild tonight. And by wild, I mean I might fall asleep on the couch." Verbena laughed.

Two hours later, Rosemary was heading out the door to work on her wedding flowers, Laurel was making a pizza, and Verbena, Lavender, and Sage were lying on the floor of the parlor, each covered in a quilt.

"What if, what if, what if, what if...hear me out." Sage paused and swallowed as if she had a hairball in her throat. "What if our soulmates don't come? It was all just a ruse! A ruse by the powers in the sky to mess with our heads? What if five years from now, Lavender and I are still sitting here, waiting around for some guy on a bright green tractor to roll down the street. And he never comes." Sage giggled and rolled onto her stomach, reaching for her glass of wine. "That would be fucking hilarious."

Verbena scrunched up her entire face. "You picture your soulmate riding a tractor down our street to meet you? How did he get the tractor on the ferry? I'm pretty sure you're not allowed to bring heavy machinery on there. They just started allowing bicycles in 2008."

"He would figure it out. And then, he'll gift me the tractor and actually be really good at, I don't know, cooking and sex? Those sound like good traits in a life partner."

"That sounds more realistic," Lavender said. "A lot of people are good at cooking and sex. Not a lot of people can figure out how to get a John Deere to Star Island."

"How did you picture your soulmate coming, Verbena?" Sage asked dreamily.

"I never really pictured it before I met him. But I wouldn't have guessed a street festival and then things being shitty for nine years." Something about saying it out loud, and the effects of Happy-Go-Lucky, made Verbena dissolve into giggles.

"What?" Lavender asked, joining in the laughter.

"Ah, it's just so fucked up. I'm so fucked up. Seriously, what is wrong with me?"

"There's a reason Mom and Dad didn't stop at number four. They needed one last chance to get it perfect." Sage put her hands behind her head and smiled smugly at the ceiling.

"Yes," Lavender interrupted, "Mom and Dad were waiting for a socially awkward farmer with very little interest in actual magic to fulfill their dreams."

"Hey! I'm not socially awkward. I don't like people. It's a different thing." Sage playfully swatted her oldest sister.

"Pizza is ready!" Laurel called from the kitchen. "And I'm going to request that everyone eat while seated."

Sage rolled off her blankets and basically bear-crawled into the dining room.

"You didn't answer," Verbena said off-handedly to Lavender.

"Didn't answer what?"

"How you think your soulmate will arrive? On a horse? On a tractor? With a brand-new kitchen mixer?"

Lavender rolled her eyes and smiled. "None of those things. He was sitting on a bench in the quad." She popped to her feet and walked into the dining room.

"Was?" Verbena repeated, tripping over her feet to catch up with her. "Wait, was? Did you already meet him in this life?"

"Pizza!" Lavender exclaimed, grabbing a slice and taking a huge bite.

"Wait, Lavender." Verbena caught up. She eyed the pizza. It looked amazing. What had she been talking about with Lavender? Soulmates? Past lives? Were they talking about Luke? Her mind was too fuzzy to hold onto anything for more than a moment.

Eh, it could wait until tomorrow. She would bring it up if she remembered. For now, Verbena was going to destroy one third of a pizza.

After too many slices of pizza, and laughing so hard she nearly peed her pants, Verbena found herself outside wandering. The house was getting louder and louder, and her head was starting to twinge. Plus, it had been years since she'd had a good ol' wander on the property. The sky was clear, the stars twinkling down on her.

"Hood?" she called, hoping her familiar was around. But after five minutes of calling her and no answer, Verbena conceded that her foxy friend was not nearby.

"Okay, I'll see you later, I guess," she called out into the sky, giggling a bit. The Happy-Go-Lucky was still swimming around in her brain, and it made her positively shine. It was like all the mess of her life didn't exist for a few minutes.

She stumbled along, ducking between trees until she was in the more densely wooded area. For a witch, Verbena wasn't really into forests. They were fine, trees were lovely, but she didn't feel super connected to them. She liked houses, homes, places where people found their little corners of the world. Nature was beautiful and wild, but Verbena had always been a little too organized for any of that.

"Who's there?" a sharp voice called out into the darkness, echoing through the trees.

Shit. Had she upset some sort of forest deity with her internal ramblings?

"Verbena Bay of the Bay line," she slurred. "House witch and amateur alchemist." She hiccupped. Hopefully, that was enough to appease the spirit.

"Verbena? What the fuck?"

Wait. She knew that voice. It was Luke! Oh, Luke! She liked Luke. She *loved* Luke. With his handsome face and blond hair and the way his shirts pulled on his forearms.

She sighed.

"Why are you in my yard?"

"I'm not in your yard. I'm in my yard," she answered, holding onto the tree next to her. Where was he? She could hear him, but her eyes could only see stars.

"Jesus, Verbena, I'm literally on my porch looking at you. Stop looking at the sky. Are you drunk?"

"Nope," she answered honestly, then smacked her lips a few times.

"Go home, Verbena."

"I will. But I needed to tell you that I like your shoulders."

A few beats of silence passed while she returned her gaze to the sky. She was pretty sure Luke was laughing now. Not loudly, but like he was trying to hold it in.

"Good night, Verbena," he finally said, a touch of scolding in his voice.

"Night, night Luke!" She turned around, her eyes still on the sky, and wandered back to find Laurel and a ride home.

Chapter Twelve

Thankfully, Luke didn't feel sick anymore. He had no body aches, no lightheadedness, no feeling like he was about to come down with something. His potion-withdrawal-July-flu was over.

On the other hand, unless he was really thinking about something decidedly un-sexy, he had a pretty much constant hard-on.

He tried all the usual things. He hadn't jerked off this much since he'd moved to Star Island and had his own room for the first time in his life.

But it wasn't helping. Sure, it was helping for an hour or two, but next thing he knew he was behind the bar, his mind would drift, and his friend was back. And at work, he couldn't just excuse himself for a few minutes. He had to think about those decidedly un-sexy things and hope it helped.

He was lucky he could wear an apron at his job without getting too many looks. An extra layer of clothing was really helpful during times like these.

The worst of it all was that he was still really pissed at Verbena. He was bone-deep mad at her, and in no mood to try to do any sort of wooing or flirting with her that might lead to them hooking up and, hopefully, a slight reprieve in his constant state of arousal. Sadly, while his brain and heart and soul were very firmly against even speaking to her at this point, his body had yet to jump on board. His body felt very weird, territorial, and primed to do downright insane things that included, but were not limited to, going to her apartment and tearing off her clothes, finding her on the street and throwing her over his shoulder to carry her to the woods where he could bang her against a tree, and having sex with her in his office.

Luke took a deep breath.

He had four tables that needed drinks, and Erin had called in sick. He had a sneaking suspicion that her friends picking her up from work at midnight the night before had to do with her suddenly being sick, but thankfully, Danny was here, so Luke didn't have to bus tables as well. He was planning to train Danny as a waiter in the next week.

Focusing on Danny was helping. Luke forced his mind to concentrate on other random stuff he could get for the apartment. There was WiFi in the bar that reached up there, and he had an iPad that he never used. He would drop it off for Danny, with his Netflix password, tomorrow. His brother couldn't still be content to just sleep, shower, eat, and play solitaire all night long.

"Luke."

He glanced up from setting a collection of drinks on a tray. "Hey, Sheriff Evans."

"Only for a few more days."

"Asher, then." Luke picked up the tray. "I'll be right back, need to deliver these. Grab a stool if you're staying."

Asher nodded and took a seat at the bar. Luke made his way around the room, dropping drinks at three different tables, taking quick appetizer orders, and handing the ticket off to Diana before heading back to get Asher's order.

"What can I get you?"

"A beer. Something dark and heavy. And if you have a free moment..." he began.

"I'm swamped. If you've been sent as an emissary from the Bay family, Owen was here before, and now is not the time. One of my waitstaff didn't show up today, so I'm bartender, waiter, and boss at the moment. Also, I'm not feeling terribly forgiving at the moment, if I'm completely honest."

"All right. I'll just take the beer then." Asher settled into his seat.

Luke got him his drink and then walked to check on his tables. Verbena

could send every single one of her sisters and their boyfriends into the bar.
He wasn't budging.

"Are most days like that?" Danny asked, wiping down the tabletops.

"Like what?"

"People just flooding in, table after table, a line outside? You've got a real
popular bar."

"Thanks, but it's only like this June through August. If you're still here
in January, we can go a week with only three customers."

"So, you're a summer bar?"

"I guess. I stay open year-round for the locals, and for something to do.
Most of my staff are seasonal. But I make the majority of my sales in the
summer. Very occasionally, you'll get a bachelor or bachelorette party in the
spring or fall, and then I'll get a little boost in visits."

"Is The Muse the only thing to do around here at night?" Danny asked
as he carried his busing bin back to the kitchen.

"What do you mean?"

"Like, is there anywhere else to meet people? My age?"

"Oh, suddenly I'm an old man?" Luke teased. Danny started to protest,
but Luke raised his hand. "Don't worry, I get it. There aren't many places
still open this late, but the campsites have a lot of kids in their twenties
usually. You could head over there, see if anyone has a fire going, meet some
people."

"Really? Can I walk?"

"Yeah, it's only about ten minutes. I'll draw you a map." Luke found
after years of living on Star Island that a well-drawn map on a napkin did a
lot more than a paragraph of directions.

By one in the morning, Luke was alone in the bar. Danny had
disappeared, hoping to find someone his own age (and Luke truly hoped he
wasn't looking for drugs, and if he was, that he wouldn't find them) and
there wasn't much left to do.

He switched off the already dimmed lights and started to head to the
back door when a loud rap on the door gave him pause. Had Danny
forgotten his keys?

Luke turned back to the front door and looked through the window. Verbena.

"Fuck," he muttered.

He could ignore her, head out the back and hope she didn't intercept him on his way to his car. Or follow him home.

He exhaled and pushed the door open.

"What do you want, Verbena?"

"I need to talk to you," she began. "And I would like to do it in private without the door open for anyone walking by to hear."

"It's one in the morning. No one is going to walk by. I don't even know why you're awake and wandering around the empty streets right now. My last patrons went home an hour ago."

"I couldn't sleep. And I knew you'd be here still," she countered. "Can I please come in?"

"Is this some weird witch thing where I have to invite you in or else you're stuck in the street?"

She rolled her eyes and pushed passed him, walking straight to the bar.

"Guess not," he mumbled.

"You can't avoid me forever."

"It's been three days. I figured I was allowed to have at least a month to be mad at you," Luke started. "But I don't know the rules when it comes to sneaking potions into someone's coffee."

"I know, I know. I did something really shitty to you. To both of us." She crossed her arms just under her breasts, pushing them slightly up in the process. Luke cursed silently. He'd been erection free for nearly an hour and just like that, back. He moved past her to fiddle with some chairs at one of the tables.

"Luke."

"What?"

"Can you look at me, please? I'm trying to apologize. Again."

"I'm not ready to accept it. Again," he shot back. Luke risked a glance at her and noticed her eyes narrowed.

"Hm," she mumbled.

Now he all out looked at her. She was dressed really weird. It was eighty degrees out, but here she was wearing a raincoat like she expected the heavens to open up.

"You feel it too," she began, raising an eyebrow.

"Feel what? Anger? Hurt? Pissed?"

"None of those." She licked her lips quickly, and he felt like someone injected desire straight into his bloodstream. She closed her eyes and took a deep breath. "Oh, you most definitely feel it." Now, she smiled wickedly in his direction.

"Are you going to tell me what you're talking about?"

"I probably should." Her arms uncrossed until her hands rested on her hips. "If you were a warlock, or an animans, or a shifter, or maybe even a sonofawitch—"

"What the fuck are you doing? Listing shit I don't know about to make me freak out even more?"

"Hush. If you were a male with supernatural powers," she continued, "you might have a heightened sense of smell. Warlocks are like witches, animans are humans with uncanny connections to animals, shifters can become small mammals, and sonofawitches are—"

"Owen told me," he interrupted. At least he knew what that one was.

"I've been working on my sense of smell for about a year, so I'm not like some witches. Some witches can walk into a room and smell out the feelings of every single person in there, whether they're magical or not." She paused and cocked her head to the right. "I can smell that you are turned on right now."

Luke was sure he pulled some sort of ridiculous face, because that was the last thing in the world he expected her to say.

"You can smell boners?"

"No, I can't. But I can smell yours." She advanced on him, and suddenly he felt like prey being cornered by one of those big cats in the jungle.

"It isn't fair," she started, "that you don't have the same sort of powers, so I'll let you in on a secret. If you were supernatural, you'd be able to smell me too."

"What do you mean, like your perfume? Cause you've always smelled like vanilla to me."

"No. Not vanilla." Verbena took another step toward him, her eyes sweeping down his chest and settling on his pelvis for a moment before settling on his eyes. "You'd be able to smell the reason I came here. Because I can't sleep from wanting you. And if I can't sleep, I know you can't either."

She moved her hand toward him, as if to stroke his jaw, but he shirked out of the way.

"Luke. Please. I know you're angry and pissed and hurt. But I'm dying here. Can you at least hate-fuck me?"

Luke froze. That sounded like a terrible, reckless, stupid idea.

And he wanted it more than anything.

Chapter Thirteen

Verbena didn't know what she was doing.

As an overthinker, overplanner, and overall confident woman, it was a position she had yet to find herself in. But here she was, standing in Luke's bar, wearing nothing but her raincoat and panties, asking him to hate-fuck her.

She definitely didn't come there thinking she would ask him to hate-fuck her. She came thinking maybe he would see her, fall to his knees, forgive her, carry her to either his house or her apartment, go down on her for forty-five minutes, and then they would have Verbena's first night of mind-blowing dick-in-vagina sex. Because while she'd given that a whirl over a dozen times, it had never surpassed "eh."

But Verbena Bay was hornier than a minotaur right now, and she wasn't leaving without Luke at least groping her.

"I'm not going to hate-fuck you," Luke spat back, a twinge of disgust in his tone.

"Why not?"

"Because." He exhaled hard, his eyes going to the ceiling. "Because one day I might forgive you, and then I'll probably be pretty pissed if the first time we had sex was a hate-fuck with you bent over a table in the bar."

"Bent over a table?" Verbena repeated. She had been certain there could be no higher level of desire than she had already been feeling, but it turned out, she was wrong. "Luke."

He turned around and started walking toward the kitchen. "What?"

"Bend me over the table. Please." She moved the ketchup and mustard off the nearest table and onto a chair.

"What?" he nearly shouted, whipping his head to her.

"Please. Do that. Right now, I want that. I want anything from you."

Luke paused for a moment, seeming to mull it over in his mind. Verbena let a small smirk escape. Had she worn him down?

"I don't have a condom."

"I don't care. Pull out."

"Are you insane? That doesn't always work."

"It'll be fine. I know you are feeling the same as me," she began. "How are you fighting it better?"

He shrugged. "I have the advantage of still being very angry with you, the person who drugged me for a decade."

"For the greater good," she interjected. "I didn't drug you out of spite or any nefarious reason. I did it so that when we got this horny and I was seventeen, you wouldn't have to go to jail for a little while."

He rolled his eyes at her, shaking his head. "Look, I get it. It sucks. We're both horny as hell, but I'm not going to sleep with you tonight, even if you pulled a condom out of thin air. No chance. Not happening, Ms. Bay."

In a swift movement, Verbena untied her raincoat and let it fall to the floor. Luke may have had an iron will, but Verbena knew what she had.

She had perfect breasts. They weren't that big, a solid C-cup most days. But she'd slept with seven guys, and every single one of them had given her the same compliment. Apparently, Verbena Bay had some of the most aesthetically pleasing tits on the East Coast.

She stood there in nothing but black panties and flip-flops.

Luke's breath caught for a moment, his gaze struggling to remain on her eyes, but losing the battle.

"God," he mumbled, his fists tightening at his sides. "Why did you do that?"

"Because I want you. And if there's a chance you want me back tonight, I'm not squandering it." She wanted more than him inside her. She wanted his forgiveness. And if it wasn't too much to ask, she would also accept love.

But if the only thing she could get from him tonight was physical, that would have to do.

"Fuck," he breathed and lunged at her. His hands were around her waist, buried in her hair, gripping the backs of her thighs. He was everywhere at once.

He backed her against the wall, then quickly turned her around, grinding his erection against her butt.

"Hell," she gasped. His mouth landed on her neck and assaulted her skin with kisses, licks, and even bites. She reached her right arm over her head, gripping the back of his head.

His hands found her nipples, teasing them into oblivion. She moaned loudly now. Her mind was a muddled mess of need and want. This felt so good, but she wanted more. She needed more. She wanted him, naked, pressed against her, inside her. Her body had been begging for release with Luke for years. She needed it tonight.

"Luke, more," she begged, her words an incantation in the air.

He didn't respond but released her for a moment. She began to protest until she felt his hands swiftly remove her underwear. She stepped out of them and kicked them to the side. She braced her arms against the wall. Verbena had never had sex standing up and from behind, but she assumed she was going to need something to hold onto. Because at the moment, her knees weren't doing too well of a job.

Luke's hands were back, one teasing her nipples, the other immediately sinking between her thighs.

"Goddess," she hissed. She leaned against him, trusting he wouldn't let her fall to the ground. His fingers slipped inside of her, then over her clit, over and over. She was so wet, so ready for him. Verbena couldn't believe how good this felt. She'd had orgasms before, even a few times with a partner, but nothing felt like this. Nothing felt like Luke on her.

She arched her back, pressing harder into all of him, his hands on her clit and breasts, his chest against her back, his mouth against her neck. She wanted to feel all of him. She wanted her hands under his shirt, on his skin, wrapped around his cock before he plunged it inside her.

"I'm going to come," she whispered. She wasn't sure why she said it. She'd never announced it before. Perhaps a part of her thought he might want her to come with him inside her, and he'd give into temptation.

He moved his hand away from her clit, trailing up to her breasts, squeezing both of them gently.

"What the fuck," she muttered, her body still too languid to do anything other than lean against him in protest.

Luke turned her around, his hands finding her waist and pushing her hips back until her butt hit the wall.

"Too fast. Give me a little longer." He grabbed a chair from a nearby table, positioned it in front of her, then sat down.

"You might want to take your pants off," she started, grabbing his shirt and pulling it over his head before he could stop her, "if you want me to ride you."

"You're not riding me," he countered. "I'm not fucking you tonight." He grabbed her rib cage, thrusting her forward so his mouth could attend to her breast. Her hands flew to his shoulders to keep her balance. She was in an awkward position: his legs on either side of hers, her butt pressed against the wall, but leaning toward him. If he let go of her, she would definitely fall over.

But she didn't think he would let go of her.

Hell, it felt good to be in his arms. It felt just as wonderful as it had nine years ago, except now she knew what she wanted. She wanted him, all of him, and she wanted it right now.

His fingers found her thighs again, dragging upward until he cupped her. He was deviously gentle, nothing but featherlight touches. She squirmed, tried to open her legs so she could sink into his hand, but she was trapped.

"Luke, harder," she panted, pulling on his hair a little. "Please."

He relented, increasing the pressure on her clit, using meaningful strokes. His fingers slipped over her now. She moaned constantly, unable to be quiet for even a minute. He released her nipple from his mouth and buried his face between her breasts, his breath hot on her skin.

She was going to come, but this time she kept her mouth shut. The last thing she wanted was for him to bring her to the edge again and then snatch it away. She'd needed this for years, and she wasn't letting it slip through her fingers again.

"Oh, Luke!" she exclaimed as her orgasm crashed over her like sea waves. The upper half of her body slammed against the wall involuntarily, but he pulled her forward, manipulating her spasming limbs until he cradled her on his lap. She buried her face against his neck, still twitching, still grinding against his hand between her legs.

He stroked her with decreasing pressure until his hand slipped away and rested on her thigh. Verbena's breath still came hard, her arms draped loosely around his shoulders for support. He gripped her thigh hard for a moment, squeezing her tender flesh, then slunk out from beneath her.

"You should probably get dressed and go home. Someone's living upstairs now. He'll be back soon." His jaw worked with every word. He turned away from her, fixating on the wall behind the bar. His hands were clenched into fists at his side.

"What?" she mumbled. "No."

"Verbena, please," he whispered.

She glared at his back.

"No," she repeated, getting to her feet. She stepped over her coat and panties and closed the space between them. She set her hand on his bare back, letting the feel of his skin tickle her fingertips. "I'm not letting you go yet."

She grabbed his hips and turned him until he looked at her again. His eyes flickered between hers and the rest of her body.

"Luke. Don't be a martyr," she teased, lifting his hands to cup her breasts. She dipped her head to his collarbone and bit him, hard. He hissed in response but didn't quit massaging her nipples into hard points again.

"We're not done," she mumbled. Her mouth trailed a line from collarbone to pectoral, pectoral to navel. Every few kisses, she landed a bite, and he reflexively squeezed her breasts hard. Her hands went before her mouth, making quick work of his button and zipper, pulling down the waistband of his boxers before he could seize her wrists away.

"Verbena," he warned.

"Shut up," she answered, settling on her knees and taking him into her mouth.

"Fuck you," he moaned. She hummed a smile in response. She slid over him achingly slow, payback for his treatment earlier. She wanted him inside her, going this slow and tantalizing every single inch, but now that her fading orgasm had her feeling a little clearer, no condom wasn't a good idea. She didn't have a patch, pill, ring, IUD, or anti-fertility spell in place, so a condom was going to be a must when he finally did bend her over a table.

"Verbena," he breathed. His hands left her breasts. One settled under her chin, barely grazing the surface of her jaw. The other stroked her cheek, smoothing the skin from her ear to her eye. "Look at me."

She fluttered her eyes open, capturing his gaze with her own. He looked so raw and broken down. She'd never seen Luke so vulnerable. Well, except that first night.

"Verbena, I—" he broke off into a silent cry, his eyes slamming shut as he came. She gripped behind his thighs, wishing none of this would end. This was their first time together. She wanted it to be perfect.

His pulsing ceased, and she eased off of him slowly, eyeing the bartender's sink. She quickly strode over and rinsed her mouth out, then popped back up. Luke was buttoning his pants already.

"Luke," she began. "We really need to talk. Can I—"

"Oh shit!" he yelled. He grabbed her panties and coat and threw them at her. "Danny's back!"

Verbena had no idea who Danny was, but she was pretty certain she didn't want him to see her naked. She hit the floor and slipped her panties back on as fast as she could, then wrapped her jacket back around her. Her flip-flops clattered to the floor beside her, and she got to her feet, sliding them on in record time.

Luke had his shirt on and ran his hand through his hair a few times.

Well, his hair is going to smell like me, she thought, suppressing a laugh. And his shirt was on inside out. Luke was a mess.

He put his hand up to wave to the guy walking up to the door.

"Come here," he said between gritted teeth.

Verbena rolled her eyes and walked to stand next to him. "Are we going to pretend we were just chatting?"

"Please, do not say anything except hello." He turned back to the opening door. "Hey, Danny! This is Verbena. She saw the light on and stopped to say hi. She's my friend."

Danny looked between the two of them, his eyebrow raising. There was no way this guy was going to buy that she popped in to say hello in the middle of the night.

"Hey, Verbena, nice to meet you." Danny was fair, lanky, and looked about her age, maybe younger. She didn't recognize him as a local, but since Luke said someone was staying upstairs, he must have been new to Star Island.

He chuckled a little, then shook his head. "I'm going to go to bed. Have a good time with your friend." Danny walked past them to the back staircase, then called over his shoulder, "Smells like someone had sex in here. Might want to open a window."

Luke rubbed his hand across his face and groaned.

"Can we talk?" She knew if she could talk to him now, after what they'd shared, he would understand.

"You should go," Luke confirmed, dashing any hopes she had of an emotional connection tonight. "This—" He motioned his hands between the two of them. "—we can't do this again."

"I'll put money on it that we do," Verbena said. "Don't worry, Luke. I don't do terrible things that often. You could do a lot worse in terms of soulmates."

"I didn't—" she heard him begin, but she didn't stay. He wanted to be mad at her, so she'd let him be mad. But she didn't need to stick around and hear about it.

Verbena Bay was going home to go to sleep and finally relax.

Chapter Fourteen

Verbena slept beautifully, like a perfectly sleep-trained toddler who had run three miles the day before. She woke up calm for the first time in years and even skipped her morning yoga. She hopped in the shower, whistling like a well-serviced fool who'd been delivered the best orgasm of her life the night before.

After she showered, she treated herself to fried eggs with sausage and bacon, a breakfast she usually reserved for special occasions. Because today was a special occasion.

Sure, Luke was still mad and basically said he never wanted to hook up with her again, but she wasn't going to let that affect her post-orgasm glow. While there hadn't been much emotional connection last night, their physicality had been off the charts.

Verbena was feeling good, and nothing would ruin her mood.

She opened her email and happily found a message from Madelynn Skado, the owner of the land on Sirius, saying she could go take a look today if she wanted. The email warned that the land there was very rough and suggested to wear hiking boots.

"This does not sound like an ideal place for a retreat center," Verbena said to herself, slipping out of her normal clothes and putting on a t-shirt, shorts, and socks. She pulled her hair up into a ponytail and grabbed a bottle of water. It sounded like she was going to have to explore this piece of property on foot, and it was going to be a scorcher today, at least by North Atlantic island standards.

Verbena loved all Star Island's little eccentricities, but above and beyond her favorite was the naming of the peninsulas. There were five, of course, giving the island the shape of a star drawn by a three-year-old from space. Each peninsula had its own personality, some of which Verbena liked more than others. Centauri was for tourists, Polaris was for the wealthy, Sagittauri and Vega were for normal people, and Sirius was for ghosts.

Not actual ghosts, the entire island was for actual ghosts. But Sirius was where people could become ghosts and disappear into the wilderness. The coast here was rugged and rocky, the waves made swimming impossible for anyone who wasn't adept, and both Solaris and Arpina were very far away. Verbena supposed if Brian Lennox, her prospective buyer, really wanted something desolate, this would be the place to go, but the land here wasn't ripe for renovation. It was rocky, quiet, and sometimes lonely.

From her apartment in Solaris, it took Verbena about thirty minutes to drive to the piece of land. She ran through logistics for Brian: cabs were inconsistent on Star Island, so they might want to look into a van to make runs back and forth from town at set times. Either that or a hoard of bikes for people to borrow, if they wanted to spend three hours riding each way. There were a few rideshare drivers on the island, but usually you had to know them beforehand and set up a ride a few days in advance. They weren't great when it came to just popping into town for lunch. Even Arpina, the smaller town on the west side of the island, was over an hour away by bike.

Verbena pulled off the gravel road to park on the edge of the property. There was no driveway, and it was over fifteen acres altogether. She parked her car and stepped out, first taking time to survey the road and neighbors. There was a solitary house in the distance, but it was barely a speck on the horizon. Shouldn't be a problem.

She took a step forward, wondering how far she would have to walk before she could see the ocean. The land was slightly hilled in the direction of the coast, but she was hoping that once she got to the top, there would be lovely ocean views and a perfect place for a building.

It was a nice piece of land. The earth wasn't nearly as rocky as she expected, and there were even some old fir trees in the distance. She would recommend putting a restaurant on the site so that the retreaters could eat there. Plus, it would give locals around here a place to grab a bite when they didn't feel like going all the way into town. It was an added expense but also added income.

Verbena paused, halfway up the hill. There was a sudden shift in the atmosphere, a stilling of the wind. Verbena felt a cold line trace her face, then flip against her ponytail.

"Ah," she said. "It's haunted."

While it was less common for land to be haunted than houses, it wasn't unheard of, especially on Star Island. There was a bloody and violent history here. The first European settlers who claimed the island had slaughtered the original inhabitants, followed by about a hundred years of murdering anyone who attempted to settle here. Especially those who were blown off course from Europe and landed on the island instead of Boston.

Verbena cracked her knuckles a few times and rolled her neck. She didn't have her supplies, but she'd taken care of so many hauntings, she wasn't worried. Verbena was a strong witch and confident in her powers. She could handle it on her own.

She set her purse down on the ground, widened her stance, and took a deep breath. She let her eyes soften and close and began to call out to the spirit or spirits that restlessly roamed here.

She was immediately hit with four separate entities. They felt very old, nearly as ancient as the island. They must have been trapped here for eons.

She teased them out, drawing them toward her with whispers of peace and promises of better days to come.

"Come here, come to me," she mumbled. She was lucky this place was in the middle of nowhere. She'd undone a lot of hauntings in town and had to do it in the middle of the night. "Come to me, Verbena Bay. I am your savior. I will help you. I will release you from this world." She felt herself turn to a beacon, drawing all restless spirits to her.

She fluttered her eyes open. They were there. Not really *there*, but she could see the four in front of her. They were like quick flashes of light and shadow, floating in the air like fog, though the sky was clear and the air warm.

"I'm going to open a path for you, so you can leave this place. Go on, find those you loved when you were alive, or at least try to. There's nothing for you here anymore."

Verbena didn't like to lie to ghosts. In truth, she had no idea what was waiting on the "other side." But with a world so full of magic, and having a sister blessed by a legitimate Goddess, she had to believe there was a great big *something* waiting for everyone.

She felt some tension on their part, which was normal, but she lifted her hand toward the ocean and felt them turn toward it.

Verbena couldn't remember the first time she'd been able to nudge a ghost out of this realm and into the next. She imagined it was when she was very young. It wasn't like she opened a door or split time in half, she just gave a little push, and they were away. She had a shadow of a memory in preschool, seeing a ghost on a playground and letting it free, but as far as she knew, infant Verbena could have been exorcising ghosts from her crib.

The spirits drifted farther and farther away from her, toward that great *something* out there, until they vanished.

She turned to continue her walk, her overall mood growing positive. Things were looking up: this land was definitely habitable, and Verbena was going to make bank on selling this lot. Luke may not have forgiven her, but at least his dick had. Her life was heading in a good direction.

A force hit her from behind, knocking her to the ground.

"Ow!" Verbena shouted, slamming to her knees. She whipped her head around, looking for an assailant but finding no one. She quickly got to her feet and brushed off her knees.

"What the hell?" she muttered. It felt as if someone had knocked her to the ground. She glanced around. There wasn't anyone in sight, and there was nowhere to hide.

Had she missed another spirit? That had never happened before. She paused for a moment and closed her eyes, searching for something that might still be lingering, but came up empty-handed.

"Bizarre," she mumbled. She shook it off and continued toward the ocean, but she couldn't help but check over her shoulder a few times. It was more than a little unnerving.

Fraochún ó ifreann, fuair mé tú!

Verbena hit the ground and covered her ears. A voice bellowed inside her head, as if someone just beside her was screaming.

Tá sé agam anois. Is tú mo phríosúnach!

Verbena jumped to her feet and took off running. She needed to get off the property. Ghosts were usually bound to something, a house, a ship, or a plot of land. She needed to put as much space between her on the property line.

Ní féidir leat éalú uaim!

Chapter Fifteen

L uke made a mistake.

It was the most enjoyable mistake he'd made in his entire life, but it was a mistake nonetheless.

Luke had slept unbelievably well once he got home, but he woke with a war in his brain.

The conflict plaguing him was twofold: he was still very angry with Verbena, and he was hard as a rock wanting her again.

Luke ran his hands over his face.

Maybe he could forgive her. She said sorry after all, and last night had been amazing... Really, what had she done? Given him a little medicine on a weekly basis for nine years and broken into his house and place of work multiple times without telling him what was going on.

"Get a grip, you fucking horny idiot," Luke mumbled to himself. He headed to the bathroom and steeled his nerves. It seemed like an ice-cold shower was in the cards for him.

The shower did little to help him. It got his body clean, but his mind remained firmly in the deliciously filthy gutter.

He couldn't stop replaying the previous night, over and over, like some sort of favorite song. He had a moment stuck in his head like a great hook, and it was when Verbena moaned his name and grabbed his hair.

"Fuck. Fuck, fuck, fuck. I am in trouble." Luke looked down at Whiskey and Jaeger, who sat at his feet, tails wagging. "Not you two. You are both good dogs. Very good dogs. It's me. I'm the one who fucked up. But..." he drifted off. Had he really fucked up? Or had he just fallen for the inevitable? Verbena had said they were soulmates, after all. And she was a witch. How was a mere mortal supposed to resist the charm of his magical soulmate?

And by charm, Luke of course meant her beautiful, naked body on display for him at his bar.

He couldn't lie, her coming in like that, slinking out of her jacket—it was sexy as hell. Luke had definitely had a hook-up-in-the-bar fantasy that hadn't been fulfilled until last night. The thrill of being in a public place, with little actual worry of someone coming upon them, had upped the tension. But there was something very particular about being with Verbena that he'd never felt with anyone before. Touching her felt like stepping off a cliff into an abyss with no ending. The world rushed around him, speeding past, while the two of them stayed completely still.

Luke walked outside with the dogs. Maybe a walk around the yard would help clear his mind.

Luke hadn't dated many women. When he was living with Boris, dates or dances or any normal high school activities had been out of the question. There was one girl, Kit Smyth, whom he had a crush on. She'd kissed him once outside of school, but he was too embarrassed to explain why he couldn't go to dances or hang out on the weekends, so he let her imagine he wasn't interested.

Once he was free from that hell, Luke was transient for a while. That didn't lend itself well to relationships. There'd been a couple one-night things, a one-week thing, but nothing serious until Jess.

Jess was a Celestial, born and bred. She used to come into the diner most weekend nights, and after a few months, Luke finally worked up the courage to ask her out. They'd gotten along just fine and fell into the rhythm of a couple who didn't have other options available. Did Luke ever love Jess? No. But she was nice, and they had the same taste in food and movies, and the sex was good, so there really wasn't a reason for either of them to leave.

Luke chuckled a little. There wasn't a reason until Matt Barnes showed up on the island. Jess took one look at him, broke things off with Luke, and disappeared to the mainland. He'd heard from her mom that she and Matt were married and living in New York City.

Now, Luke wondered if Jess and Matt were soulmates. Or maybe she'd been trying to think of a reason to leave him for a long time and had just then worked up the courage. Either way, Luke had been surprised how little the break-up hurt. They'd been together for nearly four years when she left. He should have been heartbroken. He should have been thinking about proposing to her. But marriage, kids, none of that stuff ever crossed his mind with Jess.

Luke was nearly halfway to the edge of his property now, and starting to feel like the haze of his mind was clearing. He didn't care when Jess left because Jess was never meant for him. Verbena was meant for him. He knew it when he was twenty-two, and he knew it now. He could fight it as long as he wanted, but what was the point? Really? To punish her? He didn't want to punish her. Sure, he was still mad, especially now, knowing that they could have been together for the last five to eight years.

Hell, Luke thought as he waded through the wild grasses, *I'm about to dive headfirst into the most serious and last relationship of my life.* Suddenly, the weight of it all felt unbearable, and he sunk to his knees.

What if it didn't work out?

Could soulmates not work out?

Luke wasn't stupid. He was well-aware that long-term relationships and him didn't work out. He kept in touch with Taylor, and now Danny was here, but he hadn't spoken to any other family since he left Boris' fourteen years ago. He was friendly with everyone, but no one on Star Island knew him, not really. No one except Julio from the diner knew he had a weird upbringing, and that had only been to explain his spotty employment record.

His story was what it was. His parents had him real young, out of wedlock. His dad was in the military and died in Iraq when he was two. His mom kept it together until he was twelve, when alcoholism took over her life and she shipped him off to Boris. He knew she went to prison for fraud a year after he moved in with Boris, but there hadn't been any contact since then. He had no idea where his mom was, or if she was still alive, and he didn't really care. He'd gotten used to being alone for the long run.

"Whiskey! Jaegar! Let's go!" he called. He was going to have to tell

Verbena all of this. He didn't want to, but keeping big secrets from one's soulmate sounded like a bad idea. And he intended to lead by example on that one.

"Who was that?" Danny asked the exact moment Luke walked into the bar.

He looked over his shoulder at the man who had just exited.

"Alan? He's one of the elementary school teachers."

"No, not him. Who was that last night?"

"I told you. Verbena Bay." He paused. "She's a friend."

Danny smirked. "Sure. A friend. Did she have clothes on under the coat?"

"Danny," Luke warned.

Danny put his hands up, feigning surrender.

"No other questions or comments after this one. She is fucking gorgeous."

Luke furrowed his brow, then relaxed. Danny was still such a kid to him. He was sure when they were both over fifty, Luke would still feel terribly old in comparison.

"She is. And that's enough about that." Luke headed back to his office and shut the door. He sat down and twiddled his phone between his hands.

He wanted to call her.

He should probably text, though, right? Did anyone call anymore?

Luke had her phone number, even though he'd never used it. After searching for it ten times for patrons who had fallen in love with the island and needed a realtor, he decided it was faster to just have it saved.

He pulled up her contact and opened a new text message. Then he sat and stared at the screen.

What on earth should he say?

> Luke: Hey, it's Luke. We should probably talk
> with our clothes on. The truth is, I don't want to
> be mad at you. I feel like I should be, like I
> should be madder at you than I've ever been at
> anyone before. But I don't want that. I don't
> want to be away from you anymore. We have a
> lot of wasted time behind us, and I'd like to
> keep that behind us. From now on, let's try to
> move forward, honestly. I'll start: I've never felt
> as close to another human being as I did last
> night to you.

Luke read the text four times before his sentences began to look like he'd randomly chosen words and strung them together.

"Oh my God, stop overthinking it," he chided himself and pressed send, then shoved his phone into his pocket. There was work to be done, and he'd be damned if he just sat and waited for a response. He'd been pretty cold to her last night, and he wouldn't fault her for making him sweat a bit before answering.

But he really hoped they could have it all resolved by tonight. He really wanted to see her again, as soon as possible.

Chapter Sixteen

Verbena sped down Saturnalia, the main drag that led from Sirius to Solaris. She wouldn't be happy until she had the entire length of the island between her and that ghost.

She shivered thinking about that voice. She didn't recognize the language, but it definitely wasn't one of the romance ones. She knew enough Spanish to be able to recognize its cousins. And it wasn't a Native American language either. When she first moved to Star Island, there'd been a swath of ghosts of the original inhabitants of the land, over hundreds of years, and she'd gotten used to the cadence of the languages.

The worst of it all was that it sounded familiar. Why on earth would a ghost's voice sound familiar? The only ghost on Star Island whom she knew personally who could be haunting was Great-Aunt June, and she knew for a fact that she was still fluttering around the Bay property, and she only spoke English and French. Verbena had offered to help her cross over five years earlier, but June wanted to stay and keep an eye on her girls.

Was she losing her touch? Was this a ghost she thought she'd helped before who simply transplanted to another place?

"Take a deep breath," she reminded herself. She really wanted to get into some water. Her energy felt out of whack, and a good soak in the ocean would do her some good. But that would involve getting a swimsuit from her apartment, as she didn't want to cause a stir among tourists. A bath was a good second choice.

Verbena had no problem skinny-dipping in the Atlantic, but it was generally frowned upon on Star Island. She'd learned that the hard way when she took a sky-clad dip at eighteen and was found by a local police officer. Officer Sim had been very nice, but he firmly insisted that Verbena get dressed immediately and promise never to do it again. Then, eighteen-year-old Verbena got to listen to a very long lecture about the predatory nature of some men and how she shouldn't wander around naked in the dark. Officer Sim didn't believe that invited sexual attention, but a lot of people did. Unlike Rosemary, Verbena took the warning seriously and never skinny-dipped in the Atlantic again. Well, not without one of her sisters.

A bath. Verbena focused on that. She just needed a good, long soak in some rose-scented water to recharge her powers. Then, she would think about what to do with this very aggressive ghost standing between her and a lofty commission.

Verbena pulled into her parking spot and shifted the car into park. She leaned back in her seat for a moment and closed her eyes. Between hooking up with Luke last night and being assaulted by an angry ghost, the last twenty-four hours had been more than a little intense. She might need more than a bath.

She eyed the clock on her dashboard. It was noon. Technically, she did live on a vacation island. She could pop into Luke's bar and grab a very sugary cocktail without a sideways glance from anyone. A bath, some booze, and an eyeful of Luke, hopefully blushing after seeing her at the scene of last night's crime, sounded like a lovely way to spend her afternoon.

Verbena's phone dinged with a text, and she rifled through her purse, hoping it was not Brian. She needed to get the ghost situation under control before she could recommend the property. Her lock screen said "Unknown," but Verbena was used to unknown numbers. They were usually the kind of numbers that led to hefty paychecks.

> Unknown: Hey, it's Luke. We should probably talk with our clothes on. The truth is, I don't want to be mad at you. I feel like I should be, like I should be madder at you than I've ever been at anyone before. But I don't want that. I don't want to be away from you anymore. We have a lot of wasted time behind us, and I'd like to keep that behind us. From now on, let's try to move forward, honestly. I'll start: I've never felt as close to another human being as I did last night to you.

"Holy shit," she exclaimed. She grasped her phone hard, so hard she suddenly loosened her grip, worried she might crack her screen. Luke wasn't mad at her anymore. Well, he was, but he was looking to give it up. This was fantastic news. They could be together, really together. No more wasting time, no more beating around the bush. After ten years, she and Luke could finally, truly begin their life together.

She had to respond.

> Verbena: Last night was unlike anything I've ever experienced and I'd love to repeat it, but we can do some clothes-on talking first. Maybe tonight?

Verbena held in a squeal. Her day was looking up.

She jumped out of the car, locked it, and hurried toward her apartment. She still wanted a nice soak in the bath, but this time she'd be doing so with sexy thoughts of what tonight held between her and Luke.

Ní féidir leat éalu!

Verbena's hands flew over her ears. The voice was back? How on earth had it followed her home? It should have been trapped on the property.

Tá mé cosúil leis an ghaoth mórthimpeall ort, b'fhéidir go scoirfidh tú de bheith ag mothú orm ach ní fhágfaidh mé choíche!

The voice pounded in her ears, screaming at her again and again. It was like standing next to the subwoofer at a concert. She sprinted up the stairs to her apartment. Her wards there were strong. There shouldn't be any chance of a ghost breaking through them, no matter how powerful.

She clamored up the stairs, banging into the railing as she stumbled, the voice still ringing loudly. She needed to get into her apartment.

Verbena tried to focus on her next steps as the voice thundered. Get in the apartment. Make a salt circle. Jump into the circle. Take a breather. Sprint to the armoire to retrieve basil, dill, fennel, marjoram, and coriander. She had to stay focused. She couldn't let the ghost get in her head.

She slammed into her door, keeping one hand pressed against an ear, the other ear smushed on her shoulder. Her free hand rummaged through her purse to grab her keys.

She found them, burst through the door, and dropped her purse on the ground, leaving her door swinging behind her. She could remedy that as soon as she got a break from the deafening voice.

She raced into the kitchen and grabbed her salt. She immediately dumped it into a circle around her, taking care to close the circle completely.

Silence.

"Fuck," she breathed, sinking down to sit. "That was intense." Verbena had never encountered a ghost without some sort of spatial limitation. Maybe it wasn't a ghost. Maybe this was something else entirely.

She looked up just as her couch moved across the floor, pitched to its side, and balanced against the wall.

"What the hell..." she said, just as every chair at her dining table flipped upside down.

This was a poltergeist. And now that it was in her apartment, she had to get out.

Verbena eyed the room. Her purse was still sitting on the floor next to her open door. Her phone was in there.

She picked up her salt canister, which was only about half-full. She could never make a circle big enough to get her to her doorway.

Verbena got to her feet and focused on the purse. She just needed to dash, grab it, and get back in the circle. She could do it, no problem. It was twenty feet at most, probably closer to fifteen. She'd be back in the circle before she knew it. Easy peasy.

Her coffee table flipped over.

Okay, maybe not easy peasy.

Verbena jumped up and down a couple times, rolled her neck. She still had her hiking boots on and thought they'd be better than bare feet. That way if a lamp shattered while she was running, she wouldn't have to worry about glass in her feet.

Verbena jumped over her salt, feeling the whoosh of magic against her skin as she did. Thankfully, she didn't break the circle, and she took off sprinting. She'd never run so fast in her life. She flew from her kitchen to her doorway, clamored to a stop, grabbed her purse, and turned back to the circle. The voice was back, but she ignored it. If she stopped to listen, she might falter, and she needed to keep her focus.

Her kitchen cabinet opened, pouring her dishes onto the floor. Glass shattered all around the circle, but nothing could penetrate it. She jumped over the line of salt and took a deep breath. Her apartment was being destroyed. She pulled her phone out and called Lavender.

"Hey, what's up?" Lavender asked cheerily.

"Are you at the bakery?"

"Yup."

"Can you come pick me up? I need to get out of my apartment. I have a poltergeist."

"Pardon?"

"A ghost, or I thought it was a ghost, followed me home and now it's destroying my apartment."

"And why do you need me to come get you? Can't you just make a mad dash?"

"I can also hear it. It's screaming at me in a language I can't understand and making things like walking very difficult."

"How are you talking now?"

"I'm in a salt circle. And for some reason I was fine driving. So, if you would be so kind as to escort me from my apartment to my car so I don't fall down the stairs, I would appreciate it."

Verbena listened to Lavender scurry around the bakery, speaking to people in muffled voices.

Her bedroom door opened and closed four times in succession.

"I'm coming to get you and I'm going to drive you home and make sure whatever this is doesn't follow you into our house."

"I don't think it will. Aunt June has the place locked down pretty tight."

"Still, I'd feel better knowing you were okay. I can take a break. Give me ten minutes."

Verbena tucked her phone into her pocket and surveyed the damage.

Her beautiful apartment looked like it had hosted a frat party the night before. She grimaced at the broken picture frame that held a shot of her and Mable from a few years ago.

"Damn poltergeist."

Ten minutes later, as promised, Lavender peeked around Verbena's open door.

"Is it safe?" she asked, eyeing the destroyed living room.

"I don't know. It's been a few minutes since something was thrown across the room. But some poltergeists are shy. They only show up for one person, you know, to make sure that person really feels like they're losing their mind."

Lavender ticked her brow up and sighed. "I will definitely think Verbena is crazy and destroyed her own apartment unless I see ghost activity with my own eyes," she announced loudly.

"Well, that should do it," Verbena muttered.

Lavender stepped gingerly into the apartment and waited.

Nothing happened.

"Did it leave?" Lavender asked. She walked across the room to stand beside Verbena.

"I don't know." She took a deep breath and stepped outside the circle. Silence.

"Let's go," Verbena said quickly. "I can't hear it now." She grabbed Lavender's hand and flew out of the apartment. They clamored down the stairs and rushed into Lavender's car.

Verbena felt the knots in her shoulders relax. She was with her big sister. Everything was going to be okay.

A poltergeist moved into her apartment, and Luke was open to talking to her.

It was a big day.

Chapter Seventeen

L uke sat at his desk rifling through a pile of receipts. A tourist who had patronized The Muse in June called to complain that he was certain he had been overcharged for his drinks and meal, but he didn't notice at the time because he had also been overserved. While it was a pain in the ass, Luke said he would find the itemized receipt and email it to him. He wasn't going to refund the man (unless he found a tab for over two hundred dollars, but he would have remembered a non-party with a bill that high), but seeing the receipt would hopefully give the man some peace of mind.

Suddenly, Luke felt...

He felt like his shadow had been stolen or like his heart wrapped in ice. There was pressure in his chest, and his fight or flight instinct started to kick in. It was sinking and cold, and he didn't care for it.

He shook his head a few times and rubbed his hand over his heart, trying to chase the feeling away, but it lingered. He stalked through the bar, his vision locked on the light outside. He felt like, if he could just get into the light...

He burst through the door and exhaled hard. The feeling melted away, and the normalcy of the day made him wonder whether he'd imagined the entire thing.

He grimaced. He did not like that feeling one bit. It reminded him of the pit his stomach used to fall into whenever Boris came home in a mood. Waiting for a man to start beating you was a similar feeling to waiting for a sword to fall upon your neck.

Luke walked back into the bar and shook it off as best he could. He had to concentrate on work. And then tonight, tonight, he was going to see Verbena.

Verbena: I have to cancel tonight. Normally, I would make up a fake excuse like I have a cold or something came up at work, but since I am going to strive to be honest with you, the true reason is witch stuff. Beyond that, I'm not sure how much you want to know or don't want to know. I imagine magic is kind of confusing for people who haven't been surrounded by it their entire lives. So, I have to reschedule because witch problems.

Luke reread the text a few times, his focus settling on witch problems. He'd felt off since his sudden feeling of panic this morning.

"Luke?"

He blinked several times until his eyes focused on Danny.

"Yup?"

"You okay?"

"Yeah, I'm fine." He looked back down at the text, seriously wanting to unpack it and ask Verbena a million questions. He looked back up at Danny. "Verbena cancelled on me for tonight."

"Ah, sudden cold?" Danny teased.

"No, work stuff," Luke countered. "I'm going to give her a quick call in my office," he lied, then disappeared into the back.

He exhaled as he fell into his chair. Witch problems? *Fuck*. It looked like he was in for a lifetime of witch problems. What were witch problems? Did she accidentally curse someone? Or kill someone? Or raise an army of zombies? He really should have asked Owen more questions when he had the chance.

Luke: I find I would like further information than what you have offered. Are these witch problems illegal?

Verbena: I did not do anything illegal today. I usually don't do anything illegal. Technically, I have been a witness to some illegal shit my sisters have done. But I tend to stay on the legal side of things.

Luke: Please tell me Sage hasn't made my dogs accomplices to anything illegal.

Verbena: I very much doubt it, lol. So, with being a house witch I have some affinities for dealing with ghosts, poltergeists, the occasional ghoul. I ran into a group today and one is being a particular pain in my ass.

Luke: Wait, what's the difference between a ghost, poltergeist, and ghoul?

Verbena: Ghosts are nice and people can't see them. They usually hang out very passively and don't cause any trouble. Poltergeists move shit around in people's houses. They are annoying. Ghouls can manifest physically and scare the shit out of all people, magical or not. Ghouls are the worst. They are basically zombies.

Luke: Did you see a ghoul today?

Verbena: No. A poltergeist moved into my apartment though. And he seems specifically mad at me, which is kind of weird because he wasn't speaking English and I don't think we have any connection. It was a whole thing, I found him on a piece of land on Sirius and he followed me home, and now I can't live in my apartment until I can banish him. Unless I want to get hit in the head with a lamp.

Luke leaned back in his chair. His girlfriend—no, not his girlfriend. They were not dating as far as he was concerned. She wasn't quite a hook-up either though.

His Verbena was currently being haunted, haunted enough to move out of her apartment, yet she seemed very nonchalant about it.

> Verbena: Did I scare you? Should I have just said I needed to do some moon stuff?

Luke: No, I'm wondering how often stuff like this happens though. Do you get haunted a lot?

> Verbena: Almost never. I am really good at helping spirits cross over. This one is different, and exhausting, so I thought a night at the Bay cottage to recharge wouldn't be a bad idea. Plus, I can go home now.

Luke: What do you mean you can go home now?

> Verbena: Shit. I shouldn't have written that.

> Verbena: Can we leave it at I wasn't comfortable there for a while but I am now? I promise I'll give you a real answer soon, just not right now.

Luke: Yeah. I want you to be honest with me, but you don't have to pour out your soul to me immediately. I know I'm not going to.

> Verbena: Deal. But whenever you need to pour your soul out, I'm a good listener. I lived with Rosemary for twenty-three years after all. And Laurel. Lavender and Sage have the decency to allow a little bit of mystery in their lives.

Luke: It's still weird for me to think I've lived next door to a family of witches for three years. I mean, I definitely thought you all were pagans, but I didn't think you were real witches.

> Verbena: We're pretty good at hiding, but the naked holiday parties are a bit of a tip-off.

> Luke: Naked holiday parties?

> Verbena: Not all of them. Actually, I met Asher for the first time butt-naked around a bonfire. That was horrifying. Thankfully, he was pretty much focused on Rosemary and it was dark. I was probably just a skin-toned blur as I ran as fast as I could into the trees.

Luke groaned. Now that he knew Verbena ran around naked outside, he was probably never, ever going to be able to go more than three to five hours without thinking about it. He'd been outside with the dogs on a few of those nights, when he could hear cackling and shouting carrying over the trees. If he'd known she was unclothed, her skin being tickled by the wind... he would have slept a lot less.

> Luke: Okay, I'm at work so I have to stop thinking about you celebrating your holidays.

> Verbena: Well, Lammas is coming up...

> Luke: I'm going to assume that's one of your holidays, and I repeat, I'm at work. I have to serve drinks in the next ten minutes. And food to families.

> Verbena: I'll let you go then. But thanks. Thanks for talking to me. Thanks for giving me a chance.

Luke wasn't ready to admit it just yet, but he'd give her a thousand chances. He was bound to her, no matter what. He knew it the first time he saw her, all those years ago when they were both basically kids. And he knew it now that those potions were out of his system. Verbena was his and he was hers. Their souls were entwined, and there was nothing either of them could do to outrun the other.

Luke woke with a start, immediately jumping out of bed. He glanced to his feet. Jaeger sat patiently, tail wagging.

"Did you bark?" he asked. He checked the clock. It was only eight. Usually, the dogs didn't complain unless he slept past nine. Letting them out for a middle-of-the-night piss let him sleep a bit longer.

Well, he was up now, so he might as well take them out. He pulled on the shorts that were in a heap on his floor and walked to the door.

"C'mon, Whiskey," he called, rousing his well-behaved dog from a sound sleep on the couch. He pushed open the door, and Jaeger ran out like a shot.

"Shit," he mumbled. Usually, when Jaeger made a beeline like that Luke ended up with a dead mouse or squirrel in his yard.

"Morning."

Luke's eyes snapped open.

Standing in the middle of his backyard was Verbena. She had on a dark blue blouse and tight white jeans that had his imagination flashing memories of her body pressed against his.

And he was in basketball shorts and no shirt.

"Good morning?" he answered, stepping down the stairs. Whiskey followed him, gave Verbena a quick sniff, then went about her business deeper in the yard.

"You are wondering why I am here," Verbena spoke for him. "I get up really early and I have a lot to do today, but I wanted to see you before I left." She inhaled. "I thought it might be nice to have a moment in which I am clothed but we are also alone."

"What makes you think you are going to stay clothed?" he countered.

Verbena nodded her head in the direction of her house. "Sage is right through the trees. She might not be able to see everything, but she can definitely hear, and I did tell her not to let me go in the house."

"Ah, my plans foiled by my dog walker," he said, snapping his fingers. Luke walked to stand beside her. Damn, she smelled so good. Like vanilla. Something about Verbena reminded him of everything he wanted in a cozy home.

"So," she started, "do you usually walk around the yard without a shirt on?"

"I was still sleeping until I heard someone in my yard."

"You're still sleeping at eight in the morning?" she exclaimed. "Good Goddess, Luke. You aren't a teenager."

"Yes...but I work in a bar, remember? I get in bed after two most nights."

She tapped her fingers on her chin a couple times. "That does makes sense."

"Just how early are you waking up?" he countered. Verbena looked really nice. Like shower, hair fancy, face perfect, clothes perfect nice.

"I got up at six today. Which was late for me. Usually closer to five. Or before five. Sometimes four if I have a lot going on."

"Four in the morning? Shit, we've got some things to settle on besides casting spells on one another. How on earth are we going to work if you're waking up just after I've gone to sleep?"

"Are you saying that because we're going to start going to sleep and waking up together?" She trapped her bottom lip between her teeth and grinned.

"Maybe," Luke mumbled. His mind was screaming that he was still mad at her but...but she looked so gorgeous and smelled so good, and he was aching for her again.

"It's okay. I'm looking forward to tiptoeing out of bed at sunrise not to wake you," she teased.

Luke slid his hand to her waist, smoothing the cotton shirt between his thumb and forefinger. He'd be lying if he said he didn't want to kiss her right now. He hadn't kissed her in nine years. A few nights ago...he'd been so mad kissing didn't happen. That was pure animal lust, and honestly, he felt guilty about it. Verbena didn't deserve that.

She tipped her chin back and let a small smile play over her mouth.

"Should we go check out your bed right now?" she whispered. "See how good I am at leaving silently?"

"I thought you weren't allowed to?" Luke mused. He brushed her hair away from her face and let his hand linger over her jaw.

"I'm not supposed to. But you're looking at me like you want to devour me, and I could use some devouring..." she trailed off. Her hands were on his chest, fingers wide and outstretched, trying to cover as much skin as she could. His heart thudded against his ribs in excitement.

"Verbena!" Sage's voice rang out through the trees.

Verbena rolled her eyes. "It's like she can see through the trees."

"Can she?" Luke wasn't entirely certain where these witches' powers begun and ended.

"Sage? No. She can grow food. Really well. That's her main thing."

"So, you deal with ghosts and Sage grows food? Seems unbalanced. A lot of humans can grow food really well," he pointed out.

"Not like Sage. Drought and famine have nothing on her." Verbena sighed. Luke kept his hands on her waist, slowly rubbing her sides. He didn't want to let go, feeling like any second she was going to disappear back to her property.

"I have to go. I've got a poltergeist to banish." There was a twinge of regret in the cadence of her voice.

"Is that dangerous?"

"Eh, I'll be careful." She paused and raised an eyebrow. "You worried about me?"

"Sort of. Poltergeists sound dangerous. Do they kill people?"

"I'll be okay. But I still want to have a long conversation with you. One where we sit and talk and my sister isn't babysitting us from behind the trees."

"Me too," he answered quickly. "And you didn't answer whether they can kill people."

"I'll text you later, Luke."

"Okay." Luke still had his hands on her. He couldn't quite bring himself to let go just yet. It was going to take some getting used to, Verbena off to fight in supernatural battles he didn't understand.

"Okay," she repeated and slunk away from him, trailing her hand across his chest as she did. "I'll see you later."

"Bye, Verbena."

He watched her walk away from him, into the trees, picking her way through the undergrowth. She looked back once, gave him a small smile, then disappeared.

Whiskey padded to him and collapsed on the ground.

"Shit." Luke looked down at Whiskey. "That woman is going to undo me."

Chapter Eighteen

"So, a poltergeist followed you from a piece of land on Sirius all the way to your apartment?" Laurel asked. She was in the parlor setting up a reading. She had moved out of the Bay cottage and was currently living in a small rental apartment on Vega with Owen. But she still ran her tarot card reading business out of the cottage because their new place didn't have the space.

"Yes."

"I didn't think poltergeists could move like that. Aren't they usually bound to a particular piece of land where they died in terrible violence?"

"Usually," Verbena answered. She was slowly slipping back into life at her family's cottage. She'd had two homemade blueberry donuts and three cups of tea already and had picked fresh dahlias to bring to a closing she had earlier in the morning. There were some perks to living at home when home came with a kitchen witch and an amazing garden.

"And the voice spoke a language that was clearly not English or any of the Native American languages you've heard from ghosts before?"

"Or Spanish or Italian or French. Or Polish."

"I don't think it's a poltergeist," Laurel announced. She set out her deck of cards in the middle of the velvet tablecloth.

"It has to be. I couldn't see it, so it's not a ghoul, but it moved a lot of crap around my apartment. What else could it be?" Laurel was knowledgeable when it came to the spirit realm, but Verbena was still pretty certain she knew as much as Laurel, and more when it came to hauntings.

"Maybe it's something new? We're in uncharted territory lately, haven't you noticed? I was injured in the Hedge World, dragged there without my consent, and broke a curse I had cast as unbreakable. Rosemary summoned a freaking Goddess to protect her. It's pretty clear: we're all leveling up, but so is the crap we're facing." Laurel turned toward Verbena. She noticed her sister had let her roots go a bit. Her natural brown was peeking out through the years of jet-black dye.

"So, where am I leveling to?"

"Alchemy, obviously."

Verbena shifted uncomfortably. She had managed to change the core elements of both their water heater and furnace. It wasn't part of her normal retinue of powers, and she wasn't necessarily comfortable with it.

Alchemists were not...moral magic practitioners. They were the get-rich-quick types, turning glass into diamonds, iron into gold, nickel into platinum. It was not a group she wanted to be associated with in the least.

"Don't look so dour. It's not like you're suddenly raising the dead. So you can change metal into plastic. Big deal."

"I'd rather be able to unweave a curse, like you did."

"Yeah, that was cool. But, clearly, I'm not quite powerful enough, or I'd be able to unweave the Bay curse. Maybe I'll get another boost soon." Laurel sighed. "What's your plan for the next hour? I've got a client coming, and I usually make everyone else scram."

"Bit of work, bit of research," Verbena answered. "I'll stay out of your hair."

"Thank you."

Verbena fetched her teacup, and a snickerdoodle for good measure, and headed upstairs. She did have a handful of emails to send, but that would only take a few minutes. What she really needed to do was comb the witch library for banishing spells. There had to be something in there she hadn't come across yet.

Verbena walked into her bedroom. Technically, it was her childhood bedroom, but she'd only moved out two years ago. It didn't feel that far away. She had a twin-sized bed in one corner, her walnut desk on the opposite wall. The paint was gray, of course, and her bedspread and four pillows were crisp white. She had a small bookcase that held some of the first interior design books she ever purchased and a framed picture of the five sisters from the first month they lived on Star Island. It was a strange picture, snapped by Verbena's classmate's mom, and they all looked a little worse for the wear. Sage was all-out frowning in the picture, Verbena looked super embarrassed, Laurel had just dyed her hair black for the first time and looked like a complete goth, and Rosemary was wearing a...what were those things called, bandeau tops? Basically, Rosemary had on a strapless bra as a shirt at a school function. And Lavender had a smile that looked more like a grimace plastered to her face as she attempted to hold it all together.

Poor Lavender, Verbena thought. No one ever took care of her. She had given up the rest of her youth to raise them all and move here so that they would have some financial security. She hoped once this whole Bay curse was sorted, Lavender took a very long vacation with her soulmate.

Verbena sat at her desk and opened her laptop. Rosemary had swung by her apartment after work and dropped it off so she could get some work done while exiled from her apartment. As far as they could tell, this creature was showing up only for Verbena.

She checked a couple things on the MLS, sent emails to a few of her potential clients, and ordered a bouquet of flowers to be delivered to the family that had sold their house last week. Then, she shut her laptop, picked up her cup of tea (the snickerdoodle was long gone), walked into Sage's bedroom, and disappeared into the closet and up the hidden staircase.

"Hi, Aunt June," Verbena said as she climbed the stairs. Their great-aunt wasn't always in the attic, but Verbena liked to make a point to say hello just in case she was listening in. One of the stairs creaked extra loud, as if June was saying hi back.

Verbena loved the attic, even though it went against every household instinct she had. It was beyond messy. Books were often left out and in piles, there was no organization system to the books or any of the supplies, and the pillows they kept up here for comfort were in brash jewel tones. Nothing about this room was in Verbena's style, yet she adored it all the same. Walking into the attic was like being hugged by witchcraft.

Verbena set her cup down on the worktable and collected the abandoned thyme that lay there. She brushed off any residual leaves, resolved to bring the vacuum cleaner up later that evening, and headed to the bookshelves.

They were a librarian's nightmare.

There was no rhyme or reason or even an elementary style of organization. There were books on herbology squeezed between books on love spells and curses. Piles of recently read books sat on the floor, with no intention of being reshelved. Some of the tomes had never even been used by this generation of Bay witches. When they first moved into their Great-Aunt June's house, Lavender had made a commitment to go through each book and at least write down the title and author or contributors. But life took over, and the library remained an unorganized explosion of witchcraft.

Verbena scanned the spines of the books, some with titles, some without, and pulled down about twenty. Within the first few pages, she could tell whether a book had anything to do with hauntings, and if she should keep it aside for later or replace it on the shelf.

After returning dozens of books to their places, including *Living with the Zetic Clan: How a Fire Witch Learned to Read between the Lines*, *Baneful Herbs and Their Uses*, and *A Hermit: The Upside to Loneliness and Solitary Practice*, she had a few useful titles. *Home, Hauntings, and the House Witch* was one she had read before, but it deserved a reread. It was one of the first texts she read as a teen. She would start with that tonight. There were others in the stack that she could tackle as the days went on—and if this poltergeist continued to hang out in her apartment.

It was odd, but Verbena didn't miss her apartment. When she first moved in, it had been like a safe harbor in the middle of the hurricane of her mind. Living at the Bay cottage had become unbearable with Luke so close.

His presence didn't bother her as much anymore. He might not be ready to forgive her for everything, he might never be ready, but it was all out in the open now. Her conscience was clear. She had come clean, bared her soul-crushing secret to him, been rejected, been hate-finger-banged, given him a solid blow job, and had now moved onto flirting in his yard. She took a deep breath. She could be patient. If it killed her, she could wait for him to forgive her.

She hoped it was soon.

Verbena refocused on *Home, Hauntings, and the House Witch*. She ran her hand over the cover as if she greeted an old friend.

This book wasn't June's. It was her mom's.

Holly Bay had been a house witch, just like Verbena. She was the only one who directly inherited her mother's gifts. The rest of the lot were home and hearth witches, but not specifically the same kind as their mom.

The first time Verbena laid eyes on this book was around age twelve. Her mom had climbed into bed with her one night, cracked it open, and they read the first spell together: how to throw a backyard barbecue. Verbena had rolled her eyes at the spell—it read more like a party-throwing guide—but after consideration, she realized there was magic in parties. And in bedrooms and bathrooms, front porches and backyards. The idea of home was magic in itself, and house witches were the ones to amplify it.

Verbena skipped ahead to chapter seven. While she thought it would be fun to revisit some of the first spells she ever attempted and succeeded, she needed something more powerful than how to center the energy of a home in the hearth.

"Hauntings: How to Banish Ghosts, Ghouls, Poltergeists, and Other Demonic Presences," Verbena read the chapter title. Hm, she hadn't remembered the other demonic presences part. Maybe there was something else, and that particular something else was currently breaking all her lamps.

She stuck an errant piece of paper in as a bookmark and picked up her phone.

> Verbena: We should make that morning rendezvous a regular occurrence.

> Luke: I'll wear a shirt next time.

> Verbena: You threaten things like that and I'll have to come over at seven instead.

> Luke: Jaeger isn't even up then. I'm not a scientist but I think that's before the sun comes up.

> Verbena: Lol. Okay. Just wanted to say hi. I know you are at work and a simple text from me gets you hot and bothered, etc. I'll let you go be presentable to customers.

Luke: Goodbye, Verbena.

Verbena: Bye.

Whatever this damn spirit was, Verbena needed to figure it out quickly, because it was really encroaching into the times she could spend daydreaming about Luke.

Chapter Nineteen

*Y*ou *are nothing. Not worth the dirt on the bottom of my boot. You will never be a man. A man doesn't cry or beg; he takes his beating. A man wouldn't cower in the corner. A man. A man. A man. A man.*

Boris' frame towered over him, engulfing him in the shadows. He hated this. He wanted out. He wanted a family, a real family. He wanted someone to show him how to be a man, not list every reason he didn't qualify.

The footfalls scattering in the other room gave him a glimmer of hope. Maybe they would get away. Maybe someone would save them. Maybe, maybe, maybe. He lived on maybes.

Luke shot awake. He hadn't even realized he was asleep. It had been morning. He'd gotten up and fed the dogs already. He glanced to the end table next to the couch. His coffee still steamed.

Luke didn't dream of Boris anymore. He used to. When he first got out of there—got on with his life after Boris died and he was released from that hell—he was plagued with nightmares nearly constantly. But they faded. They came less and less often, until Boris' face was a shadow in his mind.

This morning, it was like he'd never left.

He grabbed his coffee and took a long drink, trying to settle his shaky hands. Seeing Danny had stirred things up. Sure, he thought about Danny and Taylor on a regular basis, but it was different when they were together. Those terrible times couldn't help but surface.

Luke finished his coffee, waiting for the caffeine to hit and move his brain out of the muck it was stuck in. He didn't want to wallow in his past. He hated doing that.

He took a shower, got dressed, and brushed his teeth, but no matter how he tried to use his routine to make him feel better, it failed. He needed something else.

"Whiskey! Jaeger!" he called. "Come on!" He led his dogs down the gravel driveway, whistling at them to stay in line. They were well-behaved dogs, and they usually listened, though sometimes Jaeger's teenage disposition came out and she fucked off to wherever she wanted to go.

They made it to the road, then turned down the Bay's driveway. He could have cut through the woods, but it was pretty dense in there right now with all the July overgrowth. He didn't want his dogs getting covered with mud—or worse, ticks.

Whiskey and Jaeger clamored ahead, racing toward the backyard.

"Sage!" Luke yelled. "Whiskey and Jaeger are coming to say hi!" He thought giving her a bit of a warning before she got pummeled with dog kisses was warranted. He kept his pace slow though. Unlike the dogs, he wasn't here to see Sage. He wanted to see if Verbena was home.

"I thought I heard your voice." Luke couldn't hold back his grin. Verbena stood framed by the front door, one foot on the porch, the other still in the house.

"Good morning." He jumped up the steps.

"Morning? Luke Karnes, it is eleven thirty. It's nearly noon."

"Still technically morning," he pointed out.

"What would it take to make you a morning person?"

"Probably a lobotomy."

She laughed. Not a giggle this time, but a hearty, throaty laugh. She looked good. She always looked good, but he liked the feel of her this morning. She had on a plain, white tank top with jean cutoffs and her hair tied up in a bun. Luke wasn't sure the last time he saw Verbena so casually dressed, but he loved it. It was like getting a peek at the private piece of her, the version that wasn't always *on*.

"Care to walk with me? I need to get some things out of the herb garden." He looked down and noticed a pair of shears in her hand.

"Sure."

Verbena walked down the front steps, then led him around back. It wasn't the first time Luke had been in their yard. Sage had watched the dogs overnight a couple times. Plus, when he first moved in, he used to come sit around the fire occasionally. When he thought back on that, Verbena was always mysteriously missing.

"Hey," he began. "Was it always hard for you? Because you knew? Or did the spell help you?"

"Oh." Verbena stopped walking and faced him. "Well, it was always hard. The spell helped it from becoming unbearable. But you know, I knew. I knew what we could be if we were together. That made it...painful." She sighed. "But, I used it too long. That was my fault. I'm sorry."

"You've said that before."

"I really am though. I don't think I'll ever be able to stop apologizing to you. If I just gave it up when I turned eighteen, you would have left Jess, and we could have been together."

"True." His eyebrows knitted together, doing some math. "When you were eighteen, I was twenty-three, right?"

"Yeah."

"Still a pretty big age difference." He thought it over. Would have been a bit creepy for him to break up with his girlfriend and go all in on an eighteen-year-old, even if it was technically legal. Thirty-one and twenty-six was much more acceptable. And now he had means. He didn't really need means. Verbena was insanely successful. It wasn't like she was asking him to take care of her. But now, he at least knew how to take care of himself.

"You don't have to say sorry forever," he began. "I know you had your reasons. It was still shitty, but I get it."

"Thanks." She sighed, then mustered a smile. "All right. I need yarrow, lilac, wolfsbane, thistle, some cedar bark, a branch of bay leaves, and some garlic."

"Is that some sort of potpourri recipe?"

"No. It's for my phantom-banishing spell."

Luke's brow ticked up. "Wait, phantom? I thought you said it was a poltergeist? Is phantom-banishing dangerous?"

Verbena snipped her shears quickly. "I don't know, maybe. You've kind of got to look at it like this: if I were a firefighter, you wouldn't ask me every day if I was going to be in danger. The answer would always be maybe, but I would argue that the world needs firefighters, right? The world needs witches too. This island especially needs me. And if I ever want to set foot in my apartment again, even if just to collect all my stuff, I'm going to need to figure out how to get this thing out of it."

"So what's a phantom?"

"Turns out I didn't know as much as I thought about the wide range of deceased spirits haunting our world." Verbena picked up her basket and moved to the next aisle of plants. "I did most of that research when I was in high school and just after, so not everything stuck. A phantom is a ghost that is not bound to a particular place but rather to a group of people. So, it would be a longshot, but if this phantom is bound to me rather than a place, it would be able to follow me around."

"But you said it didn't follow you here..."

"Correct. Aunt June would never allow it."

"Aunt June?"

"Oh, she's my great-aunt. She bequeathed the house to us when she died." Verbena tossed another bundle of greenery into her basket.

"Did she leave some sort of protection spell against other spirits?"

"No, she haunts the house."

Luke looked over toward the Bay cottage. It did look like a haunted house, if haunted houses also looked welcoming. It was really old.

"Don't worry, she's friendly."

"Is she always hanging around?"

"Most of the time."

Luke made a mental note never to get frisky with Verbena inside that house. "Hey, is my house haunted?"

"Nope. Your land was. Crazy haunted. I cleared it when we first moved in. There were, like, twenty-two ghosts on your property."

"Really?" Damn, Luke had no idea he lived on such a populated plot.

"Yup. Big massacre there in the early 1700s. Probably ergot poisoning. One of the settlers lost his shit and murdered so many people before someone finally took him down. Those ghosts were really pissed also. Getting murdered by your neighbor really puts people off."

"Imagine that."

Verbena bent down to her knees and began snipping away at the greenery surrounding them. Luke didn't know anything about plants. Well, he knew what garlic was, and it was easily discernible when Verbena pulled up a bulb of it out of the ground.

She sat back on her heels and pushed a few stray hairs behind her ears. An errant bead of sweat escaped her, slipped behind her ear, and trailed down the line of her neck, leaving a path Luke wanted to trace with his thumb.

You will never be a man.

Luke blinked hard.

Focus, he chided himself. Look at Verbena. Be here with her. Leave the past alone.

Verbena started to smile but furrowed her brow instead.

"What's wrong?" She jumped to her feet, her eyes searching his face. "You look like you were stung by a bee."

Luke shook his head, grinning.

"No bugs." He paused. "You got anything for bad dreams?"

She raised an eyebrow. "What kind of bad dream?"

"Does it matter?"

"Yes. Dream of the future? Dream of the present? Dream of the past—"

"Past."

"On your own." She shrugged. "Dreams of the past are usually things you need to work through. Even so, I could give you a concoction, but I thought you were off potions?"

"Yeah, no potions. I thought you could maybe do some chanting over my bed to give me good dreams," Luke teased.

Verbena snorted. She dropped her shears into the basket sitting at the end of the row.

"I'm pretty sure if I stood over your bed, I wouldn't be chanting, but you would sleep better." She grabbed the basket and walked farther into the yard. "Come on," she called back to him.

Luke followed like a man hypnotized. He probably could have disobeyed and stayed where he was or even walked home, but what was the point? With Verbena leading the way, he wanted to follow.

"You want to tell me about your dream?" she asked, stopping beside a tree. It was a small, ornamental sort, with a circle of rocks around the trunk. Verbena pulled her shears out of the basket and clipped a small branch, adding it to her pile.

"No." He would. He promised himself he would, but not right now. He still didn't trust her. Not yet. He wanted her, more than he could verbalize and more than just physically. There was this loud, incessant voice in his head screaming to claim her as *his*. *His* woman. *His* girlfriend. *His* wife. He was trying his best to get that voice to shut the hell up. But that wasn't the same thing as trust.

She nodded and continued walking along the path, stopping when she got to a bunch of yellow flowers, wild and unkempt in a beautiful way, tucked behind a small stone wall.

"Want to hear a story?" She grabbed a fistful of the flowers and pulled them free, filling her basket to the brim.

"Okay," he answered. She motioned him to a pair of benches shaded by a huge ash tree.

"I've tried very hard to appear normal," she began, sitting on one of the benches. He contemplated sitting beside her, but then sat across from her instead. That way he could maintain eye contact and concentrate on what she was saying instead of the proximity of her body to his. "It's this nagging part of me. I don't want people to look at me and think, Verbena's probably a witch. Even if they really have no idea what being a witch actually means. I've never wanted to be on the outskirts of society." She inhaled. "My mom was like that. She was magical, yes, but she wasn't that flashy. She dressed like a normal suburban mom, had tons of non-magical friends, and raised us in Ohio. Not to say witches can't live in suburban Ohio, but it's no Salem."

"Or Star Island."

"Precisely. I was completely content to live that sort of life, with magic on the side. But then my parents died in a car accident when I was thirteen."

"It was a car accident?" Luke asked. "After you told me the whole witch thing I started to wonder if that was a cover-up."

"Nope. Just a regular old accident on the turnpike. Destroyed my life for a few years, Lavender's for longer probably. But otherwise a normal parental death."

"I'm sorry."

She nodded. "Thanks. It sucked. But I have an inkling you understand something about losing family. I've known you for nine years, and no one's ever visited you until Danny. You never leave Star Island, you never talk about your family. So, while you might not want to talk about it, I do understand a lot about loss. And not just the loss of my parents, the loss of everything I thought my life was going to be. I went from most likely a normal realtor in Ohio to one of five magical sisters living in a haunted cottage on an island in the middle of the Atlantic with a curse hanging over our heads."

"A curse?" Luke repeated.

"Of the generational nature. It's a lot and it's scary and it's very different than the life I expected to live."

"So, you traded a Volvo and a cookie-cutter house for curses and hordes of ghosts to deal with."

"I did. But...I'm guessing you don't have any connection to Ohio?"

"Nah. I've been there, but only passing through."

"See, it may have been horrible and hard, but it led me to you."

That was a hell of a way of looking at loss. Turning all that hurt into something a little bit beautiful. Because even if they both had to go through absolute hell, it led them to each other.

She looked down. "Luke?"

"Yeah, Verbena?"

"The bar was fun, and I wanted it very badly, but the next time we're together..." She paused and looked over his shoulder, like she was searching for the right thing to say.

"The next time we're together, I want it to be different. I don't mind waiting, if it means you'll, you know, care about me when it's happening."

"Verbena," Luke started. He could feel his heart rising to his throat.

"Don't. It is what it is. It was great, physically. And I wanted it so badly. But next time you touch me, let's make it mean something."

Luke swallowed hard. She was right. They couldn't separate the emotional and the physical any longer. It was going to be all or nothing from here on out.

Chapter Twenty

Armed with her basket of herbs, flowers, bark, and enough garlic to cook an Italian dinner for seven, Verbena exited her sensible sedan in front of the Sirius Point property. She had a full canister of salt in her purse, in case things got dicey, and Sage was swinging by as soon as she finished her produce deliveries. Once the island hit full summer, Sage personally delivered vegetables and fruits to some of the wealthier Star Island residents. They paid a pretty premium for produce straight from the Bay garden, without having to deal with the swath of tourists at the farmer's market every Saturday.

Verbena eased a foot over the property line, a bundle of lemon verbena held in front of her body. Technically, it was an herb used for purification, and she could sense that the land needed to be purified of this violent spirit, but she found that when a witch was named after an herb, they had a pretty good working relationship. Lavender, the herb, did things for Lavender, the sister, that it never did for Verbena.

"I should make a lotion," she muttered to herself. A nightly ritual covering herself in lemon verbena was probably a good idea. Especially now. She hoped the scent didn't put Luke off.

She sighed. While she hadn't *wanted* to call off the hate-hooking-up, she knew in the long run it was just another way for her to get hurt.

Disassociated orgasms are not what soulmates do. Or at least, it wasn't what she wanted to do. She wanted emotional connection, eye contact, and post-mind-blowing orgasm cuddles. She wanted mornings in bed and movies on the couch and after-dinner walks on warm summer nights. She wanted a relationship.

She needed to deal with the repercussions of her actions, not make them worse. Sure, getting felt up, down, and inside by Luke was out of this world, but she really wanted to kiss him. And she was convinced a kiss wasn't happening while he was still so angry.

So, she would wait. As long as it took.

She huffed. Verbena was not a patient person.

After a few minutes of standing on the border of the property and no contact whatsoever, Verbena cautiously lowered her bundle of lemon verbena to the ground and released it. She steeled herself for an onslaught of audio assaults.

But it didn't come.

Hm.

She had been on the top of the hill last time. Maybe she needed to be up there?

She took a deep breath and picked up the lemon verbena. If she was going back to the place where the horror started, she was going to need a little back-up.

Verbena trudged over the rocky ground, noticing a few wildflowers here and there managing to peek between the rocks. The land here was breathtaking. She wasn't a creative at heart, but it appeared to have just what the average writer/artist/creator looking to become above average needed: plenty of hiking space, stunning views, the smell of the sea, and solitude. She really couldn't turn off the realtor in her brain, even when about to face a very aggressive spirit. She made a mental note to bring Owen out here once the spirit was vanquished and see what he thought about being recommended as the contractor for the project. Now that her sister's soulmate had moved to Star Island, he needed more steady work than his current odd jobs. Laurel wanted a mountain of kids, after all, and kids are expensive.

Verbena hiked more slowly this time, watching her footfall, scanning the horizon. She hadn't seen the spirit before, but after reading up on phantoms, it seemed they were tricky bastards. Unlike ghosts, ghouls, and poltergeists, it appeared that phantoms could be seen or not be seen. They could move stuff or just howl. They could walk through walls, doorways, or open fields.

Basically, a phantom could do whatever the hell it pleased during its time bound to earth, yet dead.

Verbena finished her ascension of the hill without trouble. She grabbed her jar of salt and poured a circle, then stepped inside. She sat cross-legged and emptied the contents of her bag, lining up everything in a row.

She felt the air shift around her. The wind had been steadily coming off the coast, a cool breeze from the ocean on a clear summer day. Now, it howled, straight from the center of the island. Verbena shook her hands out and took a deep breath. She was safe in her salt circle, she only needed to concentrate.

She deftly wound the yarrow and thistle around the bay branch. She grabbed her knife and stabbed a small hole in the dirt, then stuck the base of the branch in it.

"Here to guard while I work, protect the air, the witch, the dirt," she mumbled quickly. She lined up the cedar bark in front of her, making a platter of sorts. She placed the wolfsbane and lilac on top of it, sprinkled more salt over the plants, then got out the garlic. Her knife made quick work, cutting the cloves free, crushing them into a pulp with the broad edge. She added the sticky mush to the pile.

"Guardians of the afterlife," she called loudly toward the brisk wind turning ever colder. "Take this phantom, trapped in my world. Help it get to where it deserves to go, whether it be good or bad. Guide it away from these lands and the trouble it causes for the living." She lit the bay branch with her lighter, watching as the flame turned to smoke that encircled her.

Cailleach amaideach! Scriosfaidh mé thú!

Verbena steeled herself. She could hear it, even within the salt circle. The voice wasn't deafening like before, but it was crossing the salt. That couldn't be good.

"Banish him from our realm!" she shouted. "Take him! Trap him!"

The wind disappeared. Verbena exhaled.

Did it work?

Her flame went out, as if the oxygen had been sucked away. Her eyes searched her supplies quickly. The lilac and wolfsbane blew off the cedar, cut clear through her salt ring, and disappeared across the rocky landscape.

Her salt circle was broken.

She reached for her purse. She needed to replace it.

Níl.

Verbena was slammed to her side, completely destroying her circle.

"No!" she yelled. She tried to sit up, but something pressed her down, held her fast against the ground. She couldn't see anything, but there was no mistaking the fingertips pressing against her shoulders, nor the knee on her chest.

She squirmed, tried to roll to the side, her arms flailing. If she could only reach something, anything that she had brought. Her knife was blessed and powerful. Her herbs all had banishing properties. A fistful of salt could disperse any spirit. Even if she couldn't see it, she knew where it was.

Nessa, Nessa, Nessa, plá ar mo theach. Bás.

The fingers moved from her shoulders to her neck.

Shit, Verbena thought. This shouldn't be happening. Phantoms were so rare...the ones that could actually affect the living were almost myths at this point. How had one landed on Star Island? She tried to stretch her arm farther, tried to reach the yarrow. There was a fleeting spot of yellow in the corner of her eye. If she could only wrap her fingers around it. She grasped for it, but it stayed just out of reach.

Verbena tried to roll out of the phantom's hold, but she wasn't strong enough. She needed the yarrow.

She couldn't reach it. It was too far. She was going to die on this hill. Alone.

Luke.

Why had she wasted so much time? She'd been so angry and so focused on herself, she'd wasted her only time with him. Tears stung the corner of her eyes in regret. Poor Luke. She introduced him to all of this only to leave him.

Her vision became cloudy with dark spots blotting out the sun, the perfect blue sky, the wispy clouds, the soft earth beneath her body. Her lungs felt like they were going to burst, her hands and feet were numb. It was ending.

Mom...help me, she thought before the world slipped away as if she'd fallen asleep.

She wasn't dead. She was certain that her body being dragged over rocks would hurt a lot less if she was dead.

"Fuck," she heard her transporter mumble.

"Sage?" Verbena croaked.

"Verbena!" Her legs dropped to the ground with a painful thud.

"Ow."

"You're awake! Holy shit, can you walk?" Verbena hadn't even opened her eyes yet and Sage was trying to get her on her feet.

"I don't know, ow, that hurts! Slowly," she commanded. She risked peeking her eyes open. She could see the truck in the distance parked behind her sedan. "When did you get here?"

"In time to see that...thing strangling you." Sage slipped her arm under Verbena's. "Let's chat in the car. It might be back soon. Come on, get a move on."

Verbena limped beside Sage, wishing for nothing more than to lie down on the ground and give up. But she couldn't. The phantom had tried to kill her. She didn't want to give it another chance.

"Easy does it," Sage said as she manhandled Verbena into her truck. Verbena pulled her legs into the car and slumped against the seat. Finally, rest.

"Put your seatbelt on," Sage instructed after she put the truck in drive.

"I can't."

"Do it. If I have to drive crazy, I don't want you going through the windshield."

Verbena groaned but managed to make her arms complete the simplest of tasks and buckle her seatbelt.

"You said..." Verbena tried to clear her throat. It hurt like hell. "Water?"

"Um, there's an old bottle under the seat for emergencies. It's probably warm."

"Better than nothing," Verbena managed. She fished the bottle out and took a big swig. It was more than warm, it was hot. But it still helped.

"You said you could see the phantom."

"You can't? Shit, that thing is gross-looking. Like those bodies they pulled out of the bogs in Ireland. It was disgusting. Smelled awful too, like it had been rotting for months. Blech."

"How did you get me away from it?"

"Honestly, I sort of panicked. I charged it, went a little bananas, screamed, grabbed it around the neck to get it off you, tried to pull out its eyes, succeeded in pulling out some of its hair, then I saw your salt and doused it. Disappeared into thin air." Sage paused. "Do you want me to take you to the hospital?"

"What? No."

"You look like someone tried to strangle you. Your neck is all bruises."

Verbena flipped the mirror down. She wasn't kidding. Now she really couldn't go to the hospital. There was no cover story for strangulation.

"Wait." Her mind flicked back to something Sage said. "You said something about Ireland."

"Yeah, those bodies from the bogs in Ireland. Remember? We watched a documentary about it maybe seven years ago? Laurel said she wanted to go see the bogs, that they had to be full of secrets."

"I think he's speaking Irish." It clicked in her brain. It did sound like Irish. That documentary had some people speaking Irish, and it sounded similar.

"Holy shit, Sage." Verbena's mind jumped from place to place. Nessa. He had called her Nessa. She closed her eyes and let the name wash over.

Nessa...standing against the wind...the sound of the sea on the shore, but not like here. A different place, a different time.

"I think I might be connected to this phantom from a past life. He called me by another name. Nessa. Is that Irish?"

"Hell if I know." Sage sighed. "Looks like you're up. Get ready for a shitty month. I assume that phantom will probably try to kill you a couple more times and is somehow related to the Stochs."

"But they're a Slavic family. How does that work?"

"I mean, we're English, French, and Polish, yet Rosemary had a Scandinavian life. I don't think past lives are that strict." Sage paused. "Well, at least I get a little more time before something magical tries to murder me. I think I'll celebrate with a drink when I get home."

Verbena leaned back against her seat and fluttered her eyes shut.

She was alive.

And she wasn't letting this chance go to waste. Verbena needed to see Luke. She needed to tell him how she felt.

As soon as she could keep her eyes open and turn her head without wincing.

Chapter Twenty-One

Luke pulled his car into his parking spot in town. It was one of his days off, but he wanted to check on the bar. Normally, he wouldn't have popped in on a Tuesday afternoon, but he had a nagging feeling he should check on Danny. He'd been preoccupied with Verbena since Danny arrived, what with finding out she was his soulmate and basically a ghostbuster. He hadn't given Danny the attention he should have. Luke knew what it felt like to be floating from place to place. A small part of him hoped Danny could find some peace here, settle down and make a life on this bit of beauty in the middle of the ocean. It would be nice having a brother nearby. Some real family.

Luke was used to this, a weird emptiness when important things happened. When he bought the bar, his house, got his dogs—he didn't have anyone to share it with. There were no siblings to call, nor parents to inform of huge life steps. Sure, he still emailed Taylor to keep him up to date with his goings-on, but it wasn't the same. If Danny managed to stay a permanent fixture on Star Island, he'd have family to share his good news with.

Luke walked through the normal summer flow of tourists. He spotted at least two bachelorette party flocks, each with matching t-shirts and one with a bride who was already stumbling and wearing a tacky white veil.

"Hm," he grunted. That didn't bode well for his bathroom. He really needed to add some sort of patio out back that parties could reserve and he could easily hose down.

He walked through the alley to sneak in the back. He didn't want to get caught talking to customers. If he came in the front, people always wanted to chat. In the back, they had a little more respect for the job and usually let him carry on with his business. It sounded loud, though, more than half-full. He ducked into his office, threw his keys on his desk, then turned to find Danny.

Something hit him like a block of ice.

A sinking feeling settled in Luke's stomach, and he suddenly felt like he was about to get hit from behind. He whipped his head around, expecting some unknown assailant to be hiding behind the door.

Nothing.

Luke shut the door to his office, his eyes searching wildly. His heart slammed against his chest, his breath was short. Panic attack? His fingers found his wrist, searching for his pulse. It was racing. He tried taking some deep breaths, but he felt like he was just making it worse.

Coward. Amadán. Namhaid.

Luke squeezed his eyes shut. The voice shouted in his ears. He moved to cover them, but it didn't help anything. Was this a ghost? Was this what Verbena always heard?

Salt. She had said something about salt. His eyes flew open. He moved to the door, throwing it open and trying to walk as steadily as he could while something screamed at him. He kept his eyes on the ground, made his way to the cart where they kept the ketchup, mustard, salt and pepper. He grabbed two saltshakers, then slowly walked back to his office and shut the door.

Then, he shook out that salt like it was water over a fire. The voice quieted, then disappeared.

Luke dropped the saltshakers on the floor, afraid to move for a minute.

Danny.

That voice, that voice was familiar. A voice that only lived in his worst nightmares. He hadn't heard it that loudly in years. Luke needed to get to Danny.

He burst out of his office and rushed to the front of the bar. Derrick was working, with his normal grimace and cloudy attitude.

"Hey, where's Danny?"

Derrick shrugged. "He was supposed to be cleaning up a spill around the corner, but he's been back there a while."

Luke hustled around the only blind corner in the bar. They used this section for overflow, and at the moment, none of the tables had customers.

"Danny?" he called.

"I'm right here." Danny raised his arm from behind one of the tables.

Luke ran around to face him. Danny sat on the floor with his back against the wall and his knees bent.

"You okay, man?" Luke offered his hand to help Danny to his feet.

"I think I've got the flu or something. Just got really dizzy." Danny shook his head. He looked up at Luke. He was pale, and his eyes were glassy. "You mind if I go lay down upstairs? I'll come back to work in an hour or so, wait for it to pass."

"No, take the rest of the night off." Luke tapped his teeth together. That voice. That goddamn voice was Boris. He heard a dead man's voice in his bar. Long dead. Years dead. His mind was racing. He'd never heard it before. Did Danny hear it too?

"Let's get you upstairs."

Luke led Danny to his apartment, wanting to make sure he didn't fall on the stairs and that he had food in his fridge. He told Derrick to call Erin and see if she could cover busing for the evening.

"You sure you're okay?" Luke asked again.

Danny kicked off his shoes and collapsed onto his bed. "I just need to pass out."

Luke checked his kitchen. He had bread, peanut butter, a carton of strawberries, and some pop in the fridge. He poured him a glass and carried it over.

"Drink this. Call me later." He paused. "Danny, you know you can tell me anything, right?"

"I'm not on drugs," Danny answered, shoving his pillow over his face. "I'm just sick. It's gotta be that," he added almost silently.

"I know. But anything. I'm serious. I won't judge you." Luke felt a little hypocritical. It wasn't as if he was offering his experience with a dead man at this particular moment.

"Thanks. I'm going to go to sleep now."

"Let me know if you need anything."

Luke should have stayed at work, but he couldn't. Derrick and Erin could handle it. And if it got crazy, people would go to the diner. Or go drink on the beach.

He needed to talk to Verbena. She would know what to do.

He drove straight to her house, not stopping to drop his car off. He pulled into the Bays' gravel drive, parked behind the truck Lavender and Sage shared, and hopped out. He hoped Verbena was home from her expedition. He wasn't sure how long vanquishing spirits took.

Her car wasn't there. Shoot. He was already there though. He could shoot the breeze with Sage and Lavender until she got home.

He moved to knock on the door, but it opened before he had the chance.

"Luke!"

Verbena looked like someone had tried to murder her. Her neck was covered in bruises, there was a cut on her cheek, and her hair was a knotted mess.

"What the fuck? What happened to you?" he shouted. Luke felt his blood rising. He needed to find whoever did this and...

He'd never been one for fighting, so he grabbed her around the waist and pulled her against him tightly. If he couldn't beat her assailant to death, he could at least give her some comfort.

Luke held fast to Verbena, his hands splayed across her back. She whimpered a little in his embrace. He loosened it and tried to move away, but she buried her face against his neck and tucked her arms against his chest. Her hands were shaking.

"I'm so happy you're here. Thank Goddess. I was about to call you, but then, well, I could sense you nearby."

"Who did this to you?" he asked. He couldn't focus on anything else. Verbena was hurt, and he needed to know why. The protective part of him wanted to wrap her in blankets and go on the hunt for whoever had hurt her. The logical part of him knew he should stay with Verbena.

And never leave her again.

Between the voice he heard and Danny's sudden sickness...it was like all the people who were important to him were in trouble. He couldn't ignore it.

She shook her head against his chest. "I'll tell you in a couple minutes," she said, her voice muffled. "I haven't felt a moment of clarity until you put your arms around me, and I want to bask in it for a minute."

Luke tightened his hold again, tucking his chin over her head. If she needed a minute, he could give her a minute. But he was definitely going to need the story of why Verbena looked like someone had kicked the crap out of her.

"I'm here," he breathed. "I'm here."

Chapter Twenty-Two

Verbena couldn't bring herself to leave Luke's arms. There was something so comforting, so protective, about her face against his chest, his breath on her hair. She missed this so much. She missed it more than she ever could have imagined before being back in his arms. This was where she belonged. Over years and lives and eons, she and Luke were meant to be together. She wondered how many times they had been together before, for this to feel so right so quickly.

"Verbena?" Luke mumbled. "Please, are you okay?"

She peeled her face off of his chest and gazed up at him. "I am. I wasn't for a while, but I am now."

He grimaced at her puzzling answer.

"Can we go someplace private?" Verbena asked. She knew Sage and Lavender were steps away at the dining table, and Laurel and Rosemary were probably on their way over.

"Do you want to go to my house?"

Verbena thought it over. "Sure. But I need to walk really slow."

"My car is here. We'll drive." Slowly, they made their way down the porch steps, Luke's hand around her waist. He eased her into the front seat, then ran around to his side. They were pulling into his driveway in a manner of minutes, doing the same slow easing out of the car.

He guided her into his house and put the dogs in the yard.

"I fucked up," she admitted, sinking into the couch. She waited for his response, but he only deepened his gaze.

"That phantom," she inhaled sharply, "it almost...I almost died today."

"What?" Luke shouted. He closed the distance between them, sliding to his knees, his hands going to her face. "How?"

"It could touch me. I thought I was strong enough, powerful enough, but it broke my salt circle, destroyed my spells. It was like a person, pinning me and strangling me. I thought..." She shook her head and squeezed her eyes shut. She wasn't going to cry. If she cried, she'd never be able to say everything she needed to. "All I could think about was how badly I fucked up with us. That I was about to die and I wasted eight years without you. I was going to die with the worst regret I've ever felt. I'm so sorry, Luke. It was the biggest mistake of my life, not having you."

"Verbena," he breathed. His eyes searched her face wildly, like a man being chased by a storm and looking for safe harbor. His thumbs smoothed the skin over her cheeks and down to her jaw, then brushed over her lips, parting them before crashing his mouth against hers. His tongue immediately found hers, tasting her and setting a fire in her belly.

Yes, she thought. *Finally.* She'd been wanting this since their last kiss in the park when she was seventeen. She was his, claimed by his heart and soul and his mouth. And he was hers the same. They were meant to be together, a love to span time and worlds—and death and heartbreak and joy.

She wrapped her arms around his neck, pulling him closer. She wanted to climb inside his chest and learn everything she could about him. What was his heart rate? How heavy were his breaths? What wonderful things could they do together in this life?

Luke groaned, his chest parting her legs, pinning her between the couch and his body. His hands ran up her sides, catching the fabric of her shirt and dragging it with him. She broke their kiss and moaned, more loudly than she intended to.

His mouth left hers, teeth scraping against her jaw, then traveling down her neck.

"Ow!" she gasped, her hand flying to her neck.

Luke dropped his hands and backed away, pushing away from the couch and onto his feet. "Oh shit. I am so sorry." He shook his head and stepped farther away from her. "I shouldn't have—"

"Stop." Verbena put her hand up. "Do not say another word. I have an injury on my neck and your mouth touched it. Trust me, I wanted every single minute of that." She took a deep breath.

Luke sat beside her on the couch and pressed a kiss to the top of her head. She closed her eyes and breathed for a moment. She shouldn't tumble into bliss with him yet. There were so many things he deserved to know. And she wasn't going back to the pattern of keeping them from him.

"This spirit knows me. And I think I know him, but I can't remember." Verbena looked at Luke.

"What do you mean? Is it someone who died here recently?"

She shook her head. "No. I think it's someone from another life. I think he followed me."

"Another life?" Luke repeated. He pulled her legs to rest on his lap, then wrapped his hand around her calf.

"Yes." She had to be gentle with this. While some non-magicals believed in reincarnation, many did not. They thought this life was it, and for some of them, it probably was. There had to be a few once-born souls floating around this universe.

"Are you religious?" she began.

"No," Luke answered.

"Oh, okay." She hinted a twinge of emotion behind that fast answer, but she figured now was not the time to go into a deep discussion about Luke's beliefs, especially since her older sister had summoned a goddess earlier this summer.

"Magical people, and their soulmates, live more than once. Their souls live more than once. So we've probably been together already, maybe even a few times. In the past, of course."

"We've been together before? I...I'm not magical. I'm a kid from a shit town in Indiana. I don't think I'm destined for anything great. Or have done anything great before," he said slowly.

"You believe that we're soulmates, right?"

"Yeah. It's really the only way to explain the rollercoaster of emotions and lust I've been on since meeting you."

"Good. Well, your soulmate is a witch, and we get reincarnated. And I wouldn't have a life without you."

"How do you know?"

"I just do." Verbena took a deep breath. This wasn't going how she wanted it to. "So, here's the thing. That spirit, phantom, whatever the fuck it is, I think it's from a past life. And Laurel and Rosemary have both had people from past lives come after them in the last month. I assume this guy is after me." She added quickly. "Also, we have a curse set over us that if a witch or warlock collects all the magical Bay blood, they get our powers and we probably die." There really was no reason keeping that secret, especially if this spirit turned out to be connected to both of them.

Luke pushed her legs off his and stood up. "A ghost is trying to kill you and so are other witches?"

"Warlocks too."

"Fuck, Verbena." He made a low sound, something between a growl and a sigh, then rubbed his eyes hard and turned toward the door. "I'll be back." He called over his shoulder.

"What? You're leaving?" Verbena clamored to her feet. He couldn't leave. They were in the middle of a very important discussion.

"I'm not leaving. I am going to go for a walk and come back with a clearer head. You cannot tell me all this shit and expect me to just go with it. I need a minute," he said, then left.

Verbena crossed her arms and sunk back down onto the couch.

This was the second conversation Luke had bailed in the middle of, and Verbena wasn't having it.

"Screw that," she grumbled.

Verbena sprang from the couch, her temper flaring. She was going to give him a piece of her mind, force him to listen to her. She threw the door open and saw Luke standing in the middle of his yard, his hand pressed against his forehead.

"Damn it."

She was being a bitch.

She took a deep breath and steadied herself. Luke didn't deserve her frustration. He was doing his best.

"Luke!" she called. "We were in the middle of an important conversation, and it wasn't over. I've never told anyone who isn't also magical that I'm a witch. This is a big deal to me. Talking about this stuff with you is important to me."

"Owen and Asher know you're a witch," he called over his shoulder.

"Precisely," she countered.

Luke turned around and walked back to the porch, lowering his voice.

"Owen said he wasn't a warlock."

"No. Owen is like a warlock-light. And Asher is a Guardian. Honestly, that's very mythological, and I don't really understand it so don't ask me too many questions. But I, me, your soulmate, the woman you are tied to in this life and the next, whether you like it or not, am a witch. And sometimes being a witch comes with a lot of shit, and I need to know I can talk to you about it without you running away. I love you, and I'm not keeping magical shit from you. No way, never."

Luke's brow furrowed, and he crossed his arms over his chest.

"How the fuck do you love me? You don't know anything about me."

"Then tell me. I've been looking at you with doe eyes since I was a teenager. Tell me. Because whatever it is, I'll still love you," she promised. "Tell me about you."

"You want to know about me? Okay, here goes. I had a shit childhood. Not completely, but the overarching theme of it was getting the crap kicked out of me by my terrible guardian. My mom dumped me with a distant relative who liked to beat the shit out of me and the other boys."

Verbena's shoulders tensed up, and she jumped back a little. Oh Goddesses. She knew his family wasn't in his life, but she never imagined it was that bad.

"See? Is this what you want to hear? That I've been beaten with a belt? That someone who was supposed to be taking care of me punched me in the face when I was twelve? That I had to watch my brothers take a pipe to the side, waiting for my turn? Is this what you want?"

"Yes!" she yelled back. "Yes! I want you to tell me everything! I want to know all that shit and, honestly, I want to curse the excuse for a human who did that to you." She crossed her arms and took a deep breath and shut her eyes. "Name."

"What?"

"Give me the name."

"He's dead."

She scoffed. "I can still curse a dead person. Believe me. The best curses are the ones that last life after life after life. They really drive the point home that someone fucked up."

"Listen to yourself! You sound insane."

"Maybe I am! But I don't think wanting to punish a child abuser makes me anything other than noble." She closed her eyes and shook her head. "You make me so fucking mad."

"The feeling is mutual, V." He ground his teeth together.

"I wish you would just listen to me. I'm the witch. I'm the one with magical experience."

"Wonderful. How many times has someone tried to murder you, then?"

"It's not a big deal—"

"It is a big deal! It's a big fucking deal. Whether a ghost or a witch or a mob boss or whatever. It's a big deal when someone tries to murder you, Verbena! I don't want you to die!" Luke inhaled sharply and closed his eyes. He pushed past her into the house, then turned to face her.

He stared at her for a moment, his body tense. They were like two stone statues waiting for the other to flinch.

"Come here," he managed gruffly, reaching his hand to hers and slamming the door behind him.

Her brow remained creased, but she cautiously set her fingers on his palm. He gripped her hand and pulled her against him, immediately burying his fingers in her hair and holding her head inches away from his own.

"I don't want you to die," he repeated. "Got it?"

She nodded, shifting closer to him. "I'll be careful," she promised, and she meant it. There was so much more to life now that he was in it. When she faced the phantom on the hill, her only thoughts were that she hadn't spent enough time with Luke. She wouldn't make that mistake now that she had another chance.

"Luke," she breathed. She leaned toward him but stopped just before their lips met. She was giving him an out, a chance not to kiss her.

He wasn't taking it.

Luke crashed his mouth against hers in a savage meeting. He didn't tease her or kiss her softly. He licked her lips apart and delved into her mouth. He kissed her greedily. There'd been so much wasted time between the two of them. He took kisses like they were his own, his to claim.

Luke pulled Verbena to the couch and immediately covered her with his body. She spread her legs to make room for him as he left her mouth and trailed a hot path down her chest, carefully avoiding her neck. She was wearing a t-shirt today. No easy access with a flasher's coat. He dragged his hand down her body, over the curve of her breast through her shirt, to the hem of her shirt. He flattened his palm against her belly, pausing for a moment before continuing his path. She wanted him to touch her. She wanted his fingers on every inch of her body.

He pushed her shirt and bra up, and she squirmed out of both, tossing them behind her. Goddess, she loved the way he was looking at her body. He looked like an animal about to devour his prey.

"Luke, touch me," she commanded.

"I am touching you," he laughed, placing a quick kiss on her belly.

"Touch me somewhere more fun," she countered. She wiggled underneath him and wrapped her legs around his waist.

Luke held her gaze for a moment, so soft and pleading, then set to work on her shorts.

"Whoa," Luke breathed.

"What?" Verbena craned her neck to look at him.

"You are not wearing underwear."

"Nope," she confirmed. "I changed after I got home and didn't know you'd be peeling my shorts off this afternoon."

"Do you want me to stop?" Luke asked.

"Luke Karnes, if you stop, I will fucking lose it."

Luke's face broke into a grin.

Chapter Twenty-Three

"Right there! Holy shit, do not move your mouth," Verbena panted. "Fuck, Luke. This is amazing." Verbena grasped the arm of the couch and threw her head back.

Luke's head was buried between her thighs, and Verbena thought she might die of pleasure.

Verbena had received oral exactly two times and had never come from it. She'd faked both of those times because she was twenty-two and had wanted to wrap things up.

She wasn't going to fake today.

She was holding onto her sanity by a thread. Luke was taking her, mind and body, to heights she didn't know existed. Yes, when they were together in the bar, it had been wonderful, but it was also distant and cold.

This was intimate and as hot as star fire.

"Luke, Luke, Luke," she repeated, his name the only thing keeping her from spiraling into oblivion. He moaned against her in response, his grasp tightening around her thighs.

Her pleasure built, reaching an apex it had never before, and she fell apart. She moaned, rasped, begged. Her legs trembled, and her fingers curled into fists before falling limp. She sipped air, too spent to take a deep breath.

"Are you okay?" Luke whispered, his mouth moving back to her belly, placing featherlight kisses against her low abdomen.

"Mmm," she hummed. Was she okay? She was golden. She was a puddle of limbs on his couch.

"Is that a yes?" His mouth still moved up, his tongue running over her ribcage.

"It's a hell yes. I'm amazing." She pulled herself up to sit on her elbows and stare down at him.

"Thank you." He nipped the underside of her breast.

"I'm trying really hard not to ruin the mood by asking where you learned to do that."

Luke chuckled. "If it makes you feel better, no one has ever reacted the way you just did."

"I'd hope not." Verbena stretched her arms long, then snaked them down to Luke's shoulders. "So, you didn't want our first time together to be with me bent over a table in the bar, but would you settle for your living room couch?"

"Verbena," Luke answered, his voice a warning.

"What?" She wiggled beneath him and pulled him close. "I can feel you. I know you want me."

"Of course I want you," he continued. "But it wouldn't be a good idea."

"And why not?" She slid her hands down his sides, trying to grasp his waistband so she could get him out of his pants.

"Because I don't have any condoms."

Verbena stopped moving and stared at him. "Why not?"

"I haven't had condoms in a while. Haven't needed them."

"When I told you we were soulmates, and after we hooked up in your bar, you didn't think you might need condoms? One of the big boxes? Because I bought the twenty-five pack figuring it would last a couple weeks."

Luke shifted off her and sat up. "Sorry?"

"It's okay. Take your pants off. We can still have a lot of fun without risking an insta-baby."

"What the hell is an insta-baby?"

"Oh, when soulmates get together and have a baby immediately. Insta-baby. No time to enjoy fucking whenever you feel like it because she's knocked up immediately."

"Phew." Luke rubbed his forehead. "I thought you were going to tell me you had a different gestational period. Like a baby would show up next month."

Verbena bit her lip to keep from laughing. "I don't think witches would have been able to hide their identities for hundreds of years if they were popping out babies like rabbits."

"Good point." Luke leaned against the couch and stretched his arms overhead. Verbena grinned wickedly and slunk off the couch to the floor in front of him.

"Verbena," he began.

"What?" she answered, unbuttoning his pants.

"You don't have to..."

"Luke." She paused and sat back on her heels. "Let me tell you something about myself. I never do something I don't want to do. Sure, sometimes I end up listing a house for a real asshole of a client, but know this, if I'm on my knees in front of you, it's because I want to be there." She licked her lips and set her hands on his thighs.

"Wait," Luke's hand went to her chin. "After the bar...you said you wanted it to mean something when we were together. And you wanted me to care about you." He paused and leaned closer. "This means a lot to me. And so do you."

"Oh," she answered softly as she tried to swallow the lump in her throat. "I feel the same way. You mean more to me than—"

Fraoch Ún!

Verbena jumped to her feet, and Luke bounced off the couch. He quickly did up his pants and grabbed his shirt and tossed it to her.

Cailleach salach! Salachar de mo theaghlach!

"Salt!" Verbena yelled. Luke nodded, his hands over his ears. He sprinted to the kitchen and grabbed a large canister of table salt. Verbena's head whipped around, waiting for the phantom to grab onto her and try to kill her again.

"Here!" Luke thrust the salt into her hand, then stood protectively at her back. She tossed a circle on the ground around them and hugged Luke close.

The voice stopped.

She exhaled hard. How did the phantom get into Luke's house? Other than the Bay cottage, his house was the most protected place on Star Island. It wasn't hard to protect a place when the only occupants starting at her were a pair of dogs wagging their tails at the window.

"Wait, you heard that?" Verbena's eyes flew wide open. Luke had been covering his ears.

"You could hear it?" he asked. "How? That...that was in my head."

Verbena's mouth dropped open. "You could hear the phantom," she repeated. "Speaking in Irish. Screaming in Irish."

"No," Luke answered slowly. "I could hear..." he hesitated. "I could hear the guy who was my guardian for five years. He was speaking English. To me."

Verbena relaxed in Luke's arms, her brain moving a mile a minute. "So, we hear different things. That's so weird." Her brain ticked along, trying to put pieces together. "What was his name?"

"Boris Varga."

"Is..." She didn't want to ask the next question, but she didn't see a way circumventing it. "Is he related to the Stochs?"

"I don't know. He was my dad's cousin. I only know my two cousins. Danny is one of them."

"Wait, Danny is your cousin?"

"Yes. But we were raised together, so more like a brother. But bloodwise, we're second cousins."

"Is Boris Danny's dad?"

"Yup."

"Okay." It was all starting to make sense. If he was a phantom attached to a person instead of a place, Boris probably hitched a ride to Star Island on Danny. She wasn't quite sure how the Stochs fit in, but they had to. Otherwise, they had an unconnected phantom after them, and that sounded worse.

"What is Rosemary doing?" Luke whispered. He sat next to Verbena at the Bays' dining table with the other four sisters crowded around them, while Owen and Asher were off to the side.

"I'm trying to gauge whether or not you have any magical abilities,"

Rosemary answered. "We'll all take a turn. It isn't a perfect science, but it's better than nothing."

"I'm not magical. Promise," Luke added with a grimace. Luke knew that if there was even an inkling of magic in him, it would have exploded when he lived with Boris.

"I had no idea that I was a Guardian when I arrived here," Asher cut in. "These types of things can be very dormant."

"And, like Asher, you didn't spend your formative years with your biological parents. So there really wasn't a chance for anyone to let you know." Rosemary stood up, and Sage shuffled into her seat.

"I don't know why I have to do this."

"We're all doing it," Lavender reminded.

"When have you ever been under the impression that I enjoy doing things that everyone does?" Sage looked him over. "I got nothing."

"What was his last name? The voice you heard?" Laurel asked. She had a huge book in front of her, like an ancient telephone book, but a lot creepier-looking.

"Varga."

"Do you remember his mom's name? Or a sister maybe?"

"Uh, he did have a sister. Kalina. She's my...she's Taylor's mom."

"Last name Varga?"

"As far as I know." Taylor was now Taylor Spincent. He took his wife's name when they got married in an attempt to distance himself from the Varga name.

"No Vargas," Laurel said slowly, "but..."

"But what?" Verbena asked, wrapping her hand around Luke's arm. She was extremely tense, waves of anxiety rippling off her.

"If you go back a couple generations in here, there were two Stoch witches who only gave birth to non-magicals."

By the look on the Bay sisters' faces, it was as if Laurel had confirmed the moon landing as a hoax.

"What does that mean?"

"It doesn't mean anything," Verbena began. "Do you know your grandmother's name?"

"Yeah..." Luke searched his memory. He'd met her a few times, but it had been decades. "I called her Nana, but her name was something like Chessie?"

"Chesna?" Laurel prompted.

"Maybe. But her last name was Smith. That's about as American as it gets, right?"

The color drained from Laurel's face. "Your grandpa was Matthew Smith?"

"How did you know that?"

Laurel slowly turned the book toward the table for all to see. "There were three Stoch sisters, Zora, Nadiya, and Chesna. Zora is the grandmother of Miloslav, Ivan, and Morana. Nadiya had two children, a non-magical boy and girl. Chesna had one non-magical boy. And she's listed as changing her name after her marriage."

"Witches don't usually do that," Verbena mumbled. "And since your parents never married, your mom's last name was the one you have."

"I don't get it. I'm cousins with the people trying to kill you?"

"Not direct cousins," Laurel corrected. "But you are related to them. Your dad and their mom were cousins."

Luke let this new information wash over him. His relatives were trying to kill Verbena and her sisters. As if his family hadn't been fucked up enough already, now he had second cousins coming after his girlfriend.

"Wait, did you say Miloslav? Oh shit. Milo." Luke shook his head. "I've met him. He is such an asshole." He let out a breath. "Okay, what does this mean? I'm from family of evil witches and warlocks?"

"Pretty much," Sage answered.

"Sage!" Verbena shouted. "No. It does not mean that. It means you are sort of related to some bad people."

"I'm related to a lot of bad people, trust me."

"What does it really mean to be a bad person?" Rosemary mused. "Aren't we all just working as if we are right and everyone else is wrong? Can we really blame the Stochs for their actions?"

"Rosemary, Ivan tried to kill you and Asher. And Morana tried to kill Laurel. I think we can agree they aren't good people." Lavender sighed. "Past life?"

"Probably a good idea," Verbena answered quietly. She wove her fingers through Luke's hand and pulled it against her side. She turned to face him, then smiled. "Let's go back to your house and talk."

"In the middle of a Bay family meeting?" Luke joked.

"Meeting's over," Lavender announced. "I'll get you the bread. We'll take turns peeking in, and I'll make sure the fridge is stocked for after."

"After what?" Luke asked.

"Home first," Verbena insisted.

"You're telling me that Laurel was burned at the stake in medieval France? And Asher and Rosemary were Vikings?"

"Probably pre-Viking, but yes. And from the Irish that's been assaulting my ears whenever I hear your...former caretaker, you and I are probably heading sometime on the Emerald Isle." Verbena busied herself around Luke's house, filling the dogs' dishes with water, rinsing out his coffee cup from this morning, wiping down the counters.

"Verbena, what are you doing?"

She stilled her hand and turned toward him. "Tidying helps me relax. The truth of the matter is, this is sort of going to suck, but I have to do it to help my family and I don't know a way to do it without you. If I could, I would go alone and not make you relive it."

"I don't want you to go through that alone. If you're going to see our past together, I want to also. It wouldn't be fair to make you take all of that on." Luke leaned against the wall and crossed his arms. He still felt awkward with her, like there was something blocking them, something keeping them from really relaxing in each other's company.

"Owen was beaten to death. Asher was murdered when he had two small children. It's not a great pattern."

"I assume we didn't die holding hands at ninety-two."

"I think that's a safe assumption."

Luke exhaled. "Well, let's get to it."

"Now?" Verbena exclaimed. "Like this second?"

"We should probably both take a piss before we start. Aren't we out for twenty-four hours or so?"

Verbena giggled and shook her head. "You'll be glad to know that no one has peed their pants doing this spell yet." She paused. "But yeah, I have to pee. Where do you want to set up?"

"What do you mean?"

"Do you want me on the couch or..."

Luke looked her over. She was nervous, fidgeting with her bracelet and looking around the room.

"My bed. Both of us. I'm not going to make you lay on my couch for a day. We can at least be comfortable."

"Rosemary did hers outside."

"Rosemary is a bit of an eccentric."

Verbena smiled. "Your bed is fine." She slipped her shoes off and took her hair out of her ponytail. "Lead the way."

Luke took her hand. They were both scared, because the idea was terrifying. In the next day, Luke would have knowledge of a past life he'd lived with Verbena. He would experience all the highs and lows of that life, and it would end with their deaths.

He pulled her a bit closer. There was no way he could do this without her at his side.

Chapter Twenty-Four

In a drafty castle on a parcel of land that was cold but green, Nessa lived and worked and kept her secrets. She may have been head of her staff, but she was still a serving woman to a lord who didn't care much for the old ways and the gods that came with them. So, she took care to leave her bits of bread and bowls of milk in hidden spots beneath shrubs, and she whispered her prayers rather than shout them to the sky.

The land of Éire was sacred, home to Lugh and Bríd, Morrigan and Angus. Whether in whispers or shouts, it was their land. It was far too old and haunted a place for the young Nazarene, born of scorching sun and dry deserts.

Nessa was not a stupid girl, like Shanna who'd been drowned in the lake two summers earlier. She knew practicing the religion of her people could find her locked in a nunnery if not turned into a watery ghost like Shanna. So she kept her secrets and that was it.

She walked down to the lake that morning with the washing, hoping for a few minutes of peace, but there was none to be had. Aisling was already there with her cleaning and looking to gab with whoever came along.

"Nessa!" she exclaimed, waving her over. "Has he come yet? The new lord?"

"Not yet." Nessa settled her washing beside the riverbank. "The journey from Ulster is long, and with the damp and the heavy rains three days ago, the roads must be nearly untravelable."

"How exciting! You'll have a new master. And maybe this one won't be so sour and strict. It'd be nice to have a little cheer round these parts. The sky is dreary enough."

"Lord Fergal likes things a certain way," Nessa answered diplomatically. Truthfully, Fergal could drown in a bog for all she cared, but Aisling was a gossip and Nessa needed her work, her bed, and her head attached to her body. "And his nephew is only coming to see how the estate is run. I doubt he'll stay more than a moon or two." Especially if he isn't familiar with his uncle's moods.

Nessa finished her washing and carried the heavy load back to the courtyard to hang it. The clouds were breaking up, and it looked as if a bit of sun might hasten the drying process, so she hurried up the path to get the clothes on the drying frame.

"Lugh," she whispered. "Won't you grace us with a bit of warmth and a bit of light?" The sun god could lighten her load if he chose to shine a little brighter this afternoon.

"Hello, there!"

Nessa dropped her basket and nearly jumped out of her skin.

"Apologies! Didn't mean to frighten you." A man on foot was loping toward her as if he was running a race. "My cart is stuck aways down the road in some mud, and I was hoping someone could help me."

Nessa looked him up and down. He was a nice-looking fellow, sunny yellow hair and straight teeth. He looked wealthy too. His clothes weren't worn or those of the servant class. Normally, she would have a snide remark and run away from a strange man approaching her, but something about him was familiar.

"Where's the cart?"

"I can take you," he answered, pointing over his shoulder.

"I doubt I'd be much help, but Declan in the stables would."

"Of course." The man shook his head and smiled. "I'm not thinking straight. I've been without a good night's sleep for weeks now. Where are the stables?"

"Just past that tree. Declan should be in there. He can help you." Nessa picked up her basket and turned toward the house.

"What's your name?"

"Nessa," she called over her shoulder but kept walking.

"I'm Dáire, Nessa. Lovely to meet you."

"You should go talk to Declan. No use dallying," she said firmly and disappeared around the corner.

Dáire followed Nessa's directions and walked to the stables, where Declan was indeed tending the horses. He supplied him with a mount and followed behind, and with the two horses, plus the one he'd been with, they were able to free the cart.

Dáire's travels had been exhausting. He'd ridden clear across Éire, unknowing whether or not he'd ever arrive at his uncle's castle.

The Ó Murchadha holdings were in the south and against the sea. Dáire's mother, Oonagh, spent her childhood here but hadn't returned since her marriage to Dáire's father some twenty years ago. Now that his uncle found himself without an heir, Dáire had been summoned to see the estate that would pass to him.

Having spent his life inland in the forests of Ulster, Dáire was unfamiliar with the rocky coastline and the incessant pounding of the waves against the shore. The sea raged, day and night, having no mercy upon the shore or its people. It stood by, like an angry spirit, threatening to pull the island to its watery depths.

Once he returned to the castle with his cart and solitary man-at-arms provided by his father, Dáire was shown to his rooms and promptly fell into a sound sleep. He hadn't truly slept on the road, always keeping his ears pricked for wolves or men looking to slit his throat when he was unaware. It was blissful to sleep without fear.

He woke with a start, the dream in his mind like a cloud slowly dissipating.

A woman in the sea, calling for him to join her. He had, and they became a mess of stinging saltwater and tangled limbs. Dáire quickly crossed himself, worried she was a faerie creature sent to seduce and lead him to a watery death.

He sat, glancing around his room. There was a plate of bread and cheese, a jug of ale, and a bowl of water with a length of cloth. A candle flickered against the stone walls, casting shadows across the room. Dáire fetched the candle, washed himself, then finished his meal almost as soon as he started it.

He picked up his ale and the candle and set to exploring the castle.

It was hard to imagine that this stone fortress would be his home. Or rather, it already was his home. He was to stay here and learn the land, make allies and enemies, and become the landowner. Ulster was his past. Munster was his future.

Dáire moved down the narrow halls, passing quiet, empty rooms. When his mother had been a child, the castle had overflowed with guests and relatives, but his uncle was a solitary creature. He had been married several years ago, but no children had come of the union. His wife had left and joined a nunnery after a decade of marriage, and Fergal had not married again.

The halls were drafty, and soon Dáire was wishing he had donned his cloak before leaving his room and bedding. He drank deeply of his ale, hoping it might warm him.

He found the stairs and took them, wondering if the kitchens were still working. He could do with a bit of stew or mutton, whatever might be available.

He walked through the great hall, empty and echoing even though huge tapestries hung on the walls. He would remember to study them at length in the morning with better light. The wind whipped around the room, the fire down to a smoldering glow.

"When I am lord," Dáire whispered, "this place will have a bit of life again." He would ask his parents to come, his sisters as well. Before he knew it, the castle would be alive with family, fresh with the breath of new life.

He could hear the din of quiet voices rising over the stark silence.

The kitchens.

He turned to follow the sound, and before long he could smell bread baking and the scent of chopped onions. He found a small staircase and followed it to the cellar.

There stood two women with their backs to him. One was tall, her hair as black as night and braided tightly. The other was shorter, maybe even a child, with wild red hair escaping a bonnet.

"Excuse me," Dáire began. The taller woman whipped her head around and before he knew it, she had a knife in her hand and pointed at him.

"What are you doing down here?" she demanded.

It was Nessa.

"Nessa! It's Dáire, from earlier."

Her brow furrowed, and she pushed the other woman behind her. "What are you doing here?" she repeated. She showed no intention of releasing her knife.

"I live here now," he answered quickly. "Fergal Ó Murchadha is my uncle."

"You're the heir?" the other woman stepped out from behind Nessa. "Did you really sleep all day and half the night?"

"I suppose I did." Dáire suppressed a laugh. "I find myself very hungry."

"I'll get you a bowl of porridge and a plate of venison." The younger woman wiped her hands on her apron and got to work, collecting the food.

"You didn't mention you were the heir," Nessa began as she turned to a pile of root vegetables in front of her and used her knife to chop them. "Usually, the lord of the castle doesn't come down to the kitchens. Even if he wants something to eat before sunrise."

"What does the lord do? Ignore the rumblings of an empty stomach?"

"No," Nessa smirked. "He sends a servant. Why would he leave the warmth of his bed when he could send someone and have a feast on a platter under his bedcovers?"

"Well, I have no servants at the moment, and it seems an awful waste to wake someone when I am perfectly capable of walking here myself." Dáire eyed the kitchen. It was larger than his family's, but not unfamiliar. While Dáire did little cooking, his mother and sisters often spent full days in the kitchen, making delicious treats and laughing the hours away. The pungent scent of smoke and roasted meat would always be one of comfort and home.

"Here you are, my lord." The other woman handed him a plate and bowl. "Oh, would you like me to take it up for you?"

"I will," Nessa interjected. "Ina, watch the bread and start skinning the rabbits." She turned back to Dáire. "I assume you don't remember the way back to your room?"

"I confess, I do not."

"Let's get you back to your chambers before there are rumors you've wandered off."

Nessa knew she shouldn't be speaking with Dáire.

She knew that one day, he would be her lord and she his servant, but now, now, he looked at her with clear green eyes and spoke to her like a woman.

She should stop before she came undone. Because when he spoke, it was like clean water running over her on the first warm summer day.

"Nessa!" Lord Fergal's voice was sharp and annoyed that early spring morning.

"Yes, my lord," Nessa answered, hurrying to his side.

"Bring my heir to me," he demanded. "Tell him it is important."

"Yes, my lord," she repeated, then walked purposefully toward the hall.

"He's not in his chambers," Lord Fergal called to her.

She paused, then spun on her heels, headed to the great hall.

"Not there either," Fergal mused.

Nessa suppressed a groan. "My lord, is he in the library?"

"Wrong."

"The courtyard?"

"Wrong again. Nessa, when you were elevated to head maid, I thought you would be better at this." He shook his head at her.

"Riding, then?"

"Correct. Out in the fields somewhere. I'd like him brought to me as quickly as you can manage, dear." Fergal swept a cruel gaze over her. "I do hope the ground isn't too damp."

Nessa gave him a quick bow, then headed down to the kitchen. She'd grab her cloak on the way out. The air was frigid, and the rain that had soaked the ground all morning was threatening to fall again.

With her hood pulled tightly around her face, Nessa stomped out to the fields.

The earth had been transformed to muck, the wind had a biting edge, and Dáire was little more than a speck in the distance. What on earth had possessed him to go for a ride today? If Nessa were a lady of leisure—the thought alone made her laugh—she would be bundled in blankets in front of a warm fire with a cup of mead in her hand. Why the heir to the Ó Murchadha castle would be messing around on a horse and not resting his bones and being waited on was beyond her.

She kept her eye on him. Thankfully, he seemed to be circling the area and showed no signs of bolting in the other direction.

Close to an hour later, Daire caught sight of her, mud caking Nessa's dress up to her knees and her boots three times as heavy as they were when she left. He turned his horse toward her and galloped until they were closer.

"Nessa?"

"Your uncle would speak with you," she called, holding her hand up to block the rain now falling from the sky in icy droplets.

Dáire slid from his horse and jogged to her. "Why are you out here in the rain?"

"To fetch you."

"Fergal sent you out in the rain?" Dáire shook his head. "Take the horse back, I can walk."

"I cannot."

"You're soaked through and covered in mud. I can walk."

"No, you do not understand. You are the heir to Ó Murchadha castle. I am a servant. I cannot take your mount. I will walk."

"That's ridiculous." Dáire grabbed her hand and pulled her to the horse. His hands went to her waist and turned her to face the horse. "Please. Take the horse to the stables. I'll meet you there. Unless Fergal is spying out the windows, he'll never know."

Nessa tossed it over in her mind. Her feet were aching, her knees stiff, and she could feel a headache coming on. She glanced toward the stables. They would be warm and sweet-smelling.

"Make certain Fergal doesn't see. I'll pull my hood down low and go around back. Do the same." Nessa held onto the saddle, and Dáire grabbed her around the waist, lifting her onto the horse.

"Go," he said. "Try to get warm."

Dáire took his time meeting his uncle. He warmed himself by the fire, changed into dry clothes, even had a small meal before making his way to the Great Hall where Fergal sat at a table meant for forty, with a pile of parchments surrounding him.

"I hope dear Nessa didn't tarry when collecting you," Fergal stated without looking up.

"I was on the far reaches on horseback. I'm surprised she found me at all."

Fergal raised an eyebrow and looked to Dáire. "She's a pretty thing, but worth nothing. It would be good for you to remember that. Women like Nessa are in great supply here. Take care you don't find yourself with a bastard before the year is out."

Dáire was shocked. Yes, he thought Nessa was the most beautiful woman he'd ever seen, but he would never...presume to take liberties with her.

"Besides, we need to pick a bride for you. The Ó Murchadha line needs another heir. You'll need a son or two before I leave this earth."

"I hardly think I'm in the position to marry," Dáire began. "I have no home of my own, no land, no income. I can't imagine men will throw their daughters my way."

"I have letters out with five families already, across Éire and Breataine," Fergal continued, ignoring his objections. "You'll need to make a powerful alliance. These cold years will end at some point. And we'll need strong armies to protect our lands."

Dáire regarded his uncle suspiciously. The Ó Murchadha line hadn't been a powerful one in centuries. His uncle had lived in relative solitude his entire life. Why on earth would they suddenly find alliances?

"Bring me a rose or a daisy, my dear, or hold me and say that I've nothing to fear. Give me your heart, your hand, and your sword, and I'll give you a kiss as a reward," Nessa sang softly. She was changing the bedding in the castle today. Lord Fergal was expecting guests soon and wanted every room ready for occupants as soon as possible.

The keep currently had eight empty rooms.

Nessa beat the dust out of the rugs, fitted the beds with sheets, and wiped down the surfaces. If Lord Fergal wanted to give the impression that these rooms hadn't sat empty for decades, she wouldn't be the one to stop him.

"I'll give you a kiss, I'll give you a kiss, a kiss as your reward, for your heart and your hand, your love and your sword, I'll give you a kiss as reward."

"His heart, his hand, his love, and his sword for a single kiss? He must really love you."

Nessa dropped the rag she was using to clean the bedposts and turned toward the door.

"I didn't mean to startle you. I apologize." Dáire smiled. "You have a lovely voice."

"Thank you." She stooped down and retrieved the rag. "Why are you in the guest quarters?"

"Boredom mostly. I've memorized the names of every person my uncle is convinced is coming and he's gone out riding for the afternoon. Needs to prepare to show them the sights of Castle Ó Murchadha. As if they haven't seen bogs and mucky fields before."

"Are you excited?"

"For what?"

"To meet your future bride?"

Dáire chuckled. "I'm not meeting my future bride."

"I think that will be a surprise to Fergal. He's had us racing around to make sure the castle is perfect for your future wife."

"Why would I marry a girl I've never met? Who has no interest in marrying me? I have no intention of forcing someone to bear my children and live in this despairing castle."

"The castle's not that bad."

"They say it's haunted," Dáire pointed out.

"Oh, it is haunted. There's the Gray Lord and the Weeping Lady. They're only seen at midwinter. Then the Laughing Children who run through the fields on clear spring nights. And there's the Chain-Dragger. No one knows who he is, but he's very loud."

"I cannot be certain whether you are teasing me or letting me in on a grand secret."

"Bit of both," Nessa admitted. "But if you're to be lord of the castle, you'll need to be familiar with the specters, both true and rumored." Nessa looked up from her work to find Dáire gazing at her like she was a bowl of warm stew on a cold night.

"Nessa," he began, then shook his head. "I'm sorry. I should leave you alone."

"I don't mind. Talking to you makes the work go faster. Plus, I don't often get to talk of things like ghosts and company coming. Usually, it's only Ina and myself, and we prattle the day away about food. You're a welcome distraction." Nessa didn't add that his eyes were like the sea at midsummer and when he smiled at her, she felt like a real and true lady, not a lowly servant. It was a silly infatuation, after all. Dáire would marry a fancy woman from a rich family, and they would have dozens of children and plain Nessa would serve them. She'd be grateful for the work and wouldn't begrudge him his choice. She would grow to love his wife and their babies, staying on the peripheral, as all servants were meant to. Even if he looked at her with wanting. As he did at the moment.

"Nessa," he began again, this time with conviction in his voice. "I should leave you alone, because whenever I'm near you, I can't think of anything but kissing you. And I'm the heir to the lordship, and I don't want you thinking you need to please me to keep your position..." his voice trailed off.

Nessa licked her lips. She wasn't shocked, of course. Many maids found themselves in bed with their lords, whether or not they wanted it. But Nessa...she wanted it. More than she should.

He was right, they should not push this further. If Lord Fergal found out...well, in the best case Nessa would be out of work. In the worst, she could be choking on bog water.

But Dáire stood in front of her, and she felt alive. More alive than Nessa had felt during the nineteen years she'd had on earth. She wanted him, wanted the small part of him that could be given to her. Even if it meant heartbreak, even if it meant letting him go so he could marry a lady. She wanted any small piece he could grant her, however fleeting the moment may be.

Nessa went to him. She wrapped her arms around his neck, she drew his mouth to hers, and she basked in the bliss of his lips against hers, his hands on her waist, his body against hers.

With that first kiss, it was done.

Dáire walked silently up the back staircase. It was easier, using this one. Meant for the servants and drafty, here Dáire could be certain he wouldn't run into Fergal. It was after midnight, and running into his uncle, who could waylay his plans, was furthest from his mind.

Dáire tiptoed down to the servants' quarters. He'd run into Declan once, last month, and while the stablemaster had kept his mouth shut, he didn't want to risk scaring one of the women into screaming.

He came to her door and knocked so softly it could easily have been mistaken for a tree branch in the wind.

"Quickly," Nessa breathed, her voice never raising above a whisper. She pulled him into her quarters and bolted the door behind her.

Their time together was always rushed and stifled. Dáire wished it could be different. He wished they had a cottage somewhere far-flung where he could yell to the heavens how much he loved his sweet Nessa, how the sound of her voice was the loveliest thing on earth, how her skin was softer than spring grass, how he wanted to marry her and spend all their days together. But they couldn't.

Instead, they slipped into her bed, silently explored each other, their moans smothered with kisses and hands, and enjoyed the time they shared in the dark. Their wishes for more were tempered by what they could have, stolen starlit time, silent declarations that never left their tongues.

Dáire folded his arms around Nessa and cradled her head against his chest.

"It's nearly daybreak," she said in hushed tones, her fingers tracing his hip bone. "I need to light the fires. And you need to return to your bed and sleep."

"It isn't fair," he muttered, "that I should go back to bed and you will work from now until late tonight. When I am lord..."

"When you are lord, your wife will send me away if we continue this." Nessa pressed a kiss against his shoulder and wiggled out of bed. She grabbed her shift off the floor and pulled it over her shivering body. She reached for her wool dress. Even in summer, the days were still chilly.

"Nessa, the only woman I want to marry is you," he insisted. Dáire grabbed her hand.

"Yes, but want and need are different things." She sighed. "I love you, and I would love you whether you had land and title or nothing at all, but you do not have the same luxury. You need to make an alliance with a wealthy family, if you'll have any hope of resurrecting this castle to its former glory. And if you are caught with me, Lord Fergal will rename his heir and you'll be...you'll be sent home to Ulster."

"Nessa," Dáire began. He pulled her back to him until she sat on his lap. "My uncle has no other choice of heir. If he did, he certainly would not have picked me. My parents married for love, and my father is not a wealthy man. We do not live in poverty, but our home is nothing like this castle. I will not marry a daughter of a wealthy family, because I am not going to marry anyone but you. My uncle will not live forever, and as soon as I can, I promise I will make you lady to my lord."

"Dáire, you shouldn't make promises to serving girls," she chided.

He lifted her off his lap and set her on her feet, then fell to his knees beside her. "I swear on my heart, on my land, and my God, I will marry no one but you, dear Nessa. I pledge this to you, love of my life."

"Dáire," she breathed. She fell to her knees in front of him and wrapped her arms around him. "My love, my heart."

Months passed and seasons changed, but still Dáire did not marry and Fergal did not die. Nessa and Dáire lived and loved on stolen time, moments in the dark, whispers of love that could never be shouted. When winter came again, Nessa's courses stopped. She wasn't surprised, but she was fearful. She didn't dare tell anyone, not even Dáire, for fear of being turned out into the winter. If she waited until spring...well, perhaps Dáire could take her to Ulster. Nothing was keeping her here.

Nessa kept up with her work, even if most days she simply wanted to sleep and sip broth. She couldn't let anyone know the secret she hid.

"Nessa," Lord Fergal barked at her. "I asked for luncheon. If you are unable to complete so simple a request, send the simpleton from the kitchens to help me."

"Ina isn't simple," Nessa spat out before her brain registered what she had done. She clapped her hand over her mouth and bowed her head immediately. "I apologize, my lord. I spoke out of turn. I will fetch you luncheon."

"No, no." Lord Fergal waved his hand at her. "Come here, please. Sit." He motioned to the chair beside him. Nessa sat tentatively. She'd never been asked to sit before in his presence, and she had an uneasy feeling.

"Dáire! Come in here!" he shouted. Dáire stepped into the hall from the corridor.

"Yes?"

"It seems we have an impertinent member among our staff." He nodded toward Nessa. She kept her eyes focused on the floor in front of her. She knew if she locked eyes with Dáire she would cry. "How shall we punish her? No food for the week? Turn her out into the storm?" Currently, the wind wailed and slapped sleet against the side of the castle. "Give her to Lord Aenghus? I've heard he is always looking for young women to work in his house."

"Stop," Dáire said sharply.

"Stop what? She is a servant and spoke out of turn. Would you prefer I beat her? Would you prefer to beat her?" Lord Fergal smiled wickedly.

"How dare you?" Dáire boomed. "If you so much as touch her, I'll—"

"You'll what?" Lord Fergal stood before Dáire, his eyes darting between him and Nessa. "Oh, you fool. Did she seduce you? Get her claws in you? I told you to steer away from her. She is a servant." His voice was laced with disgust.

"She will not be a servant for long," Dáire challenged. "I have betrothed myself to her."

No, Nessa thought. Why was he saying this? Didn't he know Fergal would cast them out?

"You aren't allowed to do that. You will never marry her. It's bad enough she could be carrying your bastard." Fergal shook his head. "You absolute fool." Fergal rolled his eyes. "Ina!" he shouted, his voice echoing off the stone walls.

Ina ran up the stairs from the kitchen into the great hall, wiping her hands on her apron. She bowed clumsily when she entered.

"My lord."

"Fetch Declan. I am in need of his strength."

"What are you doing?" Dáire demanded. "You can't—"

"You will not tell me what I can and cannot do, nephew. You are a guest in my house. Yes, I have named you heir, but I can take that away."

"There are no other men in your line."

"Then I suppose the line will die. If you think I would rather the bastard offspring of a serving girl take the lands of Ó Murchadha, you haven't listened to anything I've told you these past months."

Nessa sat completely still, her mind a flurry of activity. Would he turn them out? With no horses? Perhaps Aisling would take them in until they could find a way north. Or until winter ended.

"Declan. Take Nessa to the tower and lock her in it."

"Do not," Dáire stood between her and Declan. "Do not touch her."

"Declan, if you do not take Nessa to the tower and lock her there, I will have her tried for witchcraft."

"What? You would never succeed." Dáire pulled Nessa to her feet and wove his arm beneath hers.

"How little you know of your supposed love. Nessa is a pagan. She does not attend mass nor does she pray to our Christian God. The people of Munster would be glad to see a witch made to stand trial."

Nessa felt the blood drain from her face. Women were killed for less. She may still favor the old gods, but she was no witch. She had no spells or deals with the devil. She simply kept the traditions of her family alive.

"Dáire," she whispered. "Let Declan take me."

"No."

"Listen to me. We've run out of stolen time." She squeezed his hand. "Let me go with Declan. He won't hurt me." But your uncle may, she added silently.

"I love you, Nessa."

"I love you. Let me go."

As she followed Declan toward her prison, she heard a slithering in Fergal's voice directed at Dáire that turned her insides to ice.

Dáire watched Declan lead Nessa out of the Great Hall and up the stairs too paralyzed to do anything. If it were summer…he would steal her away on horseback, take her to his family lands, not this ridiculous, empty castle. He would give her a kind house, with people who loved them and didn't care if she was born a servant.

"I have been meaning to take this conversation up with you, and now seems the perfect time." Fergal prattled on as if he hadn't just imprisoned the woman Dáire loved. "There has been unrest in Limerick. Ó Brien has requested I send men to support him. His daughter is already married, so we will show our support by sending you to help. As well as a few of the young men from the village."

"You're sending me to battle? For a man I've never met?"

"I am. You will represent our family, you will come home decorated, and then you will marry a woman I have chosen for you in that time."

"And Nessa?"

"If you do these things, she may stay here, in her position. I will not cast her into the wilderness nor accuse her of witchcraft. But, if you defy me at any turn, she will be destitute or dead."

Dáire stared at the man before him: old, weakened, but holding everything he loved in the palm of his hand.

"I will go. But if you harm her, in any way, I will bury this line in the ground."

Nessa wrapped her arms around herself. The tower room was empty and freezing. The stone walls here did little to keep out the air, and Nessa only had on her wool dress.

Was Fergal going to leave her here to die? Was he going to kill her?

She and Dáire should have left months ago, before the snows started. They could have made it to Ulster, gotten away from this terrible place. Nessa thought of her mistress, driven mad by her master, sent away for failing to produce an heir that lived longer than a week. The walls of this keep dripped poison into the air. Everything beautiful was stolen here.

"Nessa?" Dáire whispered in the hall. "Nessa, can you hear me?"

"Yes!" she answered, clamoring to sit against the door. "Oh, Dáire!"

"Nessa, I have to go away. But I will return for you as soon as I can. And we will leave this place. I will take you to Ulster. I promise. Oh, Nessa, I love you."

"I love you," Nessa whispered. She ran her hands across her belly. It had been five moons since her last courses, and her stomach was bloated and hard. Dáire hadn't noticed.

"I'll come back for you, Nessa."

Nessa bit her lip to keep from wailing as she listened to his soft footfall disappear down the stairs.

She closed her eyes and breathed. She needed to stay strong. Dáire would return. She would deliver their child, and they would leave Munster. All they needed was to be together.

Dáire's father had fought in Breifné two years before his birth. He didn't talk of it often, and only said that battle brought hell to earth and that every man on the field lost his humanity and became a demon.

Dáire understood that now. He had survived battle twice, left blood-soaked and ashamed of the lives he'd taken, the men who'd cried out in guttural voices as they left this world. He'd seen brothers-in-arms killed, maimed, left screaming in pain until they finally succumbed to death. His dreams were shadowed by those calling out for help or mercy or their mothers or wives.

Only Nessa kept him from going mad. This war over lands needed to be won or finished. He did not care if his side won or lost, only that he could return to Nessa and take her away. Spring was here, and traveling to Ulster would be safer. If only Ó Brien would relent, he could leave and be in Nessa's arms.

He shifted against the tree trunk he was using as a bed for a night and closed his eyes. He willed his mind to think of Nessa, only Nessa. Her smile, the feel of her skin beneath his hands, the way she spoke to him in a stern voice when she disagreed with him.

Nessa.

He begged God to let him only dream of Nessa.

Within a month of Dáire leaving, Nessa's pregnancy was found out. Fergal put her back in the tower, giving Ina instructions to give her one meal a day, just enough that she wouldn't die before Dáire returned. Fergal hoped starving her would cause her to lose the baby, but as Nessa's time grew closer, she could feel the baby moving every day, giving little kicks and flips, reminding her of the love she held in her heart for Dáire.

Every morning, Nessa awoke hoping it was the day he would return to her and take her from this place. But every morning, she was met with Ina and a bit of bread and stew.

"Lord Fergal is not well," Ina whispered. "I promise, the moment he takes to his bed, I will free you from here. Aisling will take you in until Dáire returns."

Finally. Nessa's shoulders released for the first time in months.

"Thank you. Any word from Dáire?"

"None." Ina shook her head. "There are letters, but none from him. No one knows when it will end."

Nessa shook her head and picked up the stew to drink it. She would save the bread for later, when her stomach growled angrily and her child kicked her ribs in frustration.

Once Ina left, slipping silently down the corridor and hoping that her delay hadn't been noticed, Nessa curled onto her side. When she first came here, sleep was elusive. But now she could fall asleep whenever she laid her head down. Dreams were the best part of life now. Dreams of being held by Dáire, dreams of the child, dreams of the home they would make together. She draped her threadbare blanket over her body and drifted to sleep.

"Nessa! Nessa!" Ina shook her awake. "Nessa, please! Fergal has a fever. I have to get you out. Try to stand up."

Nessa struggled to open her eyes. Her body felt like a rock at the bottom of the sea. She could hardly move her limbs.

"Nessa, come. Declan has a horse. We have to get you out of here before Fergal comes to."

"He'll wonder where I've gone."

"We'll tell him Dáire has come home, that he's taken you to Ulster. When Dáire returns, I'll tell him where you are."

"Ina, I don't think I can walk." Nessa felt so heavy. She pushed to her hands and knees and took a deep breath. Ina grabbed her hands and hoisted her to her feet, then snuck her arm around Nessa's waist.

"I've got you. We can get you out." They shuffled to the door. Nessa gripped the wall and shrieked, grabbing her belly and falling to her knees.

"Nessa! Let me get you back up."

"The baby...the baby is coming." She sobbed. It came rushing back to her. Pains had started that afternoon, and she had passed out from exhaustion. She reached between her legs and found her skirts damp with her waters and some blood. She looked back up at Ina. "I can't walk down the stairs."

"All right." Ina inhaled sharply. "We'll hope that the fever is a terrible one. I'm going to get a blanket for the baby and some water. I'll send Declan to fetch Aisling. She'll know what to do. Try not to scream. If Lord Fergal hears you..."

"I'll try," Nessa promised. Ina disappeared down the stairs, and Nessa crawled back to her sleeping area. Her blanket was soaked through and of little use now. She tried to unlace her dress, but her fingers were clumsy. Another pain ripped through her body. She panted as quietly as possible, trying to think of anything but the agony that tore her apart.

"Dáire, please come home to me. Dáire..."

The battle raged on, though the sun had fallen below the horizon hours ago. The sky was clear—a terrible thing on a night like this. If the stars and moon were covered, the darkness would give them all a chance to run. To escape this awful hell of clanging and blood in the air.

Dáire was so tired, he could barely lift his arms, but the enemy didn't stop. They were outnumbered this time. For every man he cut down, three took his place. It was a hellish magic how the enemy fought tonight. He waited for the call of retreat, a chance to run into the woods and find some reprieve from the unending fight. Even if they gave chase, he would at least have a moment with his arms at his side. But it didn't come. He had prayed for an end to the war, and perhaps tonight was it. But he would not be on the winning side. He would not return to Nessa and save her from Fergal. He wanted so badly to have a different ending to their love. One with joy and a happy home, perhaps children in the future. Nights by the fire, joy in the house.

Sweet Nessa. He wanted to give her so much more than this. She deserved so much more than she had in this life.

Nessa knew she was dying. Yes, many women believed they were dying while giving birth, but this was different. It had to be.

The pains were sharp and stabbing, but she had no urge to push. Thick blood poured from her now with no signs of stopping. She stared at the dark ceiling, her hands on her belly.

It was better like this. She didn't want Dáire to see her die, watch her slip slowly into nothingness. He would mourn her but one day, he would find another woman, one who could give him children and survive, one who could turn this castle into a home and not a prison. He would be happy someday. The castle would shake off the poison of Fergal and be a home again.

"Nessa, oh no."

She turned her head to the blurry image of Ina. She wove her fingers through hers.

"Aisling couldn't come. Her daughter is sick...but I'm here. She told me what to do, how to help you. You need to push the baby out, you need to find your strength." Ina turned away from Nessa and shouted, "Help me! Anyone! Declan! Someone help us!"

"Ina, it's all right," Nessa breathed. The pains weren't coming anymore. A glorious reprieve. "Don't let Dáire mourn us too long. I want him...I want him to find happiness."

"Nessa, you're going to be all right. So is the baby, I need you to push. Aisling said to get on your hands and knees. She birthed her babies that way, and it was easier than lying down. Or you could stand. I can hold you up."

"I can't move," Nessa admitted. "Dear, Ina. You should leave. Get away from this cursed place. It's no place for life. You have family somewhere? Anywhere? Go to them. Find someone to love you. And stay with them, no matter what." Nessa exhaled slowly. Her mind was starting to drift away, almost like she was fighting sleep. "Ina, Ina."

"I'm right here, Nessa. I'm not leaving you." Nessa reached out her hand, which Ina took, cradling it against her chest.

"Thank you, dear Ina. You've really been like a sister to me. I hope you find some peace."

In the end, the pain melted away, and there was only the faint sound of Ina's voice drifting into nothingness. It was like a song being sung beside the sea and she was straining to hear over the crash of the ocean.

The ocean. The sea washed over her body, cold and salty and final. It would carry her to her gods, place her like a sacrifice at their feet. Her and the child. Wrapped together for eternity.

Dáire. Goodbye, love.

There was a sword in his side. The initial pain of it had been worse than anything he'd experienced, but now it faded. He lay in the field, dozens of men beside him in different stages of death and life. He felt nearer to death now than living. He still breathed, still felt the wind against his cheek. The sun would rise soon and reveal the bloodbath of the evening before.

They were coming now, looking for survivors. Every few moments, there were pleas of mercy followed by a swift silence.

Dáire looked toward the moon on the horizon and exhaled.

"I'm sorry, sweet Nessa. Don't mourn me too long. Escape Fergal. Love of my life, I wish I could see you one last time."

"Oy! There's one over here!" someone called out. Dáire felt the ground shaking beneath him with their footsteps.

"Which master do you serve?" the man asked, his sword raised high.

"Nessa," Dáire breathed. He closed his eyes and conjured the feel of her hair, the smell of her skin.

If his god was a kind one, he would find himself with her again.

Chapter Twenty-Five

"**N**essa." Luke ran his hand over his belly. It was dry and didn't hurt anymore. The blood that had been pouring from him moments ago vanished. And the air, the air was different. It was warmer and smelled like...vanilla. His eyes snapped open.

Nessa.

"Nessa!" he shouted and pulled her into his arms. "Oh God. You're here. Nessa."

She shook awake and stared at him.

He froze.

No. Not Nessa. Fuck, his mind was an absolute mess.

"Verbena. Holy shit. Verbena." Luke rolled onto his back and pressed the palms of his hands against his eyes.

"Luke." Her hand grasped his elbow. "Oh, how terrible."

"I'm so sorry," he gushed, sitting up. "I never should have gone. That was the worst decision of my life. That life. I can't believe I left you without a fight," he rambled.

"There was nothing you would have been able to do," Verbena answered. "I had run through a bunch of scenarios in my head, and childbirth was high on the list."

Luke furrowed his brow. "What do you mean childbirth?"

"Did Ina not tell? Oh goddess. Luke, Nessa died giving birth. Did they lie to Dairé? Say she left? She never left. She died thinking of Dairé."

Luke's mind raced a mile a minute. How long had it been since he left? Only a handful of months.

"You died giving birth? I don't understand. How early were you? I was gone only..."

"Nessa. Nessa was full term. And terrified to tell anyone she was pregnant." Verbena rubbed her forehead. "Nessa was me once, but she isn't me now. Just as you were Dáire, but now you are Luke." She exhaled. "So, what happened when Dairé came back?"

"I didn't come back. I died on the battlefield," Luke admitted.

"What? No!" Verbena's face crumpled. "No. He was coming back, he was going to be happy." Verbena crashed her head against his chest. "Ina promised she wouldn't let Dairé mourn too long, let life pass you by." Verbena inhaled sharply, and her hand flew to her mouth. Her mind settled on those final moments with Ina. It was an awful memory. But Ina had been there with her through it all.

"Ina was Sage! Holy shit, Ina was Sage."

"Ina?" Luke searched his memory. The girl from the kitchen, she was Sage! "Whoa, that's insane. Is that normal?"

"I have no idea."

Luke heard his front door open.

"Are you awake and decent? I'm here with the dogs and food from Lavender!" Sage called from the front room.

"Sage!" Verbena clamored out of bed and immediately hit the floor.

Luke dove off the bed to grab her but ended up beside her.

Sage walked in and rolled her eyes. "Dudes. Lavender said you'd be weak when you woke up." Sage set a cardboard box on the bed and pulled out two bags of chips and tossed them at Luke and Verbena. "Get back on the bed."

"Sage, you were there!" Verbena exclaimed. "You were in it!"

"I was in your past life?" Sage repeated. "Cool. Was I some sort of vigilante? A hired sword?"

"You were a kitchen wench," Luke answered.

"How disappointing," she replied, frowning.

"You stayed with me while I died?" Verbena offered.

"You're welcome. Well, at least I wasn't squeamish." Sage pointed to the box. "Eat a bunch of food, drink fluids, yadda yadda, Verbena knows the drill. Whiskey and Jaeger are exhausted from the five-mile walk we just finished, and they are fed. They will both probably pass out in the next few minutes." Sage paused. "Text me if you need anything. I have to go."

"You're leaving already?" Luke asked.

"Definitely. I hung with Rosemary after she woke up, and I am no longer available as point person post-past-life viewing. Too many emotions, too much death and dying of loved ones, too many regrets. It's August, and I have a ten-hour day with my plants tomorrow. But good luck hashing through it all." She turned to Luke. "If it's any consolation, Owen and Asher also had terrible deaths. Because by the look on your face, I'm guessing yours was a doozy. All right, see you."

Luke pulled himself back onto the bed, then gave Verbena his hand and hoisted her up. He opened the box Sage had left and rifled through it.

"Do you want something to eat or drink?"

"I'll take a lemonade if there's any," she answered.

He tossed one in her direction and grabbed one for himself.

"I'm sorry I called you Nessa," Luke started. "It's a lot to take in."

"It's okay. I've spent years compartmentalizing, so it's second nature to me." Verbena sighed. "I, or Nessa, had this dream that you'd come home before the baby was born and we'd escape to Ulster. We weren't so lucky." She paused. "Fergal is Boris, right?"

"Yeah, he is. He's the phantom haunting us. I can't believe he'd been... with me before. Why? Why is he so connected to me?" Luke lay back on the bed. "The day he died was the most relief I've ever felt. It was like I was tied to an anchor at the bottom of the ocean and the chain snapped. Now, the chain has wrapped around me."

"He won't drag you down again. You have me. And I might not have figured out how to banish him yet, but I will. The Stochs are strong, but so are the Bays. And I am a really strong witch." She took a gulp of lemonade. "Is he really still mad that we fell in love?"

"With Boris, it was always about control. He wanted Danny, Taylor, and I to be little replicas of him, which meant huge assholes and bullies. None of us had any friends or dated because it wasn't in his plan."

"He was probably really pissed to be born into a powerful magical family but have no magic of his own. In the wrong frame of mind, that can really mess with someone."

"Is everyone in your family magical?" Luke asked. He turned onto his side to look at her. It looked right, her lounging in his bed with her ankles crossed eating potato chips. Like it was any old night and they were about to turn on a movie before bed.

"My dad was totally human. My mom's brothers are both non-magical and married humans. A lot of men don't get the magic gene or whatever. That's why the Stochs are something. Two strong warlocks in a family is an oddity."

"But five magical sisters isn't?" he teased.

"Nope. As far as witches go, the Bay family isn't extraordinary."

"I disagree." Luke hazarded a glance at Verbena. She looked uncomfortable for a minute, like she was about to jump out of her skin. "I don't want you to go home, but I can take you home if that is what you want."

"No. I don't want to go home." She shook her head a little. "I'll snap out of it. I'm having a really hard time not focusing on dying at this particular moment. It was...a lot. And very long. When I thought about dying, I always pictured a moment. I was dying slowly for almost a full day." She chewed on her lip a bit, then turned to him. "I'm going to be really honest here, I hope you don't want kids soon, because I'm going to need time to let that fade into the background."

"No rush," Luke said quickly. "And if you don't want to ever give birth, I'm very open to fostering and adoption."

"Oh, okay." Verbena looked decidedly overwhelmed.

Shit.

"I shouldn't have said that," Luke started.

"It's okay. It seems like you've thought about it, a lot."

"I have," he admitted. "I was thinking of fostering before all of this. Now, it probably wouldn't be a good idea, what with a phantom after us and my distant relatives trying to murder you and your sisters."

"Yeah, I think we'd fail the application."

"I'm thirty-one, Verbena. I've been alone for a long time. I can't lie to you and say I don't want a family."

"Oh no, I want one too. If I hadn't just bled out from what I think was placenta previa, I'd make a baby with you in six months. But..."

"But you just bled out. And I wasn't there to hold onto you."

"And I wasn't there to hold your hand either." She scrunched up her nose and buried her face in her hands. "This is so fucked up," she said, her voice muffled.

He couldn't help barking a laugh. "It really is." Luke scratched the back of his head. This was the craziest scenario he could ever imagine. He had a soulmate, a family of evil witches and warlocks, his former guardian was haunting him, and he had a past life where he died in battle. No wonder he had freaked out when Taylor had suggested they all enlist. Some part of Luke knew what happened to him in war.

"Do you mind if I take a shower?" Verbena asked. "I have this thing with water. It calms me, recharges me, grounds me."

"Yeah, that's totally fine. Here," Luke said, standing up much slower than last time. His legs didn't feel as shaky, but like he had gone for a long run instead of a past-life trip to Ireland. "I'll grab you a towel. Do you want some clothes?" He was thinking he should probably shower and change too. They'd been out for over a day.

"If you don't mind."

Luke slowly made his way to his linen closet in the hall and was immensely thankful there were ample clean towels.

He brought Verbena a towel and gave her one of his t-shirts and a pair of boxer shorts. Then he showed her the bathroom.

"I don't have any fancy soap or conditioner or anything," he apologized.

"That's okay. I really just want to get under the water. Whatever you have is fine."

Luke nodded and shut the door behind him. He sat back on the bed and tried not to ruminate on the idea that Verbena was naked with water running down her body in his shower. Instead, he focused on Fergal or Boris or whatever the hell he was supposed to call the dead man invading his and Verbena's thoughts.

He tried to remove himself emotionally from his memories, look at them with cold logic. When he was a teen, Boris had insisted Luke ask Wendy Benton to homecoming. Luke didn't want to. Wendy was a year older and was known for being sexually active at school. Luke had no problem with anyone exploring their sexuality, but at fifteen he hadn't been ready to do anything other than kiss. When he refused, Boris had beaten him. Looking back as a thirty-something, Boris probably had a thing for Wendy's mom, who was single and extremely attractive.

Whether he was Boris or Fergal, he always wanted something from Luke. If Luke didn't deliver, there were consequences.

Verbena walked out of the bathroom, her wet hair tied in a knot on top of her head. She was swimming in his clothes, and he immediately wished he had offered her a colored t-shirt instead of a white one. It was abundantly clear she didn't have a bra on.

"Thanks. You have good water pressure. It helped." She stifled a yawn.

"Why don't you lie down while I shower?" Luke suggested. It would be good for him to give her some space. And some time without him leering at her.

"I am tired. I'll rest for a bit, and then we can talk." She climbed into his bed and slid underneath the covers.

Luke took a deep breath and left the room.

It was a lot to take in.

Chapter Twenty-Six

Verbena startled awake.

Where was she?

The room was dark, but not pitch black. She could hear something moving around...something animalistic. She slowly rolled onto her side, hoping to catch a glimpse of whatever it was.

Luke.

Her anxiety dissipated. She was in Luke's bed. Luke had dogs, and she now heard the telltale jingle of the dog's tags. She reached to the bedside table and picked up her phone. It was only six-thirty.

She was up for the day, but she doubted very much Luke was going to wake up anytime soon.

Verbena slunk from the bed and went to the bathroom to pee and rinse her mouth out with Luke's mouthwash, then tiptoed into the living room. Whiskey and Jaeger sat on the rug, looking at her with what appeared to be raised eyebrows.

"Hey," she whispered. "Want to go outside?" As soon as she said it, they both danced around, their cute bodies wiggling to and fro. She pulled on her shoes, opened the back door, and followed the dogs out. They shot into the yard, rooting out all the squirrels and rabbits that had hidden under bushes for the night.

Verbena turned to look at the house. It was a beautiful house, masculine and cozy, and perfect to live in long term. Plus, the land was lush and wooded and private.

It was a strange feeling, knowing that this would be her home, even when things with Luke felt so uncertain. His property had welcomed her the moment he purchased it, and her spellwork here was as strong as the Bay cottage. The land knew who belonged there.

After a while, Whiskey and Jaeger padded back to the porch and collapsed into heaps to sleep. Verbena walked into the house, only shutting the screen so that she could hear the dogs if they wanted to come back in. She stretched her arms overhead and peeked at the clock on the oven: seven-forty-five.

She decided starting her day with a bit of yoga was a good plan. That way, when Luke woke up, she would be completely centered for the heavy talk they were going to have. Nothing like having a past life death weighing on you to keep things somber.

She planted her feet on the wood floor and took a deep breath, raised her arms high, then slowly melted into a forward fold. A few sun salutations would set her right. She stepped back into downward dog, her hips raised and her tailbone tipped upward, her hands strong against the floor.

She fluttered her eyes open and saw Luke, framed between her legs. He was shirtless, his arms crossed over his chest.

He looked starving.

Verbena fell to her knees and twisted around to sit facing him.

"Hi," she breathed.

He didn't answer but walked purposefully to her, fell to his knees, grabbed her behind the neck, and pressed his forehead against hers.

"I was worried when you weren't in the bed." He held her tightly, as if he was afraid she would disappear in a moment.

"I'm not leaving you," she mumbled, as his mouth crashed against hers in a hungry and demanding kiss.

Verbena dug her fingers into his shoulders, pulling him closer as he guided her beneath him. She wrapped her legs around his waist, then seized his lower lips with her teeth, giving him a quick bite and soliciting a growl from him.

This was everything. Verbena felt like her body had exhaled. In this kiss, her mind had let go of the past and accepted this future, this life with Luke. They could be happy now, they could be loudly in love. After a lifetime of hiding, they were free. Verbena and Luke could be laid bare to each other.

Luke stopped kissing her for a moment and pulled back to look at her face. "Is this all right with you? If it isn't, we can stop. We can go slower, just kiss for a while. I don't want you to feel rushed."

Verbena cupped his chin with her hand, his stubble from the past two days scratching against her palm. "Luke Karnes, I want nothing more than to have sex with you right now. All day." She paused and licked her lips. "There are five condoms in my purse. I would like to use the majority."

"Fuck, yes," Luke muttered. He leaned back to his heels, pulled his boxers off her, and tossed them to the side.

"You didn't wear panties last night?"

"Nope," she answered, pulling her shirt over her head.

"If I knew that, I wouldn't have slept a wink." He drank in the sight of her and made Verbena feel positively seductive. "You are gorgeous." His voice dropped to a hair above a whisper. "God, Verbena, you undo me." Luke sunk back into her arms, skin to skin, heart to heart, mouth to mouth. She wanted to consume him and be consumed in turn.

"Touch me," she begged, her mouth against his jaw.

"Everywhere," he answered. He flipped her to straddle him, his hands on her thighs. He moved up her hips, her belly, her breasts. His thumbs teased her nipples into taut points, and she arched into his hands.

"Lean forward so I can lick you here." He pinched the side of her breast. She obeyed, bracing her hands on either side of his head. His tongue laved over the smooth skin, teasing her.

"Tell me what you want and tell me what you like," Luke asked, all the while continuing his adoration of her breasts.

"I like everything you do. I especially liked it when you mentioned fucking me bent over one of the tables at the bar. Let's do that sometime. But right now, I want you to sit on the couch so I can ride you." Verbena surprised herself with her bluntness.

"Right now? You don't want me to go down on you or use my fingers first?"

Verbena groaned. "I do want you to do those things, but I really want you inside me now. You're the only person I've ever fantasized about inside me, and I don't want to fantasize anymore."

Luke was silent for a moment, staring up at her.

"Where's your purse?"

She giggled. "On the counter."

"Get a condom out," he commanded. She did, and he walked to the couch, dropped his boxers, and sat down. Verbena handed him a condom, then straddled him. She ran her hands over his shoulders, biceps, all the way down to his forearms. She touched his chest, his belly, the creases of his hips. She took her time to enjoy looking at them. When they'd hooked up before, everything had been so frantic. Now, she could savor the moment.

"Luke, I love you," she admitted. "I don't want you to say it back right now. I want you to say it when it's natural for you. But I needed to say it. I need you to know. I love you."

"Verbena," he breathed. She shifted down and slid her body over his, drowning in the sensation.

She'd be lying if she said this wasn't the only time she'd ever felt on fire with a man inside her. Verbena tried not to get too deep into her head. She wanted to stay focused on the moment, think only of Luke and the fact that they were finally together after a decade of mess. There were still phantoms to vanquish, curses to unweave, trusts to build, but this moment, the two of them in one movement, one breath, felt like the fateful beginning of a beautiful life.

"Are you okay?" Luke asked, his hands coming up to cup her face.

"I am. Just..." She leaned her forehead against his as she slid over him. "This means a lot to me. I've wanted it for so long, it's hard to imagine it's real."

"It's real. I promise." Luke stilled for a moment and pulled her face away to look at her. "I'm so happy."

"Me too," Verbena breathed and crashed against him.

It was a frenzied race then, both of them barreling toward release. Her hands were on his shoulders, his back, his biceps—his skin hot beneath her fingertips. She couldn't get enough of him. She wanted this to last forever, this desire and lust and erupting love to live in her chest.

She buried her face against his neck as she came, whimpering against his damp skin. Luke's hands went to her hips, pumping her over and over until he found his own release.

Verbena raised her head off Luke's shoulder and eased her body off him.

"Don't go far," he mumbled, pulling her to sit beside him on the couch. They were both still panting, their hearts and lungs trying to catch up with their bodies. Verbena snuggled against his chest and blinked her eyes open.

Whiskey and Jaeger were standing at the window next to the front door, staring at them.

"Your dogs just got a very good show for this early in the morning."

Luke burst out laughing and kissed her forehead. "I suppose they did." He shook his head. "I'm going to take care of this." He gestured to the condom he was still wearing. "I'll be right back. Leave the dogs out for now. They're fine."

Verbena leaned back on the couch, sprawling out and crossing her ankles over the armrest.

Now that was sex.

Nothing against the men she'd tried to distract herself with in the years between twenty and twenty-five, but none of them held a candle to Luke. Yes, there was the soulmate magic that made them dynamite, but more than that, she had never, ever been with someone one-tenth as attentive. The way he touched her, talked to her, it was all perfect. And so damn hot.

"I would like to petition you lay like that at least once a week for me," Luke said, walking back from the bathroom.

Verbena giggled and sat up.

"I have to be honest. I'm not nineteen anymore. I'm going to need a little recovery time." He eased beside her.

"I'm good for now," Verbena said, folding her legs across his lap. "I'll let you know when I'm ready for the next round." She couldn't hold back her grin. "So that happened."

"It did happen." He paused. "Do you need anything? Food? Water? Coffee? A nap?"

"I got more sleep last night than I have in ages. I'm a little hungry though." She stood up and walked to the kitchen, where they had stashed the box of goodies from Lavender. "Want to have breakfast on the porch? There are banana zucchini muffins in here. They're delicious."

"Yes. But I'm going to put on pants. In case someone happens upon us." Luke stood up off the couch.

"I am also going to put on some clothes." Verbena laughed. "Because while I love hanging with you naked, I have a bad track record with random people seeing me naked this summer."

"Minx. I'll meet you on the porch. Coffee with milk and sugar?"

"Yes, please."

Verbena pulled her discarded shirt over her head and sighed.

She couldn't remember the last time she was this happy.

Chapter Twenty-Seven

S itting on the porch eating muffins with Verbena was the best way Luke had ever spent a morning.

She was perfect, obviously. His shirt was a little long on her, but not too long that her legs weren't on full display. The morning sun played over her skin in perfect dapples, a mix of light and shadow highlighting every lovely inch of her.

Luke smiled.

He felt like his heart was going to burst from happiness. This was it, what he wanted. He wanted to sit on his porch in the morning and eat breakfast with Verbena. He wanted to go to bed with her at night and wake up next to her in the morning and spend as much time in between sleeping with her.

Fifteen years ago, he never would have thought any of this was possible.

"You look really deep in thought," Verbena said, then took a bite of a muffin. "Are you feeling particularly pensive this morning?"

"Yes," he answered truthfully. "I'm thinking that I wish I could go back in time and show fifteen-year-old me this moment. It would have been good for him to know deep happiness was in the future."

She reached out to him and slid her hand over his forearm.

"I know it's trite and doesn't help, but I'm so sorry. I'm sorry you had such a shitty childhood. I'm sorry your parents weren't there for you and the man who was supposed to be turned out to be an absolute evil asshole. If I could go back in time, I would tell you that you wouldn't only get through it, but that you would grow into a man I am so excited to spend my life with. Someone who is kind and giving and successful." She paused. "And super fucking hot."

Luke threw his head back laughing. "If fifteen-year-old me had you tell me I was hot, I would have probably fainted from shock. And then Taylor would have hit on you." He chuckled. "Even at twelve, that kid had swag. I was not surprised when he married so young."

"Tell me about Taylor and Danny. For all the shit Boris put you three through, you all grew into good people."

"Well, Taylor was always a handful. He never wanted to take any shit from anyone. His mom and Boris are siblings, and he was too much for her, so she dropped him off. He used to come and go a bit. She'd pick him up and take him home for a couple months, but she always brought him back." Luke shook his head. "Taylor had a wild streak. Harmless stuff, but you know, slept around in high school, smoked pot, stole cigarettes. He always lived life a little fast for me and Danny." Luke exhaled. "Danny was like a puppy. He just wanted to be loved."

"He got it from you," Verbena interjected. "No matter how shitty Boris was, he didn't break the bond between the two of you."

"No, he never could. My dad died before I got a chance to know him, and Danny was slotted with a crappy father. It definitely brought us together." Luke took a sip of his coffee. "Part of me really hopes he stays here, on Star Island. But I know he has to find his place. Whether it's here or somewhere else, I want him to be happy." He looked over at Verbena. "I want him to be as happy as I am when I'm with you."

"Damn it, Luke." Verbena scrunched up her nose. "You will learn this about me, but I do not like to cry in front of people. And you are going to make me cry."

"Okay, let's think of something that won't make you cry." He strummed his fingers on his chin. "What about this? I had already masturbated three times the day you came to my bar and trenchcoated me."

She burst into a wide smile. "Three times?"

"Yup. I actually left work for an hour pretending I had to make a medical call and went home to jerk off twice. It was insane."

"And did you think about me?"

"Of course."

"What was I doing?" She set her muffin down on the table and leaned back into her chair.

"Different things each time," he laughed. "Let's see. First was you on top, not unlike the scenario an hour ago. Second was a blow job."

Verbena nodded in approval. "And third?"

"Third was me on top really nailing you." He shut his eyes. "Sorry, that was sort of crude."

"I disagree." She stood and pulled his shirt off and tossed it aside, then stepped back out of his boxers. "It sounds like fun."

"God, you are gorgeous." Luke grinned.

"Can I tell you about my fantasy?"

"Please."

"I've always wanted to have sex outside. Probably a witch thing. But the idea of me laying down on the grass right there and you nailing me, well," she inhaled sharply, "that sounds like a very fun way to spend a morning."

Luke looked at the amazing, awe-inspiring, beautiful woman in front of him and counted his lucky stars that somewhere in the universe, something or someone had decided that she was his and he was hers and he then said, "You get a condom, I'll get a picnic blanket. I don't want a grasshopper killing the mood."

Luke stumbled through his house to the hall closet where he had a picnic blanket tucked away. He hadn't used it in years, not since a concert at Emery Park, and it definitely had never been used for some outdoor naked-time.

Luke spread the blanket out, and Verbena rushed down, condom in hand. She slid beneath him, threw her arms over her head, and opened her legs.

"Nail me, Luke," she said, her eyes heavy with lust.

"In a second," he answered. Luke moved down her body, kissing her breasts, belly, hips, thighs. He moved her legs over his shoulders and smoothed his palm up her belly and settled in the space between her thighs. He licked her then, taking his time teasing her, pulling moans from her.

Around them, summer was awake. The sun shone down, rays dancing over Verbena's bare skin. The birds chirped and animals rustled, but none of it could take Luke's attention from her.

"Luke," she gasped. "I want to come with you inside me."

Not one to refuse a request, he gave her one more languid sweep, then rocked back to his heels and put on the condom before surging inside of her.

"Hard as you can," she breathed against his ear.

Luke felt that animalistic part of him—the part that wanted to claim Verbena and shout to the heavens that she was *his*—take over. He grasped her hips and thrust wildly, like he'd never be inside her again, like it was the last time they'd ever be together. He moved like he was Dairé and she was Nessa and they'd gotten one last time with each other.

Verbena moaned his name as she came, her legs bucking wildly against his hips, but he still drove into her, over and over until he was spent and exhausted and fell into a heap beside her.

"At some point, we are going to have to re-enter the world," Verbena murmured. Her cheek pressed against his chest. Luke couldn't think of another place in the world he wanted to be.

"Mmm," he grumbled. "That sounds overrated." He exhaled. "But true. I have to go into the bar at some point today. Are you ignoring your clients?"

"By the sun in the sky, I'm guessing it's only around ten. I don't get too many calls before then, but I will probably need to put clothes on soon."

Luke grumbled and rolled to his side so he could bury his face against her neck. "Do you have to?"

"Well, my original career plan was to be your housewife, but my plans changed."

Luke pulled away to look at her face. "For what it's worth," he began, "you might have been right. In keeping us apart."

"Really?" She raised an eyebrow.

"When you were eighteen, I was twenty-three. If it felt like this, we probably would have moved in together, lived in my small apartment over the bar...might have gotten you pregnant, never bought the bar. You might not have become the insanely good realtor you are." He paused. "You gave us a chance to come into ourselves. I was really mad before, but I get it. And it wasn't like we could have discussed it eight years ago."

"You would have thought I was trying to murder you with poison," she pointed out.

"Yes, I probably would have." He chuckled. "Speaking of all of that commitment..." He paused for a moment and took a deep breath. "Would you like to move in here?"

"Are you asking me to move in with you less than three hours after the first time we had full-blown sex?"

"I guess I am. I don't see the sense in waiting any longer. We've spent too much time apart, our situations keeping us that way. I'd like to put an end to that, if you don't mind. I want to get into bed with you every night and wake up next to you every morning."

"I'll be sure to climb back into bed after yoga, breakfast, and taking the dogs out," she teased. "But, yes. A million times yes. You're my home, and I'm ready to be home."

Chapter Twenty-Eight

With extreme reluctance, Verbena and Luke got dressed and departed the house. Verbena needed to email Brian Lennox and let him know that she did not recommend purchasing the plot. If the only realtor on Star Island since Sharon retired couldn't set foot there without having a fit, it would be an impossible buy. There were a couple plots, not as large as that one, in Vega that she might be able to sway him toward, so she'd head out there and take some pictures to send him as well.

As soon as she could stop ogling her boyfriend.

Boyfriend? Luke technically wasn't her *boyfriend*. He was her forever person. But, unless they got married, that was a difficult thing to explain to the general public. She supposed she could call him her lover, but that word really skeeved her out.

"Do you want a ride into town? I won't be long at the bar, just need to check on a few things, and then we could come back."

"As tempting as that is, I need my car, which Rosemary brought home, so I can drive around and attempt to sell a piece of land to someone who lives in New York City."

"I do believe you are single-handedly turning this island into a second

Nantucket. Before I know it, I'll be pushed out by some big developer," Luke teased.

"Never," she insisted. "Honestly, if it isn't walking distance to the beach, most people don't want it. They hear island destination and they want ocean views, proximity to town, and a white sandy beach, and most of those places have been sold in the past twenty years. I'd say I only have a few more years of new construction sales left, and then it will only be turnover, and few and far between at that."

"What will the number one realtor on Star Island do when there is nothing left to sell?" Luke wrapped his arms around her waist and pulled her close.

"Honestly, I'll probably turn to design. I didn't want to follow in my mom's footsteps exactly. She was a house witch too. But I'm pretty good at making a house feel like home. Or I could open up an exorcism company."

Luke chuckled. "The bartender and the exorcist. It's basically a made-for-TV romance."

"There's nothing made-for-TV about what we just did in the backyard," Verbena pointed out.

Luke groaned. "None of that or I'll never get to work." His hands slid to her bottom for a quick squeeze. "I'll never be able to look at the yard the same way. Or the couch."

"Just wait. I have plans for the entire house," Verbena quipped and pressed a kiss against his jaw.

Luke chuckled. "Hop in the car. I'll drive you to the Bay cottage."

Verbena only stayed long enough to change her clothes, grab her keys and phone charger, and wash her face, because her sisters weren't home. Without them, this cottage was turning into just another house, another stop on her journey to home. The truth was, she'd been transitioning between homes for years. Once she met Luke, this lovely cottage had begun to lose its meaning.

Verbena had felt at home with Luke, in his bed, on his couch, on his porch, standing in his shower, making coffee in his kitchen. His cabin would become theirs, and they would live and love and raise their family there, because even if she couldn't imagine that right now, she knew they would get to a place where it would happen.

Her life was with Luke. He was her home.

Verbena plugged her phone in and put on some upbeat music. She couldn't stop smiling this morning. Even with Boris hanging over their heads and the Bay curse still very much in place, for a moment the world felt full of hope.

The two properties on the Vega peninsula were not far from the Bay cottage or Luke's house. One was dense forest, but there was a clearing that could be used for a large structure, plus room for lots of trails to wander. The other was more expensive but had beach access. The Vega peninsula didn't have a sand beach, but for the purpose of a creative retreat center, a stone beach was lovely. Verbena could picture a group of artists with their easels settling in for long days of painting with such breathtaking landscapes. Between these two places, she was sure Brian Lennox could find a good fit.

Verbena pulled up to the forest property and parked her car on the side of the road, throwing her hazards on. She climbed out and looked around for a moment. There didn't seem to be any other people around to see what she was about to do.

"All right, Terminus," she began, invoking the Roman god of boundaries, "I've never worked with you before, but I need a boundary around me. Protect me from a phantom let loose upon this land. Keep him from my person." Verbena licked her thumbs, then drew circles on her ankles, knees, hips, wrists, elbows, shoulders, and neck. Terminus was a minor Roman deity, nowhere near as powerful as Jupiter or Minerva, but when a witch wanted a very specific boundary, she needed a very specific god.

Verbena stepped away from her car into the property and started snapping pictures with her phone immediately. The land here was lush and thickly forested, with an undergrowth perfect for little critters to hide and make their homes. The air smelled fresher somehow, crisper within this dense wood. This was how Verbena imagined the entire island looked when the first Bay witch came and settled.

Her memory flashed to Éire. Or rather, Ireland. When Nessa lived there, it was a wooded place, unlike the emerald green hills that now dominated. Maybe she and Luke could take a trip there once...once she and her sisters were no longer in fear for their lives.

She took a picture of the road and a good place for an entrance, then sighed. Verbena hadn't taken time to reflect on her time as Nessa. It had been a miserable existence, one she would have rather left lost to memory. Nessa's life was hard and dark. The snippets of time with Dáire were happy, but always shadowed with doubt. Everything in their world was against their happiness, and in the end they had no chance. This life would be different. They would make it work. Luke and Verbena would stay together, stick with each other no matter what crossed them.

Nessa.

Verbena shuddered. While she had set boundaries around her body to keep Fergal or Boris or whoever the hell the phantom was from physically hurting her, her mind was another story.

Nessa, the great whore.

"Not Nessa," she countered, speaking barely above a whisper. "Not anymore."

Oh yes, a Bay witch now. A poisoner, a wicked witch with powers no human should have. An alchemist, one who plays with the fabric of life.

"I'm not—" She stopped herself. Verbena was not going to argue with a phantom in her head. She licked her lips and started again. "You need to leave Luke alone. Leave Star Island."

The phantom hummed a laugh.

Do you think you can save him? That boy is mine, broken and remade in the shadow of my terror. He will never be free of me. Even if I were to dissipate into the ether, I would haunt his thoughts until his dying breath, in this life and the next. We are bound together, he and I. If he lived one hundred lives, I would be in each of them. I am the shadow of his soul.

Verbena shook her head.

"No. You are not." Verbena drew a circle with a slash over her sternum. "I declare Star Island my home, and I its protector. I banish you from this place, from the side of Luke Karnes, Dairé, and any other name that soul has answered to or will. I send you to the afterworld."

The phantom rumbled, a low and menacing sound, slowly transforming into a laugh.

You have no jurisdiction over me, witch. You do not control the tides of the afterworld. I am not bound to you, Nessa.

The air shifted, and he was gone. It was humid now, every breath full of heavy damp. Verbena looked around for a moment, then panicked.

Was he going to find Luke?

Chapter Twenty-Nine

L uke walked into the bar, his face covered by a goofy smile.

He had never been so happy in his entire life.

First of all, the sex. God. Sex with Verbena was mind-numbing.

More than that, she had agreed to move in with him. Verbena was moving into his house. He was going to live with someone. Forever. It should scare him, the finality of it all. There would be no more dating, no more living life on his own terms and schedule, and no more sleeping until noon when he felt like it, from the sound of things.

But he wasn't scared. He was thrilled.

"Luke!" He snapped his head to the back hall leading to his office and saw Erin frantically waving him over.

"What's wrong?"

"I don't know. Danny is upstairs and he's freaking out. He might be having a panic attack? It sort of reminded me of when my sister didn't get into Columbia and she went ballistic for about an hour. Either way, you should check on him."

"Shit." Luke moved to run upstairs and then stopped. "Who's working right now?" Usually, he had the schedule imprinted in his brain, but at the moment he couldn't think of anything other than Danny.

"Diane, Derrick, and me."

Luke glanced around the bar. There were customers, but not too many. People would have to wait today.

Luke bounded up the stairs to Danny's apartment, pushing through the swinging door.

Danny was curled into a ball on the floor, his hands pressed against his ears.

"Danny!" Luke dropped beside him, reaching out to touch his back.

Danny flinched, curling further in on himself.

"Danny, it's Luke!" he shouted.

Because he knew. He knew that right now Boris was in his head, screaming at him, making him feel like a broken little kid again while the man who was supposed to protect him did everything in his power to terrorize him.

"Luke?" Danny blinked open his eyes. His irises shifted around wildly, then steadied, focusing on Luke's face.

"I'm here. Let's get you on the bed." Danny nodded and let Luke lead him to the bed, but he kept his hands over his ears.

"He's here," Danny whimpered. "Boris. He's in my head. Am I going crazy?"

"You aren't," Luke soothed. "You are not crazy. I hear him too."

"You don't understand. He's in there more than he's not. It's been so long, I can't even remember what it was like without him in there...it's never quiet." Danny squeezed his eyes shut.

"You're going to be okay," Luke reiterated. "We'll get help."

"Luke?" Verbena called as the door creaked open. She slipped into the apartment, her eyes flashing between Luke and Danny.

"I can't. I can't live like this. It's all the time. It wakes me up when I'm sleeping. I had to stop driving." Danny choked back a sob. "Help me." He grabbed at Luke's forearms.

"Luke," Verbena said sternly. "Can he...hear him?"

"Yes," he answered.

She hurried to the kitchen and opened the cupboards and pulled out a canister of salt, giving it a shake to weigh the contents.

"Can you sit him up on the floor? As small as possible?"

"Danny, I'm going to move you to the floor. It will help, I promise." Danny nodded his head and let Luke lead him to the center of the floor. He arranged Danny sitting up, then sat behind him so he could lean against him. He felt like a little kid again. So small against Luke, even though he was nearly as tall as him. Danny's weight sagged against him, his hands still cradling his ears.

Verbena slowly poured a circle of salt around Danny and Luke, mumbling, "Hestia, block out his demon. Settle his mind, give him some peace." The circle was completed, and Danny stilled. He dropped his hands from his ears and looked between Luke and Verbena.

"How...how did that happen?" His eyes cleared and stared at Verbena.

"I'm going to get some more salt from the bar, get a circle around the bed so he can sleep," she whispered. "Stay with him there."

Luke nodded and turned back to Danny. "I'm here, Danny. You're going to be okay."

"I don't understand."

"Verbena is sort of like a healer," he said slowly. He wasn't sure if he was allowed to tell anyone she was a witch, so he'd keep it vague. "Like in old stories, those people who lay their hands on the sick and they get well. Well, Verbena's a little like that."

Danny nodded and closed his eyes. "I'm so tired."

"She'll get you set up in the bed in a minute. We're going to figure it out. You're not alone, Danny. You've got me."

Chapter Thirty

Within the hour, all five Bay witches were in the apartment over The Muse. Danny was still unconscious or sleeping—it was hard to tell which—but he seemed peaceful for the moment. He wasn't twitching or whimpering. Just out.

"So, he's Luke's cousin slash brother?" Sage asked in a hushed voice in the corner that housed the kitchen. As a studio, there really wasn't much room for six people to gather without being on top of Danny or in the bathroom.

"Technically, they're second cousins, but they were raised together for five years," Verbena answered.

"But the phantom is his actual father? Shit." Lavender sighed. "We need to figure out where all Luke's relatives are. If it isn't only the Stochs coming after us, we'll need a wider net when it comes to being prepared."

"Luke doesn't think any of the other branches are magical, and according to the Compendium, they aren't. And by the way he describes his other cousin, Taylor, there's no chance any latent magic is hiding in him. Too passionate of a teenager. Something would have bubbled up." Verbena looked back at Sage. "You getting anything?"

"Me? No. Why would I be getting anything?"

Verbena looked from Danny to Sage and back again. A small part of her had wondered if they were soulmates. They were around the same age, and him showing up on Star Island when two of her sisters were still waiting for soulmates seemed a little coincidental.

"You don't recognize Danny?"

"The guy from Indiana passed out on the bed? No." Sage furrowed her brow, then rolled her eyes. "He's not the one for me, Verbena."

"Just checking. Lavender?"

Lavender pulled a face. "No, that young man is not my soulmate. Good Goddess, Verbena."

"I'm five years younger than Luke," she pointed out.

"Yeah, and I'm about twelve years older than him. That's a bit of a bigger gap. What should we do with him? He can't stay in that bed forever."

"I'll make a salt path from the bed to the kitchen and the bathroom. I wish we could salt the whole building, but there's no way a pedestrian wouldn't cross the path and disturb it. And I don't want Danny to go from calm to a complete onslaught of Boris in his brain. Trust me, it's very jarring and uncomfortable."

"Maybe we could get a ghost to move in here?" Laurel whispered. "Get their territory settled?"

"Boris is really strong. I don't think a ghost that isn't extremely rooted here would work."

"We could bring Danny to our house? Aunt June has done a good job keeping Boris out," Rosemary offered.

"Maybe. For now, I think he needs to sleep." Verbena glanced at Luke, who sat on the floor beside the bed. "I'll talk to Luke about it. See what he thinks would be best."

"Luke, we'll figure it out," Rosemary said. "You've got the whole Bay crew on the case. And since I haven't had a chance yet, here's your official welcome to the family. I'm sorry it's not under better circumstances. But I know you and Verbena are going to be very happy together. And I can tell you already had amazing sex more than once. So good on you."

Luke shot a look to Verbena.

"Sorry. Now that you are going to be settling into your official role as my soulmate and life partner, you'll have to get used to Rosemary asking extremely personal questions and letting you know any sort of sexual energy she picks up from us."

"Okay?"

"Don't worry. I'll also be very open with my own personal matters." She paused. "Asher and I have really good sex. Out of this world. We fixed our street by banging."

"Rosemary...not now," Lavender breathed. "His brother is being terrorized by his own father. Let Luke be."

"Sorry! Oh! I have an idea!" Rosemary exclaimed, then slapped her hands over her mouth. "I'm going to run home. If I line the boundaries of the apartment with my best protection flowers, it'll hold for at least a day. Not a permanent solution, but at least Danny won't have to worry about crossing salt if he has to pee."

"Will that work?" Luke asked.

"It will," Rosemary insisted. "I'll be back in under an hour. Why don't the rest of you do your thing in the apartment while Danny is still out? Couldn't hurt to have a bunch of protection spells everywhere."

An hour later, Verbena had reinforced all her protection spells, Lavender had a pot of herbs simmering on the stove, Laurel had peeked into Danny's mind to make sure he was sleeping soundly (he was), and Rosemary had lined the outer walls of the apartment with flowers.

Sage had done nothing, as there wasn't much a harvest witch could do in terms of protection outside of her own lands, so she offered to stay until Danny woke up.

She flopped on the couch and crossed her arms over her chest. "It's like a day off. I'll nod off for a bit and let you know when he wakes up."

"What if he attacks you because a strange woman is in his apartment?" Luke asked.

"Luke, no offense to Danny, but I can handle myself. And before he went to bed, his brother's girlfriend poured salt around him, and it helped him sleep. I'm sure he's in the frame of mind that things are a little bit sideways at the moment." Sage settled into the couch and closed her eyes. "You two get out of here. He's probably going to sleep for twenty hours. Especially if Boris has been waking him up every night."

"She's right," Verbena said, wrapping her arm under Luke's. "Let's get the bar situated for the night and then we can go home."

She was right. As much as he didn't want to leave Danny, Luke had a business to run and a plan to make. Because if Boris was running loose on Star Island, the last place any of them should be was here.

He tucked Verbena against his chest and kissed her hair quickly.

"We're going to figure this out," he said softly.

"We are. We're a team now, and there isn't anything we can't face together."

Chapter Thirty-One

"How do we help him?" Luke needed a plan. Boris was going after the two people he couldn't live without. He needed this man out of his life, for good.

They pulled into Luke's driveway and climbed out of the car.

"There's some really strong magic I can try, but I haven't done it before."

"Is it dangerous?"

"Honestly, yes." She paused. "You remember how I told you I turned metal into plastic? Well, I think I could turn Boris into a ghost or a ghoul. If I can change the make-up of his being, we might be able to get rid of him."

"How do you get rid of a ghost or a ghoul?"

"Exorcise a ghost. Behead a ghoul."

"Behead? You want to behead someone?"

"Not someone. A ghoul. A dead creature. Same thing if we were suddenly overrun with zombies. We'd be chopping off heads left and right. But I'd prefer a ghost. I've exorcised dozens of ghosts. Never cut off a ghoul's head."

Verbena rubbed her forehead. She wasn't even sure if she could change him. She'd never done it with a...well, not living but thinking creature with free will to an extent. There was something inherently different about transforming a furnace compared to a phantom.

Luke stopped walking and turned to her. "How am I supposed to protect you from Boris if he operates in a way I can't begin to understand?"

"You're not," she answered. "I'm the witch. I'm supposed to protect you from him. And Danny."

"Still. He's my problem. I should deal with it." Luke paused.

"Luke," she began slowly, "he's getting through wards. I already had your bar and the apartment protected. Not as strongly as my house or yours, but...I don't know why he's so strong. It might be because of..."

"Danny." She nodded. Luke felt so defeated. He needed to fix this.

"Danny told me he couldn't hear him until he left Indiana. It's gotten worse since he came here."

"We're all here. Minus Taylor, everyone Boris is connected to is concentrated in one place. I'm sure that has made it easier for him to cross into our thoughts and world."

Suddenly, Verbena's hands flew up to her ears. She shook her head a few times, then licked her fingers and started drawing symbols over her skin. She fell to the ground, like she had been knocked over and rolled onto her side.

"Verbena? Are you okay?" Luke dashed to her side and grabbed her shoulders.

Her eyes popped open. "Be gone from this place." She exhaled and looked at Luke. "That shouldn't happen. Your house has stronger wards, but your yard is protected. It's like the magic is fading." Luke pulled her up to sit.

"What did he say to you?"

She barked a laugh. "Same old same old. I'm Nessa, the big whore, he'll never release you. Blah, blah, blah. I'm going to destroy him. But I need to figure out how."

Verbena tripled the wards around Luke's property. She made it impossible for anyone other than Luke, the Bays, and Danny to enter the premises, even with permission. While it was inconvenient in the long run, it made the wards air tight. There was no way Boris could break through those lines, or so Verbena insisted.

"I'm exhausted," she admitted as soon as they walked into the living room. "That took a lot out of me." She stretched her arms overhead.

"Do you want to lie down? Try to sleep?" Luke asked.

It would be better if she was sleeping while he figured things out. He didn't want to fight if his plans weren't achievable.

"Actually, yes." She slipped her shoes off and left them by the door. "You'll wake me, though, if Sage calls?"

"Danny's going to sleep for hours, but yes, if you manage to sleep that long, I'll wake you."

"Thanks." She raised to her tiptoes and pressed a kiss against his neck. "Come and snuggle me if you want."

"I will in a bit."

Verbena disappeared into his bedroom.

Luke's chest ached.

He didn't want to do this. He never wanted to leave her. But she said it: Boris was stronger with the three of them together. And Danny had said the voice didn't follow him in Indiana.

Luke and Danny were going to Indiana. He'd get Danny someplace safe, set up in an apartment. Luke would pay the rent for the next few months, let Danny get back on his feet without Boris in his head. Then, he'd drive west, put as much distance between himself and Verbena. With the three of them spread thin across the country, Boris would have to dissipate. There'd be nothing holding him together.

He and Verbena needed to bide their time, just a little longer.

Luke sat down at his computer and pulled up driving directions. He and Danny could be on the evening ferry and on the mainland by eight-thirty tonight. Verbena had protected the car, so Luke would drive as far as he could before he needed sleep, then nap on the side of the road in the car. They could get to Indiana by tomorrow afternoon.

She'd be mad, of course. Verbena wouldn't be Verbena without her need to control every situation. But he was doing it for her, for them. If he could give her time to figure out how to stop Boris, it would be worth it.

Luke would live with Boris in his head forever if it meant Verbena and Danny were safe from him.

"You never came in." Verbena slunk out of the bedroom. Her hair was piled on top of her head and messy from sleeping.

"Getting some stuff done," Luke answered quickly, closing his laptop.

"Any news from Sage or Danny?"

"Still sleeping. Laurel relieved Sage so she could go home. I'll go check on him in a bit." Luke inhaled. There was no use in letting this beat around inside him. "I'm going to take Danny to Indiana."

"Indiana? I'd think that'd be the last place he would want to go."

"He said he couldn't hear Boris there. It was the only place his mind was quiet."

Verbena sat on the couch beside him, tucking her feet under his thighs.

"Does he want to go?"

"It's the best choice available."

"So, you didn't ask him." She rubbed her forehead. "What's the plan then? You and Danny get to Indiana, and Danny never crosses state lines again? Does he know anyone there?"

"I'll get him set up in an apartment until we figure it out."

"So, you'll leave him and come back?"

"No. I'll keep going," Luke answered. He stood up and walked into the kitchen. It was cowardly, but he couldn't quite face her at such a close distance at the moment.

"Keep going where?"

"Seattle, I think. Maybe Portland."

"What the fuck is in Seattle or Portland? In case you haven't noticed, it's summer, you own the only bar on Star Island, and without sounding conceited I hope, your hot soulmate is here."

"Yeah, and my hot soulmate is also being physically and mentally attacked by my...whatever the hell Boris was. My uncle, my cousin, I'm sure there's a life in my past where he was my father or brother. Whatever he is, he is connected to me, and he is a monster. I won't let him close to you. Not again." Luke could feel rage building in his chest. How dare Boris fuck with Verbena?

"So, you'll let him keep us apart again?"

"Better than one of us dying," Luke spat. "Verbena, I'm doing this for us."

"This isn't for us. We need to stay together. Luke," she closed the distance between them and put her hands on either side of his face. "Listen to me. This is what Boris wants. When we are together, we are stronger. I am a strong witch. Powerful even. I can figure this out."

"Figure it out and get yourself killed in the process? You said it yourself, you've never done this kind of magic before. I know I'm not magical, but I can tell: you're scared. It's not normal, alchemy. Has anyone ever even attempted to transform a phantom?"

"No one writes down failed attempts. And I'm not normal. The moment I succeeded in alchemy, I became something different. I wouldn't think it mattered to you though."

"It doesn't. I want you safe. I want you away from all of this. If Boris wants to torture me with visions and his voice, he can go ahead. But not you. I couldn't protect you from him last time. I know dying in childbirth was commonplace then, but he made your life hell. I'm not letting him get to you this time. Shit, Verbena. I love you. And it's fucking killing me." He thrust his hands into his hair. He hated this, he hated all of it. He wanted the past to leave him alone and stop poisoning them.

"Can't you give me a chance? Morana tried to kill Laurel, but she didn't. Laurel was strong enough to trap her. Ivan tried to kill Rosemary, but she made a fucking plant attack him. I know I can do this. I know I can gather up all the power I've ever had, in every life, and exorcise Boris. I can do it."

"But if you can't? If you fail and Boris..." he swallowed hard, "kills you? What then?"

Verbena ran her fingers down his jaw to the side of his neck and settled her palm against his chest.

"Please, Luke. Stay. Trust me to fix this." She leaned her head against him, and for a moment, Luke thought he should stay. He could stay in this bubble of his house, protected from Boris, happy with Verbena. He could figure out how to live with the incessant shouting in his brain, the jolts of panic when he heard that god-awful voice.

He slid his hand up her back until he cradled her head against him. He wanted so much with her. He wanted years and years of happiness, a true family. He wanted love and passion and the deep bone-shattering connection he felt when he was close to her.

"Don't make me let you go again," Verbena whispered. She looked up at him, her eyes wild and searching. "Please."

The floodgates broke apart as he brought his mouth down to hers. She gasped at the force of him against her, but she didn't recoil. They crashed together in absolute madness. There was no Luke without Verbena anymore. She had become a piece of his soul, one he could not live without.

He peeled her shirt over her head, his movements frenzied. He needed her—needed her skin on his, her breath in his ear, his name on her lips. A whirl of chaos saw her shorts discarded, his clothes as well. He pulled her to the ground, splayed her legs before him, and plunged into her without a second thought. He hadn't given her much foreplay, but she whispered "yes" the moment they came together. He needed to be inside her, to be with her. This moment, the last two days, those memories would serve him when he was gone.

Verbena wrapped her legs around his waist, a stubborn tightness in her thighs, as if she were trapping him with her. Her hands reached over her head, grasping the doors of his cabinets for support. He braced his weight on his elbow, then ran his thumb over her jaw to tip her chin toward him.

"Tell me what you want," he commanded.

"This. You. I want you. Forever and ever," she breathed.

"Say you love me." Luke tried to keep his voice steady, but it cracked at the end. God, he didn't want to leave her. He needed her more than he'd ever needed anything before.

"Luke," her eyes locked on his, her hands on either side of his face, "I love you. I love you." She trapped her lip between her teeth and fought to keep her eyes open. "Tell me. Say it to me."

"I love you with all of my bleeding broken heart, Verbena Bay." He gripped her hips like he'd never touch her again.

She let go of his face and threw her arms around his neck, frantically grabbing at his back as she came. Her panting turned to moans and then to sobs of pleasure.

Luke's eyes snapped open. He wasn't wearing a condom.

"Fuck," he mumbled and pulled out of her before he spent himself. He leaned back on his heels and buried his face in his hands.

God, he loved this woman so much his skin ached.

"Luke." Verbena reached for him, her hand gripping his bicep. It would be so easy to fall back into her arms. "Please, don't leave me." Her eyes brimmed with tears.

"I'm so sorry." He got to his feet and turned away. He needed to leave before she begged him again. Because then he might stay, and that would be the worst thing for all of them.

Chapter Thirty-Two

With a suitcase, Danny, the dogs, and a full tank of gas, Luke left on the evening ferry.

Verbena felt like her heart had fallen through her feet and buried itself in the ground. She didn't go to the ferry to see them off. She didn't wish them well or kiss Luke goodbye or beg him to stay.

She stood up off that kitchen floor, put her clothes back on, and walked home to the Bay cottage.

She needed Luke to come back, apologize, tell her he was wrong and that he would never leave her. This was supposed to be the life they got to be together in.

But he wouldn't do that. If he could leave her freshly fucked and in tears on the floor, his conscience wasn't getting the better of him anytime soon. So, Verbena trudged up the stairs of her family home, ignoring Lavender and Sage's greetings in the parlor, and climbed into her old bed. She pulled her white comforter up to her chin, even though it was hot as hell outside, and burrowed down for a long and thorough wallow.

She was trying not to hate Luke, but at the moment, her brain could not stop shouting, "ASSHOLE!"

Her door opened and hit the wall, jarring her back to reality.

"Hello. Uh, you want to come downstairs and explain why the hell you walked in here looking like death and got in bed? Do you have a head injury?"

"Go away, Sage."

Sage did not go away. Instead, she sat on the foot of Verbena's bed, elbowing her feet to the side.

"Do you have a UTI from too much sex? There is an herbal concoction for that. Or good old-fashioned antibiotics. We have some cranberry juice if you want a glass."

Verbena rolled onto her back and pushed the blankets down. "My urinary tract is fine, thank you."

"Then why are you here? Aren't you supposed to, I don't know, want to spend every waking moment with your soulmate?"

"My soulmate is gone," Verbena confessed.

"Did he go to work? That is going to happen. No reason to fall apart." Sage patted her leg awkwardly. "Chin up, Verbena."

"He left, okay? Luke left. Gone. Off Star Island. On his way to Indiana."

"Why didn't you go with him?"

"Because it's all part of his big plan." The volume of her voice was rising. "He's going to drop Danny in Indiana, then drive until he can see the Pacific and hopefully drag Boris along for the ride." Verbena pulled her covers back up and turned toward the wall.

"Hm. Guessing by your reaction you did not agree with this course of action." Sage sighed. "Well, we made a pork tenderloin and roasted some potatoes and peppers, plus there's a bottle of rosé on the table that isn't going to drink itself, if you're interested."

"I don't think a good meal and alcohol are going to make me feel better about my soulmate abandoning me."

"Suit yourself. But adding hunger to all the reasons you are pissed might not be wise."

Verbena huffed and nestled deeper into her bed.

"Fucking hell, I cannot believe I am going to have to deal with this shit," Sage muttered as she walked out of the room and down the hallway. "Come down if you change your mind!"

Thirty minutes later, Verbena was tired of wallowing, and her stomach betrayed her with a growl so fierce she jumped. She still felt like absolute shit, but it seemed that didn't stop her from needing dinner.

"Oh look, the banshee is up," Sage said dryly. She picked up the bottle of rosé and poured some into an empty wineglass beside her.

"I was not wailing," Verbena retorted, snatching the glass and taking a gulp. "I may have let a dignified cry slip, but nothing loud enough to foretell a death."

"Do you want to call Luke?" Lavender asked gently.

"Why? So he can reiterate that he's stuck in his stupid plan?"

"Well, you could see how the drive is going."

"Lavender, he left two hours ago. He's still on the boat." Verbena flopped into the dining chair and finished her glass of wine.

"Okay, I'm getting you food. Please don't go crazy tonight. I have a busy day tomorrow, and I don't want to be up all night with a puking sister."

"I'm twenty-six. I can puke alone if need be." Verbena reached for the wine bottle.

"Goddess, this sucks," Sage said, slumping in her seat. "Why do I need a soulmate right now? I don't even want a boyfriend."

"I'm sure the universe sends women too."

Sage rolled her eyes. "I don't want a girlfriend either. If I'm going to have sex, I would like a dick but that's it. I don't want relationship shit. I don't want *this*." She nodded at Verbena. "Rosemary almost got herself killed because she was in a daze so heavy after fucking Asher, which by the way, gross, that she thought her children were running around Star Island. And the two of them are way too open about when they are fucking and how it went. I do not want to hear about some guy railing my sister nightly." Sage shuddered. "Laurel and Owen are attached at the hip. If Laurel is alone, it's only because Owen is thirty feet behind her ready to pop out from around a corner. You, who I haven't seen show an ounce of emotion in years, are acting like a sixteen-year-old whose boyfriend left after the first time they fucked. No one is selling the soulmate shit to me. From my view, it looks like a jumble of heartache and orgasms."

Verbena sighed. "It sort of is." She took a gulp of her wine.

Lavender set a plate in front of Verbena. "Eat. Give your stomach a fighting chance."

Verbena stabbed a potato with her knife and brought it to her mouth.

Stabbing things felt good.

Chapter Thirty-Three

Verbena woke up at four in the morning with her heartache replaced with rage. The soreness between her ribs had transformed into a red-hot fire of anger. And every last drop was directed at Boris. Boris Varga, bane of her fucking existence, was going down. Today.

She needed to face him today, because she didn't want to have to wait. She didn't want Luke to get all the way to the Rocky Mountains before she could give him the all clear. She wanted her soulmate by her side as soon as possible. Being apart from Luke didn't suit Verbena, and she had no intention of ever going back to that life.

And, on the off-chance Luke was right, she needed Boris to show himself here so he wouldn't be stretched too thin for her to do anything about it.

Verbena Bay was going to change the material make-up of a once-living being.

Goddesses protect her.

There wasn't much preparing for Verbena to do. When she changed the furnace and water heater into plastic, it was a whole lot of will, a smattering of Latin, a healthy dose of abject terror, and repetitive motion. It wasn't like she'd asked for a blessing from a goddess or twisted herbs between her fingers. It was all in her. Alchemy wasn't something a witch could learn. It was a part of her being as much as Laurel's ability to travel to the Hedge World was a part of hers. Alchemical magic could change the make-up of things. There was no reason Verbena couldn't at least try to turn Boris into something else.

She had used Latin instead of English when changing the furnace. Spells in languages other than a witch's native tongue were always more powerful. Something about the time it took to imbue those words into their souls put more magic in them. Now, Verbena could suddenly understand medieval Irish, but she wasn't sure if it would count as an inherent language. She'd stick with her high school Latin. The hours she spent doing conjugations alone should protect her.

"Wouldn't Ms. Bierbower be so proud?" Verbena had always liked her Latin teacher. Little did she know, she was still practicing phrases but also turning metal into plastic.

Verbena did a quick protection spell over her body, licking her thumbs and circling her joints. Menstrual blood would have been better, but she didn't have any on hand, and she recoiled at the idea of covering herself with blood, even if it was her own. It wasn't like she *wouldn't* do it, but it was definitely a worst-case scenario type of action to drench oneself in blood, even for witches.

Verbena was going to change Boris into a ghost. She knew ghosts. She saw them, heard them, helped them. She'd exorcised dozens of ghosts on Star Island, and while there were a million reasons why he could be different, it still sounded easier and safer than letting a ghoul loose. If she didn't manage to decapitate it immediately, it could lead to a whole new way of thinking for the entire world. If a non-magical person managed to see a ghoul, which was a real possibility as they weren't protected by some magical haze, they'd have a zombie on Star Island. Ghosts were safer. If Boris' ghost managed to escape her, well, at least he wouldn't baffle scientists everywhere.

Verbena checked her watch. The sun was rising in thirty minutes. Transitional times of the day—dawn, noon, dusk, midnight—they all held power for spells of transformation. She needed to be on the border of land at a border time. Her power would magnify exponentially. She could do this.

Verbena took a steadying breath and closed her eyes.

She was terrified. She shook her head and clenched her fists, digging her nails into her palms.

"I am Verbena Bay. I am a witch. I am an alchemist. I am power and love, and I will not let a phantom steal the love of my life away from me again. Luke deserves happiness. So do I. And Danny and Taylor and anyone else this phantom tortured in this life or others. Boris Varga, I will banish you. You will be wiped from the ether this morning, and no one will ever be tormented by you again." She tied on her sneakers, tightened her ponytail, and stepped out of the house. The wards were strongest around the house, weaker in the yard, and nonexistent at the property line.

She walked toward Luke's empty house with a razor-sharp focus.

She could not fail.

Chapter Thirty-Four

Sometime around three in the morning, Luke pulled to the side of the road outside Rochester, New York. Danny had been sleeping in the backseat, still catching up after weeks of interrupted nights. It had been a messy thirty minutes—groggy brother, last-minute packing—but they were off the island as the summer sun hit the horizon.

Once night truly set in, Luke knew he needed a couple hours or they'd be drifting off the road. He couldn't risk a hotel. Boris had to be following them. The last thing he wanted was he and Danny to be bombarded by his voice without Verbena to contain him. They needed to stay in the car, which had a boundary on it laid by Verbena, and get to Indiana as fast as possible.

He slept fitfully, his seat slightly reclined. His body was dead tired, but his mind couldn't relax. Only hours ago, he'd been in bliss with Verbena.

He'd never thought it would have been stolen so quickly. He wanted more time. He wanted her. Verbena had been a light in the peripheral for so long, but now that he was free of spells and potions, he knew that she was meant to be his. And he wouldn't let Boris take her this time.

Luke blinked against the rising sun, groaning. He should have thought to throw a t-shirt over his face so he could sleep longer. He wanted to disappear back into his empty dreams.

He rubbed his hands over his eyes a few times, then rummaged for his sunglasses. Once in place, he turned back to see if Danny was awake yet. He had granola bars for breakfast, and once they ate they could get to a gas station, fill up as quickly as possible, and get back on the road.

Danny wasn't in the back seat.

Luke jolted up, threw his door open, and searched wildly.

"I'm right here," Danny called. He was sitting away from the road on the small hillside, waves of green grass around him, Whiskey and Jaeger on their leashes beside him.

"Danny, get back in the car. We have to keep going. We'll get to Indiana soon."

"I was pretty out of it when I agreed to this road trip," Danny answered, showing no signs of budging. "Why are you taking me to Indiana?"

"Because it's the only place you can't hear Boris."

"You think my mental illness understands state boundaries?" Danny shook his head. "Luke, I haven't been back to Indy since it started. I'd guess it will follow me right over the Ohio border."

"Danny...what's going on with Boris isn't normal."

"Yeah, no shit."

"No, I mean, our family isn't normal. Like there are supernatural things going on."

Danny exhaled and draped his arms across his knees, then shook his head smiling. "Is this about my grandma being a witch?"

Luke felt the color drain from his face.

"You know?"

"Shit, Luke, I lived with her. Of course I know. I'm not magical, neither are you or Taylor. Boris wasn't either." He paused a beat. "How did you figure it out?"

"Verbena."

"Ah, she's a witch? Makes sense. The way she knew how to pour the salt around me. I remember my grandma doing shit like that, blessing my bed, laying herbs around the house." He sighed and raked his hand through his shaggy fair hair. "So, you think that because I couldn't hear Boris in Indiana there's some sort of border there that will protect me?"

"Yes. Also, once you got to Star Island, Verbena and I could both hear him too."

"Verbena? Why the hell would Boris fuck around with her?"

"It's a past-life thing."

"Okay." Danny sat silently for a minute, watching the cars drive past. Traffic was picking up now. The rest of the world was waking up, and thankfully, no one thought anything of a pair of guys sitting on the side of the interstate. Luke felt so far away from Verbena right now, on this patch of grass in New York. Everything felt wrong.

"You love Verbena, right? She's your girlfriend?" Danny finally spoke.

"She's my soulmate. So more than a girlfriend, I know she's the one. Yeah, I love her."

"Wonder if I get one of those," he muttered. "But you left her, on that little island, to take me to Indiana."

"Danny," Luke started. "Look. You are my little brother. Or my second cousin, or whatever. But I love you too. I always will. I don't want to see you in pain. Seeing you writhing around with Boris in your ear...I couldn't protect you from Boris when he was alive, and I'm sure as hell not going to leave you to him when he's dead. It's my job to watch over you. I don't care what our actual relation is, you are my brother, plain and simple. I would get hit by a train for you."

"Please don't." Danny turned to face him. "Luke, it's not your fault. I had a shitty father. No matter what, he was my shitty father. Without him, I wouldn't be here. And we both had moms who couldn't...they couldn't do it. They couldn't be there for us or raise us, and I've made my peace with those facts. Does that mean I feel good? No, of course not. Every day I wish my mom was someone stronger. Someone who could have turned her life around for me. I still struggle with all of it, even before I started hearing him."

"I should have gotten us away."

"You couldn't. Boris had that damn silver tongue. Remember when I went to school with a black eye and he told the principal Taylor hit me? Everyone fucking believed him. Taylor was only thirteen then. It was clear I'd been hit by a man. He was a monster. We were kids. We were only kids." Danny exhaled. "You did protect me. You're my big brother. But you weren't superman. You couldn't go up against a man and win." Danny chuckled. "Too bad we aren't warlocks. We could have taken him out with... I don't know. My grandma was a garden witch. Maybe an herb of some sort would have turned him either catatonic or into a good person."

"If Taylor had any magic, he would have burned the whole town to the ground," Luke laughed. "Thank God, he met Jenny and calmed down when she got pregnant."

"Nothing like impending fatherhood to stop Taylor from fucking around so much." Danny smiled. "Remember when he snuck Karina Leman into the garage after that dance? And you and I thought someone had broken in?"

Luke let out a belly laugh. "That poor girl. I ran in with a fucking ruler over my head because it was the only thing I could find, and there she is sitting in her bra with Taylor struggling to get it undone. She screamed, you panicked and rushed them, Taylor starts swearing up a storm." Luke shook his head. "Poor Taylor. He was about to see boobs for the first time, and we thwarted it."

"Taylor's fine. He has two kids and a hot wife. I'm sure he sees her boobs all the time." Danny cracked himself up, laughing so hard he laid down on the hill and wiped tears from his eyes.

There was so much pain. But Luke gained two brothers he could never give up.

Luke leaned back on his hands, turning his face to the sky. The sun was warming up, the grass soft. If it weren't for his growing unease, it would have been a beautiful morning.

There were years between Luke and Indiana, but he still hadn't made his peace with it. It was like a weight he couldn't let go of, and he didn't know if he'd ever be able to. He had buried it deep for years, but it was back now and pressing on him.

He looked over at Danny. His eyes were closed, and he was smiling.

"You notice that?" Danny said.

"What?"

"No Boris. I can't hear him. Hasn't made a sound, and I've been out here for over an hour. Maybe you were right. We got on the road and he disappeared. You should call Verbena, have her meet up with you out here. You can ditch me at a motel and have some alone time."

Luke froze.

Danny was right. Luke couldn't hear Boris either. It was like his voice dropped out of his mind completely. This whole time they'd been talking about him, and nothing. Not even an inkling of him in the background.

"Do you think he didn't follow us? That he stayed with her?" Luke started to feel panic rising.

Danny shrugged. "Maybe. But she's a witch. She can handle a ghost, right?"

"He's not a ghost, he's a phantom. He's hurt her before. Physically. He almost killed her. And she couldn't get him to leave before."

"But she made the safe places, right? So I could sleep? Is her house like that?"

"Yeah." Luke pulled out his phone and called Verbena. It was well after seven now, she had to be awake.

No answer.

"Hey, I know you're mad at me, but Danny and I can't hear Boris outside of the car. Is he still on Star Island? Or did us leaving do enough? Please call me back. Or text me. Or have Sage call me." Luke ended the call and flipped the phone nervously between his hands. Every breath without a ding on his phone was a little more panicked than the last.

"Do you want to go back?" Danny asked.

"Yes." Luke stood up. "We need gas. And food. I only have a couple of bars in the car."

"We'll be fine. Let's hit up the closest gas station, I'll grab food while you fill up. We'll be back...what, around noon?"

"Noon. Okay." They rushed to the car. Luke found the closest exit and turned around, heading east again. His chest was tight, and his hands ached from gripping the steering wheel too tightly. He needed to keep his head clear. He had to focus on the road, focus on getting back to Verbena and making sure Boris wasn't with her.

But, in a part of his mind, he knew why she wasn't calling him back. Boris was with her and she was alone. She wouldn't make him worry like this for no reason.

He had abandoned her when all he wanted was to keep her safe. Now, she was on her own with Boris.

Alone with a phantom who could kill her.

Chapter Thirty-Five

There was a break in the wards between the Bay cottage and Luke's house, and Verbena was staring at it.

It looked like any old patch of wooded land, the sun shone no differently than it did ten feet in either direction, the animals chattered away, the moss grew up the tree trunks.

This was the spot, the place where she would take down Boris. For Nessa, for Dairé, for Luke and Danny. For trying to kill her on the Sirius peninsula. He would not go on after this.

Verbena would destroy him.

She walked to the property line with her head held high, her feet sure in their steps. She would not cower as she faced him. She was a Bay witch, strong and powerful, and she would protect the one she loved above all else. Boris Varga was a powerless man, twisted by his own inadequacy. He would not fell her.

Verbena took a deep breath, then stepped into the pocket between the wards in the middle of the woods. It was a lovely August morning, clear and warm with a few fat clouds passing in the distance through the deep-blue morning sky. Verbena found it unfair that the world could look so perfect when everything was shit. It was one of the great tragedies of life, that the weather refused to match her feelings. She wanted skies heavy with gray clouds, dismal fog and rain.

She stood with her back against the tree, brandishing her spell knife. Her eyes fluttered closed, and she exhaled slowly. It was time. There would be no turning back, no running away. One of them would not leave this place today.

"Fergal Ó Murchadha, I call thee to me. Teacht orm." *Find me.* "Come to my side, Fergal. Nessa is here, young and tempting, bringing your nephew to his doom through love. Veni ad me, phantasma." *Come to me, phantom.* She tried to honey her words, but she couldn't help a sarcastic sharpness from coming through. "Invenire pythonissam." *Find the witch.*

The chatter of the birds fell silent, and the wind stilled against her cheek.

Here he comes, Verbena thought. She took the knife between her fingers and pinched it, then circled her wrists quickly. A bit of blood over saliva couldn't hurt.

Nessa, with skin like milk and hair like night, he began, his voice lazy over his words. *Where is Luke? And my boy?*

"Safe," she answered, her mind already beginning the spell. She took Fergal in her mind. She didn't know him as Boris, and hopefully, their appearances were not too different. She thought of his face, the way he carried himself, the cadence of his voice.

They left you so unprotected? He hummed a laugh. *I will not squander my chance.* Verbena felt an icy grasp around her bicep.

"I bind you to this place, the soul known as Fergal Ó Murchadha, Boris Varga. You are trapped between the wards, as you are trapped between worlds. You cannot leave this place without my allowance." Her voice was steady, though her heart thumped against her ribs and her arm ached where he held it. She could do this. She could change him. As long as she could keep him still, she could do it.

Verbena squeezed her eyes shut, keeping him in her mind, picking apart what made him a phantom and trying to weave him back together as a ghost. The fibers of these creatures were thin, like spider silk or the cotton of seeds. She grasped at the edges with her mind, tried to work them to her will. There was nothing solid to reach. It wasn't like metal or plastic, those were firm and solid. With Boris it was like grabbing at wisps of fog—there was nothing to hold.

Nessa, Verbena. If you bind me here, I bind you to me, silly girl. You believe a phantom does not have magic of its own? I have traveled through air and sea, lived among the woods and the water for more than a decade. My power grows with every moment I stay on in this realm.

Verbena felt her chest clench, like she'd been slammed with a hammer. A sharp slash traveled down the center of her being and she couldn't hide her wince.

Stitched together, Boris said. *If I am stuck here, you are stuck with me. I plan to make you pay for your sins.*

Verbena was torn asunder.

Her eyes betrayed her, for when she glanced down at her chest, all was well. There was no gaping hole, no needle points, no knives delved into her flesh, carving patterns of searing pain. There was only her t-shirt and the skin beneath it. As freckled and smooth as it had always been.

But all of the pain was real. The sharp, biting invasions, the pulling and prodding. She swore her ribs were being slowly wrenched apart. But she didn't drop her knife. She held it so tightly the handle bit against the skin of her palm.

Tears stung her eyes, sweat ran down her neck, but she was trapped.

Why had she allowed herself to be so stupid? Of course, Boris had power. He was a phantom. That alone should have scared her away. In her decade of exorcising creatures, she'd never come across one like him. Never felt the power that coursed around him, never fought and lost against anything supernatural. Why had she believed she would do anything but fail?

Luke had been right. He was too strong for them. He was a knife wedged between the two of them, keeping them apart life after life after life in an unending cycle of loss.

Boris was from a powerful line. Even if he hadn't had magic in this last life, it didn't mean his soul was without it. This phantom was stronger than any warlock she'd met, binding them together, knitting the dead with the living. The two were like oil and water, naturally repellent of the other. Yet he wove their souls so tightly, Verbena felt that she'd never be free again. His weight locked around her soul like an iron chain dragging her to the bottom of the ocean.

She wanted to see Luke, wanted to tell him how he was right. Boris was too strong. They couldn't defeat him. She was a sham. Her alchemy a fluke. She wasn't strong or powerful or special. She should have fled, stealing moments with him, kisses when they passed like ships in the night, their love a silent, heavy burden never to be shouted or proclaimed, only kept buried within her heart.

You dream of Luke even now? He will not come, nor will you survive long enough to see him. Your fragile human heart, under this much duress, will falter and fail and you will join me. I've stitched us together into one being. We will float this world together. I will keep you here for eons, never to find him again. Nessa with the plump lips and daring eyes. You will be mine.

"No," she forced out.

Your attachment to Luke betrays you. I can feel it radiating off you. How badly you need him, how you wish he would save you. He will not. He has no magic, no bravery, no drive to stand up and fight, yell. He is a coward, through and through. He runs when he should fight, bows when he should stand. He is no man.

If her attachment to Luke made Boris stronger, she would let it fade from her mind. She let the memories of him become shadows in her mind, like the wisps of spider silk in the morning wind, like the composition of Boris himself. His kisses falling into brushes of dust, her name on his lips becoming a silent whisper. She watched him drift away like dew on the grass under the sun.

She would let him go.

Her body became heavy, and she fell to her knees, even with Boris' icy grip on her. The grass on her skin was a welcome, if only momentary, distraction, before she lost consciousness.

"Verbena." The voice was clear, and stern. She couldn't move or open her eyes, but somewhere in her brain, the recognition was niggling her. She knew that voice. It was important and familiar, and she had wanted to hear it for so many years.

"Verbena, listen to me. You have to listen. I don't have long."

Mom.

Verbena's eyes shot open. She was still in the forest, and Boris' form still held her, but she couldn't see him. All she could see was her mom's form blotting out the sun above them.

She was there, Holly Bay, looking as she did thirteen years earlier, wearing her favorite mulberry sweater, her brown hair cut to her chin with blunt bangs.

"Mom? How?" Her mind flew a million directions. "Did I die?"

"Not yet. But you might. You have to fight him, turn him. You can do it. You are an alchemist. It is in your blood. The Bays in France have secretly practiced alchemy for centuries. You must change him. Do not give up. Come on, my girl. You can do this. You have the strength, you have the power. You have so much to live for. Don't give it up."

"Mom," Verbena's chin began to quiver. "Mom, I'm not strong enough. I don't know how to do it."

"Pull it from within, Verbena. My house witch. We are much more powerful than anyone gives us credit. Banishing ghosts, making people feel welcome, turning pieces of earth into homes. It is powerful magic. As powerful as quelling a forest fire or calling the sea."

"I need you, Mom. Help me," Verbena sobbed.

"Not—" her mother's voice faltered, and she began to fade.

"No! Mom, Mom, please stay with me. Please, I'm so scared. I don't know what to do. Don't leave me. I need you!"

Her form shadowed slowly, turning into grays and whites, melting into the background.

"Mom!"

"Not ghost!" Her mother's voice rang clear before disappearing completely.

Verbena blinked hard. Her mom was gone, Boris' face now becoming sharper over her. He did look like Fergal, but younger. When Nessa died, Fergal was an old man, but Boris looked to be in his early fifties.

Not dead yet, I see? We shall have to work a little harder.

Verbena winced against the worsening pain. How was she staying conscious? This body had never been through trauma like this, but Nessa had. She was a breath away from what she'd experienced while dying of childbirth, yet her mind would not let her fade into the blackness. She strengthened her resolve and took a shaky breath.

"You will not have me. I am a Bay witch, a woman of house and home. I protect the boundaries of the living, and you are not welcome here," she spat.

Hubristic witch. I will end you.

Chapter Thirty-Six

L uke couldn't ignore the damning feeling in his heart.

What if he was too late? What if Boris got to her and Sage wasn't there this time? What if leaving was the biggest mistake of his life?

He never should have left her.

They arrived at the port midday. The ferry didn't run again until three in the afternoon, and Luke couldn't wait.

"I am going to charter a boat," he said, a split-second decision. "I'll have to leave the car, but she needs me now." He and Danny had been standing outside the car for a full ten minutes, and neither had heard Boris. The only explanation was that he was with Verbena.

"How are you going to get to her once you get there? It's not like you can take a cab home," Danny pointed out.

"If I can't find anyone to drive me, I'll bike." He would carjack someone if it came to it. He had to get to Verbena.

Luke pulled his phone out again, hoping beyond hope that he'd have a text from Verbena explaining that she'd been with a client or was mad at him or somehow still sleeping. Anything to let him know she was okay. He had called Sage also, but he knew her schedule. Once Sage got into the fields, she was unreachable until her work was done or until she was physically removed from her plants.

Luke took Danny to the private charter desk at the port. There were a few people who ran boats throughout the day for a hefty price. Not everyone wanted to wait for the ferry, or wanted to share their space while traveling.

He booked them passage on a smaller boat that could make the trip in an hour rather than two. The boat had three other passengers, but it was scheduled to leave in thirty minutes, and it seemed like the best option.

Once they boarded, Luke's panic rose rather than settled. The space between them was too great. It was like he could feel Verbena slipping away from him, even as they closed the distance between the mainland and Star Island.

Luke began to fear the worst.

If Boris did anything to her, hurt her, he would...well, he couldn't very well kill a dead man. There were curses, but Luke wasn't magical.

He would hunt him down forever. No matter what life he lived, no matter how many times Boris tried to control him, Luke would hunt him like an animal. He would force himself to remember—remember Fergal threatening to beat her, sending him to war and away from her, remember Boris hitting him with the crowbar, destroying his childhood, driving them mad with his voice in their minds. He'd remember the bruises on his soulmate's neck.

Verbena was a piece of himself, a precious and irreplaceable soul, and he would fight with everything he had to keep her.

After disembarking, Luke ran frantically around town, trying to find someone he knew to drive him. It was as if the fates were against him still. He couldn't find anyone he knew. It was like the island was surrounding him with strangers on purpose.

"Here." Danny handed Luke the bike he'd rented. "If I can find a ride, we'll grab you on the way, but start." Luke took the bike gratefully and, without a word, started toward the Bay cottage.

He rode faster than he ever had, his legs throbbing with the effort. The whole world felt against him in that moment. He rushed down the street, not pausing for cars, and still it wasn't fast enough. He needed to get to her.

Luke pulled into the Bay driveway and dropped the bike to the ground. He jumped up the stairs and pounded on the door.

"Verbena! Sage! Lavender! Anyone?" He remembered what Verbena said, about his house never locking her out. Maybe it was the same with the Bay cottage. He tried the knob, which first stuck but then opened under his hand. Luke burst into the parlor, clamoring through the downstairs, then upstairs, before he was satisfied that the house was empty.

If she wasn't here, she had to be at his house. He left his bike on the driveway and began the run through the backyard.

The Bays had a lot more land than he did, but most of it was cultivated. After Rosemary and Sage's gardens, there was only an acre or so of wooded land, and the majority of it fell between their houses. Luke sped toward the copse of trees, willing his body to move faster than it ever had. He dove into the woods, dodging between sharp branches and jumping over roots. Only a few more steps.

He could see her.

Verbena was on her knees, hands braced in front of her, eyes squeezed shut.

She was in pain.

"Verbena!" he shouted, tearing toward her. She didn't move, didn't react to the sound of his voice at all. He didn't stop running, sprinting, until something stopped him a few feet away. It was like he bounced off thin air, knocked to his ass.

Came back for your whore.

"Fuck off, Boris!" Luke growled. "Verbena. Look at me. I'm here. You're not alone. Come on, baby, open your eyes."

She blinked them open for a moment, glanced at him, then shut them again.

"At least," she bit out, "at least I get to say goodbye this time." She swallowed, her voice barely audible. "I love you."

"No! Don't you say that." Luke scrambled to his feet. "Boris, you sick asshole. Leave her alone. You didn't torture me enough when I was a kid? Well, here I am. Do your worst. You know what? Taylor and I dreamed about a thousand ways to kill you. We were going to run you over with the car, burn the house down, stab you with a kitchen knife. Little did we know, all we had to do was leave a boot on the stairs and your sorry ass would break your neck like a little bitch. You think you were a big scary man? You terrorized children. You call me a coward? You'd rather beat a scared twelve-year-old than live the life of a man. You wanted the three of us to grow in your likeness? Wanted to raise a bunch of pathetic assholes in your image? Well, we all chose to be men, not cowards. You were nothing to any of us, a by-blow that made Danny. You'll never hurt any of us again. We wash our hands of you. You are nothing."

You ungrateful brat. I should have left you with your mother. What happened to her? She still alive? Still bouncing from meth head to meth head, too busy chasing her next high to raise her son? Your father wasn't even dead in the ground before she jumped onto the next man. Tumbling between the hands of the men who used her and used her until she was nothing but a sack of flesh. The shame she brought upon herself, upon you—

"My mother doesn't hurt me anymore," Luke interrupted. "Neither do you." He looked at Verbena. Her eyes were clearer, and her pain seemed to have lessened. Boris couldn't concentrate on both of them. "You're dead. You might be floating around here for a bit, but you've got a lot to atone for, from this life and Éire. You afraid to cross over? To face every last thing you've done? I've never been one for religion, but I've got a witch girlfriend and a phantom cousin. It's all starting to fall into place for me. I bet there's a big angry god just waiting to get his hands on you. Waiting to push you down into a bog or lock you in a tower. The torture you dealt out is about to come back to you one-hundredfold. You will not beat us, not this time. There's no war to send me away to and keep me from Verbena. Let's even the fight."

Luke watched Boris' face flicker into Fergal's, then back to Boris.

I will destroy you.

Chapter Thirty-Seven

Verbena could breathe again. Luke was distracting Boris, talking to
him about the past, and with the focus shifted off her, the pain
lifted just enough so she could think.

Her mom...her mom had been here. Her face in front, her voice loud
and clear. Verbena swallowed a sob. She could mourn and bawl later.

Her mom had said not ghost. Boris should not be a ghost.

She pawed around the ground and grabbed her knife. She twisted the
blade between her fingers again, then brought her bloodied fingers up to her
forehead, her lips, her neck, and her heart.

"Hestia, be with me," she muttered, invoking the goddess her mother
spoke with most often. The Greek deity of the hearth, the home, the sacred
spirit Verbena needed to bless her. She pushed up to her knees and fisted her
hands at her sides.

She looked at Boris. He came in and out of her vision now, splotchy
shades of gray among the greenery surrounding them. She fluttered her eyes
shut and let herself only think of Boris. Only his face, his eyes, the sound of
his voice. She let him crowd every corner of her mind.

Then, she began to change him.

He was phantom, powerful yet non-corporeal, a shade in the world. She
threaded the wisps that made him, the snakes of gray dust, weaving them

tighter and tighter until the air became thick and heavy and weighted with substance.

And she made him corporeal.

A grotesque face formed first, a twisted mess of what he must have looked like in life, but truer to the form of his soul. His skin tinted a grayish blue, his hair was a dull brown, like the light of the world had been sucked out of it. His limbs came next, fingers with gnarled knuckles, elbows and knees pointing the wrong way. The skin of his back stretched tightly over bones, like there wasn't enough to contain the skeleton and at any moment it might split.

Verbena had never seen a ghoul. It was an unholy sight to behold.

The bind he'd created slipped too—without his phantom status, his magic faded. Ghouls were crude creatures. They held no power over witches.

She felt Boris' power over her fall and jumped to her feet, knife in hand.

"Luke," she warned. Ghouls could touch, grab, kill. They were as deadly as humans but without the fear of death themselves.

As Boris regained some semblance of human form, he towered over Luke, a smile twisting across his face.

"This...I could get used to this," he boomed. Boris reached across the barrier, grabbed Luke around the neck, and dragged him toward them. Luke's hands clutched at Boris', trying to pry him off his neck.

"Hold his arms!" Verbena shouted, jumping onto Boris' back. She tackled them both to the ground, his grip on Luke loosening, but Luke holding tightly to him.

Verbena grabbed a fistful of Boris' hair and tipped his head back, exposing his neck. With all the strength of her body, she stabbed his neck, over and over while he fought, then twitched against her. She didn't stop. Though her body felt drained of every ounce of energy and all she wanted was to roll to the grass and give up, she still stabbed and sliced, over and over.

"This knife isn't working!" she shouted. She wanted it to be over, she wanted Boris gone from their lives forever.

"Give it to me," Luke said, his voice even.

Verbena handed Luke the knife and fell to the side. Luke rolled Boris to his back and took a deep breath.

"This is the end." Luke lifted the knife and methodically sawed through Boris' neck. The moment his head detached from his body, he disappeared.

Luke dropped the knife and sunk back on his heels, inhaling sharply.

"Is he...gone?"

"Yes," Verbena answered. She rolled onto her back and let her eyes close. Damn, she was exhausted. Utterly, deeply, just vanquished a fucking phantom and murdered a ghoul bone-tired.

"For real this time?"

"For real. When ghouls dissipate, they don't come back." Verbena rubbed her chest a few times where she and Boris had been bound. She was sore, like she'd taken more than one punch to the sternum, but there weren't any wounds. Their connection had been severed when she made him a ghoul. Now, she only needed to let herself heal.

Luke knelt beside her and took her hand in his. "I'm so sorry I left. It was the worst decision of my entire life, and I will never do anything like that ever again."

Verbena gripped his hand and nodded. "We stick together."

"Forever. I will never run away or try to solve a problem without you. We're a team."

"The best team." Verbena pulled herself to sitting. "I can't believe I did it. I was so sure I was going to fail, that I was going to die."

Luke snaked his arm around her and pulled her against his chest. "You are amazing. You figured it out."

She shook her head. "My mom came to me. Told me what to do."

"Was she a ghost?"

"No idea. But she was there." Verbena snuggled against Luke's neck. "I'm really tired."

"Do you want to go home?"

"More than anything. But I need to tell my sisters what happened. And you should get ahold of Danny. But then, I want to get into our bed and sleep next to you and forget that we faced a phantom and vanquished a ghoul."

Luke pulled her to her feet and against his chest. "Let's go find your sisters."

"For fuck's sake, Verbena!" Sage yelled from her place at the dining table. "I was a quarter mile away. You couldn't have said, hey Sage, I'm about to face a phantom that might murder me, would you be a doll and watch over me? You don't even have Rosemary's orgasm goggle excuse. I know you slept alone last night."

"Sorry," Verbena answered. "But it worked out. Another Stoch has been taken care of. And this one in a very permanent sense."

"Hm." Lavender strummed her finger against her chin. "What if there are more ghosts?"

"What do you mean?"

"Sage said it before, each of us has been connected to a Stoch. Miloslav is the only living magical Stoch."

"Boris wasn't magical, not when he was alive," Luke pointed out.

"True," Lavender answered, "but clearly his soul had magic." She picked up her cup of tea and walked toward the stairs. "I'm going to do some research. Sage? Do you want to come?"

"Not particularly," Sage said.

"Aren't you interested in who might be coming after you?"

Sage shrugged. "They're going to come whether I know their name or not. I'd rather be surprised."

"Suit yourself," Lavender called, walking up the stairs.

Verbena snuck her hand across the table to wind around Luke's forearm.

"All right, that's my cue. You two go to Luke's house, I'm going to bed." Sage paused and looked at her sister. "I'm glad you didn't die."

"Me too."

"See you later."

"Say it one more time," Verbena asked.

Luke huffed. "You were right, I was wrong, and I promise from now on to defer to your judgment." He pulled her toward the porch.

Verbena raised an eyebrow. "On all things?" This would be a good time to get some long-term agreements out of him.

"All magical things."

"What about interior design?"

"As long as you don't turn our house into a haunted house, I'm sure I'll like it." Luke unlocked the door and moved her inside. He kicked off his shoes and set them on the doormat.

"You know, when I was twelve I redecorated my room in all black. Black walls, black rug I found on Craigslist, black frames with macabre pictures hanging on the walls," Verbena teased.

"Is this your way of telling me you have terrible taste?" Luke pulled her against him, his hands resting on the top of her butt.

Verbena laughed. "No. I took it all down a week later. Too dark. Laurel kept the rug and pictures though." She snuggled against his chest. "I like your house. Our house. It's cozy and inviting and has a very comfortable couch, and the yard and kitchen floor are both great for sex."

"Holy shit," Luke laughed.

"What?"

"I've never had sex with you in the bed." He grinned. "What a terrible soulmate I've been. Come on." He grabbed her hand and took her down the hall.

"I'm so tired."

"Let me take care of you. Get you in the shower. Tuck you in for a nap. We can be together after you sleep."

Verbena giggled. "Well, maybe I could muscle out a quickie before I pass out. But you'll have to go on top."

"Whatever you want, Verbena Bay. Love of my goddamn life."

"I want you to join me in the shower."

"I was waiting for you to ask." Luke grabbed her around the waist and pulled her shirt over her head. "Let's get you out of these clothes."

Verbena smiled. Her body hurt, her mind was fried, but she couldn't help feeling like the luckiest woman in the whole world.

A Few Weeks Later

"When I bought this house, I definitely didn't think the third bedroom would be turned into a library," Luke moaned, carrying yet another box of books through the front door. "I also didn't think the library would be a cover for a spell room."

Verbena walked in behind him, with an indiscreet brown box in her hands, which held her ceremonial knife and several small idols of house and hearth deities.

"I had plans for a man cave," he added.

"A man cave? You do not seem like the man-cave type. Maybe a nice bar, but why would you need one of those in your house? You have the best bar on the island a few miles away, and it also has a deep fryer. And a staff." They walked into the third bedroom and set their boxes down. They had set up a new bookcase yesterday, and Verbena's armoire from her apartment had been moved in this morning. Now that all the furniture she was bringing was in place, the two of them were taking their time bringing over the boxes in their cars. So far, the kitchen and bedroom were in their respective places, but the "other" category still needed unloading.

"Some bring shoe collections, I bring witchcraft paraphernalia." Verbena stretched her arms overhead. "How many boxes are left?"

"From your apartment? I think five. But we still need to swing by the witchy neighbors' house to get the rest of your things." Luke sidled up beside her and wrapped his arms around her waist.

"We can get the stuff from the house tomorrow. It's only a few things." Verbena leaned into his arms and rested her head against his shoulder.

She was tired from moving. At least work was quieting down at the moment. Spring and summer were her crazy times, but once autumn kicked in, no one wanted to take a cold ferry out into the Atlantic to look at homes. She only had two active clients, and they were Rosemary and Asher. And she had the perfect house lined up to show them on Saturday.

In the end, Brian Lennox's funding had fallen through. All that life-threatening work for nothing. But she wasn't sad. Parts of the island needed to stay wild.

"I'm ready for bed," she admitted.

"Verbena. It's five-thirty. We haven't had dinner yet. This is the problem with you insisting on waking up so early." Luke pressed a kiss to her forehead. "Why don't you order pizza and get in the shower. I'll finish bringing the boxes in, and you can unpack them before the sun comes up tomorrow."

"Deal."

Luke unloaded the boxes and let the dogs run around the yard for a bit while Verbena showered. He knew there was only a fifty-percent chance she'd be up for pizza, as she often showered in the early evening and got straight into her pajamas and then bed.

And that was okay. He didn't mind climbing into bed a few hours after she did. She always noticed him and snuggled close until he drifted off, and then woke up to the sounds of Verbena making coffee, talking to the dogs, or occasionally having a hushed conversation with someone looking to buy a slice of Star Island.

The dogs collapsed on the porch in an exhausted heap just as Peter, the solitary pizza delivery guy, walked up the stairs.

"Here you go, Luke. Verbena paid over the phone."

"Thanks, man," he answered and ducked inside with the boxes. The dogs were used to Peter and wouldn't chase him down the street, and Luke didn't want to look at Whiskey or Jaeger's puppy eyes while he enjoyed a slice of pizza.

"Verbena, if you're awake, pizza's here," he said softly.

"I'm up," she called from the bedroom. "Set it down for a minute and come back here."

Luke did as she said, wandering down the hall, trying to ignore the piles of boxes along the way. Verbena was a house witch—she'd have this place feeling cozy in no time. Hopefully, for the sake of the dogs.

"What's up?" he asked, pushing the door open. "Oh."

Verbena was sprawled out on the bed, her wet hair like a crown around her, her hips dipped to one side, and her arms loosely above her head.

She was also naked.

"I may be tired, but there's no way I'm not getting naked with you on our official first night living together. House rules."

"You've slept here every night for two weeks," Luke pointed out as he pulled off his shirt and tossed it aside.

"It wasn't official though." Verbena stretched out her legs. "I've changed my address and everything."

Luke nodded and crawled between her legs, inching them apart as he did. He sunk back to his knees and ran his hands over her thighs. "Well, I would never argue with you over anything like a change of residence. As I said, I defer to you on all house and witchcraft-related matters." He hummed against his smile. Damn. The woman he loved was a creature to behold. Especially when she looked like a goddess for him to worship. "Just how tired are you?"

"Why?" she asked, a smile curving over her mouth.

"I'm trying to gauge how thorough I should be," he teased. He hooked his hands under her knees and slid her to him.

"Never too tired for you."

Three days later, Verbena slid back in bed around nine and snuggled against Luke's back until he rolled over and wrapped his arms around her. She breathed him in as she sank into the hollow of his shoulder, their house pulsing with old magic.

The ancient promise they'd made in a lifetime before had finally come true: a peaceful cottage together, without anyone left to drive them apart.

Thank you for reading! Did you enjoy? Please add your review because nothing helps an author more and encourages readers to take a chance on a book than a review.

And don't miss more from Colleen Delaney's *The Witches of Star Island* series, coming soon.

Until then, discover PRECISE OATHS, by City Owl Author, Paige E. Ewing. Turn the page for a sneak peek!

You can also sign up for the City Owl Press newsletter to receive notice of all book releases!

Sneak Peek of Precise Oaths

BY PAIGE E. EWING

People who knew about Others thought spider-kin seers couldn't be surprised, but even Liliana could only see what she looked for. No one wakes up and wonders, *Will a Celtic werewolf accuse me of murder today?*

Liliana simply looked to see what the weather would be, just as she did every morning. When her fourth eyes showed her a fast-forward movie of clouds gathering and drizzly rain, she put on warm blue knit tights under her purple velvet skirt.

Her only plan for the day was to clean and organize before her favorite client's appointment. Janice Willoughby had been her client for over a decade. The room-bot that kept her floors spotless and dusted everything it could reach was a thank you gift from Mrs. Willoughby. Something to do with Liliana's advice helping her to become Mrs. Willoughby. She even invited Liliana to her wedding ten years ago in the Fayetteville Community Church.

The spider-kin seer didn't go of course. Weddings were filled with crowds of strangers. But it was still nice to be invited. And the room-bot was marvelously useful.

Unfortunately, the handy bot's telescoping arms couldn't reach to dust the highest shelves in the room where the spider seer conducted business. Liliana balanced on her ballet-slippered toes between the back slats of a wooden chair and the edge of a shelf while she dusted. Out of boredom, she let her fourth eyes wander. Large and cat-slanted, the eyes opened on her forehead above her eyebrows, lavender and teal opalescent colors swirling.

She saw three strangers on her front porch. The shortest one would knock on the front door—very soon by the sharp, barely future shading of the vision. She glanced at the nicely dressed short woman's wrist phone as she lifted her hand to knock.

She had only a minute or two until they arrived, depending on how accurate the time on the woman's wrist phone was.

Strangers.

Liliana twisted the dust rag in her hands. Strangers often laughed at her or spoke to her slowly as if she were stupid.

Her clients understood that Liliana had trouble sometimes remembering to follow social rules. Strangers expected her to already know and follow all the rules.

Who made up the social rules anyway? How does everyone else always know them?

She sighed in frustration, balanced on one toe tip on the chair's back for a moment, then hopped lightly down to the hardwood floor. She tossed her dust rag onto the corner shelf next to the pile of unfolded scarves.

There was no avoiding it. The three people did not look like they wanted her to convert to their religion or to sell her anything. She would have to answer the door.

Liliana closed all six of her inhuman eyes out of careful habit and brushed her thick, black hair forward with her fingers on both sides. Her hair would help obscure the tiny crinkles from closed spider eyes on her forehead and temples. Her appearance should now be indistinguishable from a young adult human. All three of Liliana's parents had worked hard to teach her how to blend around humans. Normals could sometimes be violently intolerant of those who were different, and Liliana didn't want to have to kill anyone today.

She cracked the door just as the short woman's knuckles were about to touch it. That let in the traffic noise of the busy street in front of her house.

The three strangers were taken aback for only a moment. Lots of people had door cameras these days and might have been warned by their house AIs watching through those mechanical eyes.

Maybe these people were driving by and saw my sign.

The big sign outside said, "Madame Anna Sees All." It wasn't true, since no one could see all without going insane, but her second mother urged her to paint it five decades ago. Ixchel said that advertising did not have to be accurate, only catchy.

Curiosity tickled the back of every part of Liliana's mind. Some part sent her a thrill of possible danger, but she couldn't trace it. Perhaps the warning was from a part of her mind that used one of her closed sets of eyes. She would check after her strange visitors left.

A brief glance with her first eyes, her dark blue human eyes, told her only one of the three people on her doorstep was a man. He wore jeans, an open synth-leather jacket, and a black T-shirt with white letters and a stick figure that said, "Stand back. I'm going to try...science." Disproportionately large, shiny black combat boots stuck out from his ordinary jeans.

She stared at them. He must have very big feet.

Those look like actual leather, made from cows.

Taxes on leather and other animal products had made them an expensive rarity since 2036, when the Green Party swept the elections toward the end of the Energy Wars.

The short woman in the blue synth-silk suit held up a shiny gold badge in the general direction of Liliana's wandering gaze. Her skin was perhaps the darkest shade Liliana had ever seen on a human, and she wore her hair in neat, shoulder-length braids. Her stature put her face nearly level with Liliana's. An agreeable coincidence. There were not many people as petite as she was.

Keeping her smile carefully small so her fangs wouldn't show, Liliana smiled at the woman's sensible but dressy flats.

"Good afternoon, ma'am. I'm Detective Shonda Jackson. This is the CID liaison with Fort Liberty, Sergeant Zoe Giovanni, and special CID consultant, Doctor Peter Teague." She indicated the other two people, who nodded in turn. "We'd like to ask you a few questions."

"Questions," Liliana repeated. The tightness in her shoulders relaxed. Everyone came to ask her questions. They must be new clients then. She waited for them to ask.

"Yes," the police detective confirmed.

Liliana considered opening her third set of eyes to look at these new people properly, but she couldn't risk her inhuman eyes being noticed. There were about a hundred Normals for every Other, so the likelihood was high that any new strangers she met were Normal.

The third stranger, a tall, pretty soldier with Army sergeant's stripes, looked at the sky. She had no makeup, an athletic build, and a pained expression.

Liliana looked at the sky too, but saw only the clouds and drizzle she had already seen with her fourth eyes that morning. There did not appear to be anything unusual up there.

"Ma'am, could we come in?" the soldier asked.

"Oh!" Clients asked questions at the table, not on the front steps. Liliana had forgotten to invite them in, and strict social rules prohibited them from entering without her permission.

The soldier's name was Zoe Giovanni, but her customers taught Liliana that social rules demanded she call soldiers by their rank and last name. She didn't know about civilian police officers, though, since she'd always avoided interactions with them. She assumed she should use the policewoman's rank, but should she use the detective's first name, Shonda, or her last name, Jackson? It was probably different from the military.

"Yes, Detective Shonda, Sergeant Giovanni, Doctor Teague. Please, come in." She opened her door wide, bowed gracefully, and gestured for the three strangers to enter her work space with her usual flourish of flowing sleeves. Dramatic motions were expected from seers.

"That's Detective *Jackson*." The short woman crossed her arms and pressed her lips together.

Liliana's cheeks heated. That had to be a new record, even for Liliana. It usually took more than a few seconds before she managed to annoy someone that much. "I am sorry, Detective Jackson."

She closed the door, muffling the traffic noises. The formal dining room Liliana had converted into her business was not ready to receive visitors. The pile of new, unfolded scarves lay messily on the shelf near the closed door to the rest of her house. The goddess symbols, crystals, and other arcane bric-a-brac on the higher shelves were still dusty. And the large crystal ball was off-center on the round table in the middle of the room.

Hastily, Liliana moved it two inches to the left.

The three people stood among her scarves and clocks and mystical knick-knacks peering around curiously, filling up a lot of space.

The spider-kin suppressed an instinctive urge to squash herself tiny in a corner of the room. "Sit down."

The strangers started at her abrupt order.

She winced at her own tone. She'd meant that to be an invitation but didn't get the voice inflection right.

To fix her social mistake, Liliana added a graceful gesture with one arm accented by the butterfly sleeves of her hibiscus-print silk blouse. She might not be good with her voice, but after growing up dancing on the high lines of a circus, no one could fault her physical grace.

They sat in the three client chairs around the far side of the round table.

Liliana chose a sheer, rose-printed scarf from a shelf and sat in the chair opposite the strangers. Now they wouldn't feel insulted because she didn't make eye contact. It was expected for her to stare at the crystal ball. She sighed with relief.

In the dramatic singsong that she'd memorized, Liliana said, "Madame Anna sees all. Pay me what you feel is fair for truth that cannot be seen by other eyes. I see what is, what has been, and what might be. Ask and the truth shall be yours."

She watched the strangers in the crystal reflections. Amused smiles played around their lips.

"Well, we did say we wanted to ask questions," Peter Teague said.

Sergeant Giovanni rolled her eyes.

Oh. They must expect a charlatan's show.

Liliana would have to prove to them that her sight was genuine before they would ask any questions of substance. She kept her smile small so as not to show fangs. They would learn what she could do. "Who chooses to be seen?"

Sergeant Giovanni grinned wide and shrugged. "I'll bite." She glanced at the detective for permission or confirmation.

Detective Jackson sighed, then nodded. "Fine." Liliana didn't know why the detective was still so annoyed. It seemed like a small mistake and Liliana had apologized. "I suppose we can start with that. It'll be interesting to see what the lady can do."

Liliana draped the scarf over her head as a veil to obscure her face. If they were Normals that didn't know about Others, she had to make sure they didn't notice when her inhuman eyes opened and closed. She waved dramatically over the crystal ball. When they looked at her gesturing hands, the spider-kin opened her third set of eyes just below the inner corners of her human eyes, like glossy black tears.

The sergeant's soul shimmered with color and energy, but not the distinctive, feral shine of a beast-kin, the cool green overlay of a plant Fae, or the hard edges of a mineral Fae.

A Normal. I was right.

Sergeant Giovanni's heart pulsed richly red, a passionate person, impulsive, someone who falls in love easily and deeply. Her inner self was riddled with the dark purple cracks of past heartbreak. A shell of pale yellow cynicism guarded her tender, wounded heart. "You have loved unwisely, Sergeant Giovanni. More than once, you chose forever, but forever didn't last."

The soldier with her long brown hair up in a neat twist at the top of her head arched an eyebrow. "Will I meet someone tall, dark, and handsome?"

Her cynical shell sought to hide the genuine question behind humor, but the answer mattered to the soldier. Liliana risked a quick peek with her fourth eyes, making an extra fluttering motion with her hands to distract the strangers.

Will Sergeant Giovanni meet someone tall, dark, and handsome?

Images solidified of a very tall man with strong, memorable features that Liliana found exceptionally handsome. Scars marred the smooth, dark brown skin on one side of his face. On one temple, a few strands of wiry gray mixed with black in a military short haircut. On the other, his ear was lost in scars, and a white streak marred the neat black hair. He wore a U.S. Army colonel's uniform, and he shook Sergeant Giovanni's hand in a vision with the only slightly faded shading of the recent past.

"A tall, handsome man with dark hair and skin and a burn scar on his face is already part of your life. He is someone you respect, an officer."

Liliana tilted her head, considering. This man intrigued her. The colonel's handsome face shimmered slightly, a sign that it hid something else, something Other.

What is he?

Some years in the past, he walked in a dry, barren land, armed and careful. Sergeant Zoe Giovanni followed, guarding his back.

"You follow where he leads."

A dying bush brushed the bare skin on the back of the colonel's hand. The bush bloomed.

Oh.

Liliana blinked her fourth eyes in shock. To affect plants so profoundly with an unintentional touch, the colonel must be Sidhe, the royal Fae who had the strongest ties to the Green. She hadn't thought there were any Sidhe on this continent, and yet, someone who obeyed a Sidhe sat across the table from her.

Her hands gesturing around the crystal ball faltered. Sidhe from the seelie day court were indirectly responsible for the near extinction of her species. She swallowed hard.

He is only a vision.

To keep from leaving a trail of blooming flowers and greening grass everywhere he went, a Fae with that level of power would have to suppress his aura constantly. That required an intense level of vigilant control.

Why does he hide his power?

Instead of looking for visions, Liliana thought about the veil over her head and the Normal woman with the passionate soul who sat across from her.

There are many good reasons to hide what you are.

For the merest moment, she considered telling Sergeant Giovanni what her tall, handsome colonel really was, but then winced at a scolding voice in her memory. "My daughter will be a woman of discretion, an *ehemythos*, not a tale-teller blaring the secrets of others as if she had the right." Her fourth eyes helpfully supplied a glimpse of her father's swarthy face, grim with anger.

"He has a will of iron," Liliana said carefully. That was probably not a secret.

DoctorTeague nudged the sergeant with an elbow. "You gotta admit, Zoe, 'a will of iron' fits Colonel Bennet to a tee, and he's tall, dark, and handsome with a burn scar on his face."

"Oh, you think the colonel's handsome, huh?" the sergeant teased. "Should I tell him about your crush? Should I warn Ben he's got competition?"

Liliana shuddered, only half listening. This powerful Fae colonel must live right on the Fort Liberty Army base, mere blocks from her house. The vividness of his face in her vision indicated a high probability she would encounter him in person in the near future.

More visions of Sergeant Giovanni and the dangerous Fae colonel flashed rapidly in Liliana's fourth vision. "You have served with him in many battles. He has killed to protect you, and you to protect him." *And in addition to possessing powerful magic, he is a formidable warrior.*

While the spider-kin hated even the idea of moving away from the clients she had guarded for years and her cozy home and routine, Seattle had the advantage of being on the other side of the continent from the Sidhe.

These people followed him. Perhaps that had been the hint of danger she sensed earlier?

Detective Jackson raised her eyebrows. "Is all that accurate?" she asked the other two.

"All true," the red-headed scientist confirmed.

The detective whistled low. "Impressive."

"Forget about it." Sergeant Giovanni waved a hand carelessly. "Anyone could listen to the scuttlebutt and know all kinds of things about our unit. Soldiers gossip like old ladies."

"There's one problem with your theory," Detective Jackson pointed out. "In order to brush up on you and your CO's past, Madame Anna would have had to know who was coming. I didn't call ahead. Did you?"

Uncertainty swept over Sergeant Giovanni's face. "It's some sort of trick." Her dark eyes narrowed in suspicion. "Aren't you supposed to tell me I'm going to meet the man of my dreams and live happily ever after?"

Liliana put aside persistent visions of the sergeant's dangerous commanding officer and peeked at her romantic future. What she saw made the spider-kin cringe. "You will meet a man soon who will give you chocolate and jewelry, but he is dishonest. He desires another." Sergeant Giovanni did not seem very skilled at choosing her mates. "Do not trust the man with the silver rose. Absolutely do not wear the locket."

The sergeant shook her head and laughed. "Seriously? You need to go back to fortune-teller school or whatever. That fortune sucks."

This objection Liliana had heard before. In her practiced singsong voice, she said, "I see only the truth of what might come to pass, not what you wish the truth to be."

"She's got you there," the detective said with a chuckle.

Liliana glanced with her third eyes quickly at the policewoman from under her veil. She saw grudging respect dawn in her sharp eyes, along with a firework sparkle of suppressed laughter.

The spider-kin smiled back. This police detective was also a Normal, with deep moral principles. The rich, dark blues of profound courage interlaced her aura, shaded generously with the softer green of compassion.

Detective Jackson's smiling eyes turned to a squint as she tried to see the spider seer's face better through the obscuring veil.

Quickly, Liliana closed her third eyes.

Peter Teague nudged Sergeant Giovanni with an elbow. "We didn't actually come here to talk about Zoe's terrible taste in men."

Sergeant Giovanni's wry face reflected in the crystal ball.

"You have questions. Now, ask and I will answer." Liliana waited patiently.

"Right," Peter Teague said, but he didn't ask her anything. The soldier and the man of science looked at one another, as if each expected the other to speak.

Detective Jackson rolled her eyes. Perhaps the annoyance she kept expressing was not Liliana's fault. "Ma'am, we're investigating a string of murders. Soldiers from Fort Liberty have gone missing. Some have been found dead. We thought you might be able to help us."

Liliana stood up so quickly she knocked over her chair. "NO!" She tore the veil off her head and faced the corner, turning her back to the strangers.

Her second set of eyes, the domed green eyes that shone like polished chrome on her temples, opened without conscious thought as they always did when Liliana felt threatened. They allowed her to see in nearly 360 degrees, although in spectrums different from her human vision.

The man slipped one hand into the sleeve of his jacket to the hilt of a knife. The two women both had guns.

Liliana knew better than to startle armed people. She knew better. She shouldn't have done that. She wished these strangers would just go away.

The spider-kin picked up one of her new scarves from the messy pile on the corner shelf. "No one asks me to see murdered people. I don't want to see murdered people." Her nightmares were rich enough. "Please, don't ask me to see murdered people."

She ran the scarf through her fingers, facing the corner of the room next to the inner door that led to her living room. Burnout velvet cloth was her favorite. The sensation of silk then velvet trailing in patterns between her fingers always calmed her.

"It's all right," Detective Jackson said gently. "You don't have to look at the murdered soldiers." Her voice soothed like someone talking to a frightened child. "We just want to ask you a few questions. That's all."

Liliana swallowed and nodded at the corner. It was all right. She'd misunderstood. They wouldn't make her watch people be murdered. "Okay."

Talking to people with her back to them was a violation of a strict social rule both her mothers had ingrained in her. "Okay. You can ask." She took a deep breath to steady herself and turned around, still holding and staring down at the burnout velvet scarf in her hands. "But I won't look. Okay? I don't want to see murdered people."

Peter Teague followed the spider seer to the corner of the room.

Liliana tried to step back from him, but her heel touched the wall next to the door.

"Right." His voice wasn't gentle like Detective Jackson's. "Tell us where you were last night."

Don't stop now. Keep reading with your copy of PRECISE OATHS, by City Owl Author, Paige E. Ewing.

And sign up for Colleen's newsletter to get all the news, giveaways, excerpts, and more!

Don't miss more from Colleen Delaney's with *The Witches of Star Island* series, coming soon, and read all her books at www.colleendelaney.com

Until then, discover PRECISE OATHS, by City Owl Author, Paige E. Ewing

Even though spider-kin Liliana sees the past, the future and into men's souls, she can still be surprised. After all, no one wakes up wondering if they'll be accused of murder by a werewolf.

Wolf-kin Peter Teague of Fort Bragg's Criminal Investigation Division analyzes the venom in six dead soldiers. The victims were killed by a spider-kin, and Liliana is the only spider-kin in Fayetteville.

Pete's handsome boss, the dangerous fae Colonel Bennet, watches Liliana with burning ember eyes, but refuses to call his investigator off.

It's up to Liliana to keep Pete from executing her and convince the skeptical scientist she's not the murderer, all while keeping her new friend from getting eaten by the real killers. And if that's not enough, she might even have to socialize!

How will she survive the paranormal mystery that puts her as the prime suspect?

Please sign up for the City Owl Press newsletter for chances to win special subscriber-only contests and giveaways as well as receiving information on upcoming releases and special excerpts.

All reviews are **welcome** and **appreciated**. Please consider leaving one on your favorite social media and book buying sites.

Escape Your World. Get Lost in Ours! City Owl Press at www.cityowlpress.com.

Acknowledgments

A few years ago, I went to a new therapist for my life long anxiety and she began my first appointment by saying, "tell me about your relationship with your husband." I went on for about five minutes describing my best friend, the person I rely on most in this world, and the love of my life. My therapist responded, "Well. That isn't how that question usually goes." So thank to my mister. I seriously couldn't do any of this without a partner like you.

Thank you to Tee Tate, my wonderful editor. Working on this series with you has been a wonderful privilege and I truly believe you have made these books better with your guidance. Thank you to City Owl Press for taking a chance on me and the Witches of Star Island. It has changed my life.

Thank you to my dear writing friends who are always available for the following: listening to me whine about copyedits (you truly have no idea how much a friendship with me involves this), telling me I am not a terrible writer, reading versions of these books that are nowhere near good, and being all around good friends. Thanks to Jen, Abigail, Katy, Tova, Natalia, and Charish.

Thank you to the Dark Tomes and Tombstones book club! I love coming to chat and getting basically all my insecurities as a writer washed away by you all.

Thank you to my whole village—my mom, siblings, friends, neighbors. I am spoiled for support.

And thank you, reader, for sticking with this series until book three! I truly hope you are falling in love with the Bay sisters and their soulmates. It's been a joy to write them. Now there is a sarcastic farmer who needs my attention...

About the Author

COLLEEN DELANEY is an author, librarian, gardener, and occasional baker. She likes being outside in every season except winter, which she prefers to enjoy from a window. She currently lives on the shores of a Great Lake with her husband and four time-consuming children.

www.colleendelaney.com

instagram.com/colleendelaneywrites

x.com/cdelaneywriter

tiktok.com/@colleendelaneywrites

youtube.com/@ColleenDelaney

threads.com/@colleendelaneywrites

About the Publisher

City Owl Press is a cutting edge indie publishing company, bringing the world of romance and speculative fiction to discerning readers.

Escape Your World. Get Lost in Ours!

www.cityowlpress.com

facebook.com/CityOwlPress

x.com/cityowlpress

instagram.com/cityowlbooks

pinterest.com/cityowlpress

tiktok.com/@cityowlpress